Dear Reader:

Every writer hopes that their work will last and that it will reach as many readers as possible. That's why I am so very pleased that One World/Ballantine chose *Love's Deceptions* to be among the first of its new Indigo Love Stories. I am equally thrilled that, by reading this book, you will be a part of this very special moment.

In writing African-American romances, I try to create love stories that all women and *men* can identify with. I also believe that it is important to portray both men and women in the most positive light possible. In *Love's Deceptions*, Rachel, Mattie, Lesa, and Stacy experience love and heartache, joy and sorrow, in search of what we all hope for in a relationship—a love that will outlast time itself.

So come with me now, inside the pages of *Love's Deceptions*, where the heat of passion and the chills of danger and intrigue combine into an enticing sensation sure to leave you breathless. Rest assured, though, there's always someone's hand you can hold on to or a shoulder to lean on. Together we'll prove strong enough to brave *Love's Deceptions*.

Enjoy!

Charlene A. Berry

By Charlene A. Berry:

SECRET OBSESSION
LOVE'S DECEPTIONS*

*Published by Ballantine Books

Books published by The Ballantine Publishing Group are available at quantity discounts on bulk purchases for premium, educational, fund-raising, and special sales use. For details, please call 1-800-733-3000.

Love's Deceptions

Charlene A. Berry

One World
THE BALLANTINE PUBLISHING GROUP • NEW YORK

Sale of this book without a front cover may be unauthorized. If this book is coverless, it may have been reported to the publisher as "unsold or destroyed" and neither the author nor the publisher may have received payment for it.

Ballantine Books
Published by The Ballantine Publishing Group
Copyright © 1996 by Charlene A. Berry
Cover photo © Roger Lee/Superstock

Excerpt from *Shades of Desire* copyright © 1996 by Monica White.
Excerpt from *Dark Storm Rising* copyright © 1996 by Chinelu Moore.

All rights reserved under International and Pan-American Copyright Conventions. Published in the United States by The Ballantine Publishing Group, a division of Random House, Inc., New York, and distributed in Canada by Random House of Canada Limited, Toronto.

http://www.randomhouse.com

Library of Congress Catalog Card Number: 97-97049

This edition published by arrangement with The Genesis Press, Inc.

ISBN 0-345-12222-8

Manufactured in the United States of America

First Ballantine Books Edition: April 1998

10 9 8 7 6 5 4 3 2 1

Chapter One

A deserted California beach ... sounds of chirping seagulls whirling and gliding above the churning surf ... distant joggers silhouetted against the rising sun ... the smell of salt and seaweed on the breeze spawned by the incoming tide ... a little bit of heaven on earth!

Why was the chirping of the seagulls suddenly so loud and insistent? Dazed, Rachel Grier rolled over and hit the alarm's off button. Waking groggily, she took a long breath, slowly rolled out of bed, and walked to the bathroom down the hall, pausing only to peek into the small bedroom. Slipping in, she stared with wonder at the little bundle buried deep beneath the covers. There was a lot wrong with her life, but her four-year-old son Nicky was the rightest thing that had ever happened to her. Though he could be mischievous, his face in sleep was that of a cherub. She smiled as she picked up Oscar, Nicky's teddy bear and best friend, from where it had fallen to the floor. Placing the teddy bear beneath the animal-patterned designer sheets, she waited for the predictable. Yes, once more in sleep Nicky pulled the bear close and then smiled as she gave him a soft kiss on the forehead before slipping out the door.

Staring at her reflection in the bathroom mirror, a still pretty but somewhat worn-looking black woman with lines and circles around her eyes and deep grooves bracketing her mouth, all the things that were wrong in her life came back to her. Dear God, what has happened to me? What happened to that bright, motivated twenty-five-year-old who, armed with her college degree, planned to conquer the corporate world, to be profiled in the business section of *Time*? Stanley Grier happened to me! When I first laid eyes on him, he was the handsomest black man I had ever seen and he had ambition to match mine. Articulate, ambitious, and single—he was the kind of man who crosses a woman's path only once. Or so I thought. As for his entrepreneurial endeavors, maybe it wasn't his fault that he didn't have enough money to branch out on his own at first or that clients were leery about a black man running his own business in such a short time. Sure, it had to be a blow to his ego when his new accounting firm went under and he had to go back to his old job. But that was no excuse to take his failures and shortcomings out on me!

I've settled for less than my dreams. I threw them all away when I married the man I share my bed with. There'll be no five-bedroom house, white picket fence, two-car garage, no beautiful rings and bracelets for anniversaries, no discovery that the man I married is even more of a man than he seemed when my eyes were filled with stars every time I saw him. I guess I'm lucky that he doesn't come home every night even though he must be cheating on me. At least when he's not here I don't have to walk on eggshells for fear I'll antagonize him or worry that Nicky will see his father striking his mother in anger. What kind of childhood is that? I'll do anything, bear anything—even this horrible marriage—to protect my son.

I envy my friends at work. They've got their lives on track. Lesa has a dream life—high-rise condo, beautiful clothes, more money to spend than she knows what to do with. She didn't settle for less! Even Mattie doesn't seem like a woman who settled for less. Maybe at fifty, she does not have a lot of material things, but she has memories of a wonderful marriage, before she lost her beloved Charles.

LOVE'S DECEPTIONS

And I'll bet she's got plenty of beautiful memories to keep her warm on long, cold nights. I'll never be able to say that! Well, maybe I don't envy Stacy. How does she manage to be a single parent and make ends meet? She's only twenty-eight, but where is she going to meet a man who'll be glad to raise two sons of another man, a man she wasn't even married to? She has so much to do as a single parent that she hardly has the time or energy to come to work, much less to socialize! No, as bad as I have it, Stacy has it far worse.

Somehow, thinking of all the problems Stacy faced every day of her life made Rachel's problems more manageable, at least for now. She gathered her energy to go down and fix one more breakfast for the husband she feared, maybe even detested, and the son who made enduring this marriage possible.

The overly crowded bus came to a screeching halt, and the passengers began hurriedly making their way to work. People were rushing out of taxis and cars to make it to their offices on time. Across the street, in front of the California Medical Insurance Center, a gold Mercedes Benz pulled up.

Salt-N-Pepa's "Whatta Man, Whatta Man" spewed out of the Alpine speakers as the passenger door opened. The aroma of jasmine floated into the morning air as Lesa stepped out.

At twenty-five, she was a vision of beauty, every man's secret fantasy. She caught the eyes of both old and young men. She had a solid, toned body, and she knew it. Women envied her. She wore formfitting clothes that were always in style, and she looked like a million dollars in anything she put on. She read every fashion magazine on the newsstands. Lesa would have sought a modeling career, but at just five feet in height, she had a hard time getting her foot into modeling agency doors. So Lesa started dating men who didn't mind buying her things that cost three hundred dollars or more, like big-time drug dealers.

She wore her brownish red hair in a French roll most of the time, accenting her beautiful African features. With her high cheekbones, heart-shaped face, medium-sized nose, and naturally plum-colored pouty lips, Lesa was definitely a looker.

"Are you coming to pick me up this afternoon?" she asked, leaning into the car.

"Hell, Lesa! I've got some serious business to attend to. Can't you catch the bus?" Tony said, placing a call on his cellular phone.

"Bus! If I felt like catching a bus, I wouldn't need you, would I?"

"Watch your mouth, girl."

"C'mon, Tony. I sure don't feel like waiting for no bus in this heat."

Tony exhaled a long sigh as Lesa waited for a response. "All right. Damn! I'll try to be here by five," he said with a slight attitude.

"You better do more than just try. You better have your slick ass sittin' right here when I walk out these double doors."

"Look, stop trying to tell me what I should and should not do. I'm my own man and what I say goes, and don't you forget it, aw'right?" He turned the radio up full blast. Sometimes Tony wondered whether it was worth it, putting up with Lesa's smart mouth. He thought about how it was when he first met her. There he was, a man who was making plenty of money, but without any real idea of how to add class to his life. Then he met Lesa, whose every move said class. Thanks to Lesa, he lived in a ritzy town house with classy furnishings—a long, long way from his years in Watts. He knew quite a bit now about spending money to impress folks. Maybe he really didn't need her anymore. Still, there was something about walking into a room with Lesa hanging on to his arm.

LOVE'S DECEPTIONS

"Your dumb ass is gonna go deaf," Lesa hollered as he skidded off. Luckily she had stepped away from the car or he would have run over her feet.

The elevator doors opened. Lesa rushed inside and pushed the seventh-floor button. As the doors began to close, a man started running toward the elevator.

"Hold it!"

"Sorry! Catch the next one," Lesa yelled back as she punched the "Close" button. *No way I'm gonna ride by myself with a strange man, with what's been happening in this building! I got more sense than some of these sistahs, like that file clerk who decided to take the stairs down and got herself raped last week right there on the stairwell. My mama didn't raise no dummy!*

The elevator sped to the seventh floor where she got off.

"Sheww!" she sighed in relief, wondering if Stacy was there yet. She glanced down at her watch again and then made her way through the exit to the eighth floor.

The doors swung open and she sauntered through.

"Mmm. You're early. What's up? Are you planning on sneaking out today?" a mature, firm female voice asked.

It was Mattie Thompson, the eighth-floor office manager, who was Lesa's good friend.

Mattie was older, the one who'd been with the company the longest. She began working after she and Charles Thompson, an insurance salesman, had moved west from New York; not because she wanted to, but because her husband's health had depended on it. The stress and pressure of the job had been too much for a man who smoked and drank heavily. And when Charles died of cancer a year ago, Mattie hadn't been prepared.

"Mattie, chill out. You act like I can't come in early for once in my life." Lesa plopped down on the corner of Mattie's desk.

"Oh, don't get me wrong. It's good to see you putting your priorities in perspective for a change," Mattie said.

Lesa knew Mattie was right, but she didn't want Mattie

to know she was right. Lesa had a hard time getting to work on time. In fact, she had only been on time twice in the last two years.

The elevator doors opened. Rachel stepped out.

"Good morning, people. What are you doing here? Don't you have a home?" she said to Lesa in one long breath. As she walked over to her desk, Rachel placed a small package in Mattie's hand. It contained cookies she had made the previous night for Nicky.

"Thank you very much. I'm glad somebody loves me," Mattie said with a grateful smile, taking a bite from one of the chocolate chip cookies.

"Oooh! You never brought me anything good when I worked up here. What makes Mattie so special?" Lesa whined.

"You used to freeload off everybody else. That's why," Rachel said smugly. Lesa sucked her teeth and whipped her head around to ignore Rachel's comment.

"Forget you, Rachel."

"Shouldn't you be downstairs? Or did you put all of your work into Stacy's tray again?" Rachel asked.

"Stacy isn't in yet. I guess she had trouble finding a baby-sitter again this morning," Lesa answered.

Stacy was twenty-eight, a single mother of two sons, age six and one. Her boyfriend Clyde walked out on her when she got pregnant, but she let him back in when he got laid off from his job. Stacy couldn't stand to see him in a slump, even though he'd left her with a baby to rear alone. She was the type who hated to kick a man when he was down. But after knocking her up with their second child, Clyde walked out on them. Again.

She and Clyde had talked a lot about making their relationship a permanent one, but Clyde couldn't make up his mind about whose bed he wanted to sleep in. He kept accusing Stacy of being more of a mother than a girlfriend. So after putting up with his comings and goings for five years, Stacy finally made the decision for him.

LOVE'S DECEPTIONS

When he left the second time, she was determined it would also be the last time.

Everyone around her knew Stacy had it rough. Being a single parent and trying to make ends meet every day was a nearly impossible task in itself. She hardly had time for herself—let alone a relationship—and she hadn't had any male companionship in a long while. For Stacy, the bottom line was her fear that she never would. She didn't believe she'd ever meet a man who wouldn't mind raising somebody else's kids.

Stacy wasn't a bad-looking woman, with her petite frame and medium-length hair which she wore pulled back in a bun. But finding the time and the money for a new hairdo and shopping to improve her wardrobe were luxuries Stacy seldom had.

"I don't know why she just don't take a couple of days off from work and try to find a good day-care center for her kids," Lesa said, as she looked at her reflection in a picture on Mattie's desk.

"Lesa, I don't think Stacy would appreciate your analysis of her situation. Besides, you don't know what it's like to have to live your life from paycheck to paycheck. I tell you, you young girls have a lot to learn about life and responsibility," Mattie said.

"Young? Young? Mattie, please. I've had enough experience in my young life for two people. I've been on my own since I was eighteen trying to 'make ends meet' as you put it." Lesa fell silent as she thought about how she had left home at the earliest opportunity because she was sick and tired of living in a house of lies. True, she didn't have children, but in every other way she had had a full course in "life."

"Good morning, ladies," said Terry, one of the technicians, as he walked past.

"Good morning," they said in unison. Terry was an enigma to them. Although he wore the required dress shirt and tie, he seemed always to be wearing a shirt one size too small to show off his muscular torso and narrow waist. His Sansabelt slacks always seemed in danger of splitting across his heavily muscled thighs. Clearly, he spent a lot of time working out. Although there had been rumors that he had been "involved" with various women in the building, no one could supply a name or actually remember seeing him with anyone.

"Don't you think he acts kinda odd?" Lesa asked as her eyes followed Terry all the way out the door. "He sure finds lotsa reasons to pass through this office and sometimes he don't look right in his eyes, as my granny used to say." Living with Tony and his drug business, Lesa had had plenty of opportunities to size men up. And while she could not have named any particular thing, something about Terry bugged her.

"Your problem, Lesa, is that you think every man should look like he just stepped out of *Ebony Man* magazine," Mattie said. "I think Terry's just kinda shy. We're all running a little nervous because of all the trouble in this building. Thank the Lord that girl did some screaming the other night!"

They fell silent, thinking of the most recent occurrence. Two nights earlier a file clerk on the fourth floor got the scare of her life. She was the last one leaving the office and had just flipped off the lights when a muscled-up brother walked in and asked if she was the only one there. When she started screaming, he managed to disappear before the building guards could get there.

"I'll bet he figured out that was the wrong time and the wrong question to ask that nervous sistah," Lesa said laughingly.

"Laugh if you want to, but me, I say good for her! Now, Lesa, I know you girls think you can handle anything, that bad things just happen to other people, but you gotta be careful. This is a terrible world we live in," Mattie cautioned.

"Hey, don't worry about me," Lesa said. "I know the score."

"You know why you can't find a decent man? You think you've got all the answers," Rachel blurted out.

"Rachel, you're just jealous 'cause your swinging days are over. I don't see you turning any heads," Lesa said with a smug look.

"That's right. I'm a married woman. The only head I turn is my husband's. That's the only head I'm concerned about."

"Yeah, right! If you had the chance, and you wasn't married, I'd bet you couldn't keep a lid on those buck-wild hormones of yours. You've probably been married so long that you forgot you have a sensual side."

"Lesa, you have the right to think what you want and do what you want. Just don't do it at the expense of others, that's all," Mattie retorted.

"I'm going back downstairs. You all are gettin' too cynical for me."

"Good! Go earn your day's pay," Rachel shouted as Lesa left.

As Lesa got down to her floor and settled in at her desk, Stacy rushed off the elevator.

"Did Mr. Simmons ask about me?" she asked, huffing and puffing as she placed her jacket on the coatrack.

"No, I covered for you again," Lesa told her.

"Thanks, I owe you."

"You damn right. If you owed me money, girl, I'd be one rich sistah by now. I could quit work from all the times I've covered for you." Lesa leaned over and whispered, "You had trouble finding a sitter again?"

"Trouble is puttin' it mildly. I swear, Lesa, it's getting harder and harder every day. I don't know if I can make it on just this income alone. I may have to start looking for another job or a part-time job pretty soon," Stacy said.

"Why don't you call your social worker and get them to put a tail on Clyde?"

"The only way they'd find that bastard is if they laid down and got up with him every day. I swear Clyde is like Houdini. You think he's in one place, and it turns out he's in another."

"Have you seen him lately?"

"Have you seen Elvis? That should answer your question," Stacy said. "If it weren't for him putting me in this predicament, I would have a bank account full of money."

"Girl, the next time you hear from him, I would get the number traced or something. He's probably living high off the hog by now. The no-good bastard."

"Maybe. He wouldn't tell me one way or the other. I wish I could hit the lottery one time in my life. Wouldn't that solve some problems? But if I didn't have bad luck I wouldn't have any luck at all," Stacy said.

"If you need money, Stace, you know you can ask me," Lesa said.

"Thanks, girl. But I would hate to start borrowing money from people 'cause I wouldn't know when I'd be able to pay 'em back."

"I didn't ask you that. I may have a couple of hundred stashed away here and there."

"Lesa, how can you have more money left over at the end of the month when I have more month left over at the end of the money?" Stacy asked.

"That's because I make it a rule: no cash, no sex."

"Sex isn't the problem with men, it's when they have to start dishing out money. They all got a problem with that."

"Let me run it down for you, Stace. There are only three ways to get anything in life: one, you can work for it; two, you can wish for it; and three, you can get it by any means necessary."

Stacy laughed as Lesa worked her neck back and forth like the true sistah she was. "I'm afraid to ask you which way you're going," Stacy said.

"Number three. If one don't work, I have two more choices."

They both broke out in laughter.

* * *

"Good morning, ladies. How is everybody this morning?"

"Fine, Mr. Wilson," Mattie and Rachel greeted their boss.

Fred, an older black man in his late fifties, was one of the directors at the company. He'd been there for ten years, and he was very fond of everyone on his floor. But he took special interest in Mattie.

"Mattie, everyone knows Mr. Wilson has a thing for you. There isn't a day that goes by he doesn't make it a point to speak to you personally," Rachel said with a devilish grin.

"Don't you start with that again. You hear me?" Mattie said quickly.

"Come on, Mattie. The man is crazy about you. I don't know why you keep playing this 'I'm not interested' crap. If I were you, I'd be sucking it all up. Who knows? You could get a raise out of it," Rachel said, smiling, though she knew Mattie wasn't that sort of woman. In fact, Mattie was just the opposite.

"I don't call going to bed with the boss a means of moving up the corporate ladder. I'm too old for sex games," Mattie said.

"Oh, really? And when did you get too old for sex, Mattie?" Rachel asked.

"When I found out that I couldn't stay awake past *60 Minutes*."

Rachel snickered at Mattie's playful attitude. It was good to see her laugh again, considering the trauma she had gone through a couple of years earlier.

Chapter Two

When I walked through the door this afternoon, I could have sworn I heard voices talking to me. But that's impossible, considering that no one lives here but me. That's one of the reasons I hate to come home; I am all alone when I get here, Mattie thought. Since Charlie passed a year ago, I haven't known how I would make it without him. But there isn't enough money in the world to substitute for the loneliness I feel inside. I never dreamed of being alone at my age. I always thought fifty was the golden age and the doorway to living a full life. So why do I feel like an old brass bell that hasn't been rung by a strong hand in a long time? No one told me that growing old and being alone would be so painful and depressing. It's been really hard for me to get back into the swing of things, in every sense of the word.

I come home every day, take out leftovers for dinner, go upstairs, and take off my clothes. Most of the time I feel so useless that I don't even bother to turn on the television. The only time I can handle what the world has put on me is when I get a stiff drink in me. A nice, tall Long Island iced tea. It always does the trick. Lord knows that iced tea has more kick to it than the regular tea Grandma makes for Sunday dinner. I don't drink all the time. I'm more of a social drinker. The only difference is that I socialize with myself.

When night falls, I sit for hours, listening to my private collection of Nancy Wilson's recordings and crying. I don't know why. Sometimes I think I'm losing my mind or I'm so drunk that I have no control over anything.

At daybreak, I wake up and find myself passed out across the bed in my slip. The record player is playing nothing but static, and I'm embracing an empty liquor bottle.

Tonight it's worse than usual. I'm not only lonely, but a little scared, too. That trouble at work must have me a little on edge. Why else would I be wondering who'd find me if something bad happened during the night? This is one time I'm gonna be sure the doors and windows are locked. And maybe I'll play my music so loud that I can't hear boards creaking as this old house keeps "settling."

"Come on, Nicky. You're going to make Mommy late," Rachel yelled from the bedroom.

"Rach, have you seen my belt? I thought I hung it on this doorknob last night," Stanley said in a frenzy. He, too, was running late.

"No, Stanley. Are you sure that's where you put it?" He always thinks he never misplaces anything, Rachel thought. If he put as much energy into doing things around the house as he expends on his friends, maybe he'd know where most of his things are!

"I know I laid it right here last night. Nicky! Did you move Daddy's belt?"

"Stanley, you know he didn't move it," Rachel snapped.

"Well, where in the hell is it then? I swear! I lay things down and suddenly they sprout feet and walk away."

"Just put on another one," Rachel said, annoyed with his whining. "Did you check the dirty-clothes basket good? You may have left it on the pants you had on yesterday."

"Rachel, you haven't heard a damn thing I've said, have you? I told you where I put it last night, and now it's not there." Stanley began pulling out and throwing dirty clothes all over the room. "I wish you'd wash on a regular basis, so clothes wouldn't be piled to the ceiling!" He was yelling.

Rachel rushed over and shoved herself between him and the hamper, picked the clothes up, and placed them back in the basket. "Just move," she told Stanley.

"Don't push me!" Stanley said through clenched teeth. "I told you about putting your hands on me."

He had acquired a terrible temper lately. When it came to doing things his way, he didn't tolerate any argument.

"I'm sorry. I didn't mean to shove you. But sometimes you act like you only have one of everything in this closet. Here it is, right here, right on the same pair of pants you had on yesterday," Rachel said. She held up the pants.

Stanley snatched the belt out of her hand and proceeded downstairs, mumbling to himself.

"Blind bastard," Rachel said under her breath. "Nicky, let's go!"

Stacy arrived at 2331 Subbrook Lane, the home of her parents, the Reverend Otis and Mrs. Hilda Carr.

"What took you so long? I could've still been in bed," said Hilda, in rare form as usual.

"I forgot to get Terrence's medicine. He's been sniffling for the last couple of days," Stacy explained, rushing to get the kids' jackets off.

"He wouldn't have a cold if you gave him that cod-liver oil."

"I told you, Ma. The doctor prescribed Children's Tylenol for him. It's what he recommends for infants," Stacy said.

"Well, I guess your mother doesn't know what she's talking about then, huh? I raised you on the stuff, and you never caught a cold. But no, what kept you from getting sick isn't good enough for my grandchildren," said Stacy's mother, standing firm.

"Ma, I didn't say that. I just said . . ."

"I know what you said, and I know what that so-called doctor said as well, but I've been around long enough to know what works and what don't. I tell you," her mother continued, "you new mothers swear you know what's best. Humph, not in my book you don't." She grabbed the baby from Stacy's arms.

I hate it when she starts preaching on everything, Stacy thought. It's bad enough having a father who is a preacher. I get sick of having to watch what I say and do around them. They refuse to accept change. She relates everything I do to a verse or a scripture in the Bible. If I hold in my sneeze, damn if she don't have a Bible verse for that. I'm sick of it. It's not that I don't believe in God, I just would like to find Him for myself. That's why I'm so glad I got my own place. I don't have to live the way they want me to or listen to their Bible stories. It had been exactly this sort of narrow-mindedness that had driven Stacy into Clyde's arms. Like many young girls who had grown up in a very strict household, she was an innocent who was ripe for the picking. She had welcomed Clyde's easygoing attitude and the excitment of dating a man her parents would never have approved of. And, like others before her, she had paid the price for her innocence.

"Are you still looking for a permanent sitter?" Hilda asked, bouncing Terrence on her knee. "I told you that I don't mind watching these boys."

"As soon as I can find a part-time job. I've been checking the papers and talking to friends about some night work."

"How in God's name are you going to work two jobs, knowing these boys need a mother?"

"Look, Ma, I don't know. But I'll manage. Find that in the Scriptures," Stacy said abruptly.

"How dare you play with the good Lord like that! Oh, Father, please forgive this evil child," Hilda said as she stretched her arms toward the ceiling. Then turning to Stacy, "The Bible says . . ."

"Oh, Ma, please. Just stop it with the holy word for once," Stacy said angrily. "I don't need you to remind me of my responsibilities. I'm reminded of them every day I look into these kids' faces."

"You made a mess of your life. Huh!" Hilda said finally.

"Look, Ma, I gotta go. I'll be here after five to get the kids. Thank you for watching them on such short notice."

"Tony, get up. Come on. I need a ride to work. I'm late," Lesa called out as she jumped out of bed. She jetted into the bathroom of the two-bedroom town house where she and Tony lived. "Tony! Getcha black ass up now," she called again, holding her hand under her mouth so the toothpaste wouldn't drip on her Persian rug.

Tony just moaned and covered his head. Lesa went back into the bathroom and gargled her mouth out, blitzed to the closet, and snatched down a pink pleated skirt and matching blouse.

She wiggled her firm beige-colored body out of the red thong teddy, her long thick hair falling in her face.

"Tony! Get up!" Lesa yelled, ripping the sheet from his dark chocolate form. Suddenly, for some strange reason, Lesa wasn't in a hurry anymore. Although they had their differences and at times couldn't stand the sight of each other, there was a certain chemistry between them.

Why does he make me so weak? Lesa asked herself as she stood staring at his nakedness. Sometimes Tony can be a real jackass. But he still has the handsomest body I've ever seen, she thought.

When I first met Tony, he was a bit flashy and too self-assured. He talked about how money was never a problem for him and bragged that whatever he wanted, he did not hesitate to get. I admit, I really have a thing for men who know how to take charge and go after what they want. Maybe that's what drew me to Tony. It probably was the only thing we had in common. When I saw him at the happy-hour spot, I knew he was gonna be my man.

Just seeing a well-dressed man with a great body and charisma, too, does something to me. But I'm no fool. I've met a lot of men who had potential, who wore fancy suits, sported fancy cars, and had pockets full of business cards they didn't hesitate to flash. But potential couldn't buy me a damn thing. Tony had his own business, a drug business. If Mattie knew the truth about Tony, she really would be worrying about me. It does cross my mind that Tony might get so stoned that he'll send one of his drugged-out pals to check up on me at work. Who knows what cute ideas they might get?

Lesa walked around the bed, enjoying Tony's maleness. Naked, he was like a beautiful black stallion. Every muscle had a character all its own. She couldn't help but get warm and moist all over. Between her legs she felt a throbbing. A quickie would really start her morning off right.

She knelt down beside him and began to stroke his penis, and in seconds his body came alive. Tony moaned and slowly rolled over on his back while his eyes remained shut. This bastard ain't asleep, Lesa thought as she squeezed his manliness.

Time ticked on as Lesa positioned her sultry body on top of his.

"Come on, Tony, stay up," Lesa demanded as their bodies connected.

Tony's eyes slowly opened. He seized Lesa's hips and began thrusting into her. She felt her nipples harden with every thrust. Tony let out a deep sigh as she rotated her hips around and around, faster and faster. Their bodies pulsated with excitement. Lesa broke out in goose bumps. That was a sign that they were both about to explode.

"Hold it, baby, hold it," Lesa managed to blurt out between each intense thrust. She looked at the clock on the nightstand. It was already after eight and counting. Her workday would begin at nine. But there was nothing like reaching the top of the mountain together, Lesa thought, a wide smile of gratification enveloping her face.

Chapter Three

"Stace, I may have a lead for you to follow up on. It's a part-time job," Lesa said as she walked into the office. Stacy was skimming through the morning paper, checking out the classifieds.

"Oh, yeah? What is it?"

"Well, to start, it pays two-fifty to three hundred bills a week, and you can set your own hours. The best part of it is that you can work right out of your apartment at night."

"What! Girl, where do I apply? I'd be really set if I could get that job, plus keep this one," Stacy said excitedly.

"One of my girlfriends does some work for this company, and he said you could start the job right away if the interview goes well."

"Wait a minute. You said he. I thought you said your girlfriend told you. You just said he."

"Chauncy's a homosexual. He'd rather have people address him as she," Lesa said as she went through some papers on her desk.

"Well, I'll be damned. He—I mean, she—likes it when people introduce him as a she? Why, when he was born a man?" Stacy asked, confused.

"Truthfully, I could care less what he wants to be called. Either way, he likes to get screwed like the rest of us," Lesa said nonchalantly.

"Ehew!" Stacy squinted.
"Here's the number, if you're really interested."

"Package for Rachel Grier," Terry cried, carrying a rather large box to Rachel at her desk.

"Package? From whom?" Rachel asked with wide eyes.

"I don't know. I was downstairs when the delivery man brought it in. Maybe it's from a secret admirer," Terry said, raising his eyebrows. As he edged over to place it on her desk, his shoulder brushed lightly against her breast.

"If he's admiring me, then that really is a secret. Let me see who it's from." Rachel took the box. "Thanks for bringing it up, Terry," she said, moving over and wondering just how accidental the brushing was.

"Whatcha gettin' now?" Mattie asked as she returned from a meeting with Mr. Wilson.

"I don't know. Oh, wait a minute, I do know. It's the hand-embroidered curtains I ordered from Macy's," Rachel said, ripping through the package like a little girl at her own birthday party.

"Why didn't you just go to the store and buy them?"

"I saw them in a catalog, so I called the store to hold two sets for me. The salesperson told me they were out of stock, but I could order them over the phone by using my credit card. And when they came in, they would be shipped directly here. Besides, if Stanley caught me sneaking another bag into the house, he would have a fit." Rachel rolled her eyes.

"Oh, my, Rachel, they're gorgeous! The large tassels hang so elegantly to the side. Are they silk?" Mattie asked, admiring the detail and design of the material.

"Yeah, girl. They looked so nice in the book. I just hope they look this nice when I hang them up."

"How much did they cost, if I'm not being too nosy?"

"That's the clincher. They cost half a paycheck. They were imported all the way from Paris and I haven't even been there myself."

"How are you going to explain them to Stanley when he sees them?"

"I'll think about that when the time comes," Rachel said, not giving much thought to what lie she would tell her husband. Either way, Stanley was going to hit the roof.

As Rachel approached her house, she knew she had to duck and dive so Stanley wouldn't catch her bringing in another shopping bag. She had to be extra careful, in case he made it home first.

She carried a couple of bags of groceries, while Nicky brought in her purse.

"Nicky, set Mommy's bag in the chair and go upstairs and wash your hands for supper."

Rachel rushed about, throwing dinner together. It did not take long, considering Nicky's favorite dish was pizza and veggies. Whenever Stanley was late, he ate out. That meant she had more than enough time to take down those old, dingy curtains and put up her new ones.

Hours passed, and Stanley wasn't home yet. As she cleaned up the kitchen, Rachel started the wash. Each time she passed the living room, she couldn't help but smile at the wonderful change the new curtains made. She wished Stanley would find the time to paint those tired walls. They didn't do anything for the curtains. But knowing him, she'd probably be the one painting the entire room.

Rachel was down in the basement when she heard the front door slam shut. It was well after nine o'clock, but for her, it wasn't long enough. She was praying that Stanley would be too tired to want to do anything but take a long, hot shower and go straight to bed.

"Rachel!" he yelled from upstairs. There goes my prayer, she thought. She dropped the dried clothes into a basket and carried the load upstairs. When she got there, Stanley had already gone through the mail.

"What is it, Stanley? And hello to you, too," Rachel said as she stepped into the kitchen.

"I thought I gave you the money to pay off this Visa bill."

Oh, no, Rachel thought. She knew she had forgotten something. She hadn't checked the mailbox when she got home. How was she going to tell Stanley that she had charged her brand-new curtains on their Visa, after he'd made it clear that they were going to cut back on unnecessary spending? Rachel thought quickly, then said nonchalantly, "I did. But you know I needed some new curtains."

"Yeah. But what kind of curtains cost four hundred and twelve dollars?" There were beads of sweat on his temples. That was always a sign that he had had a rough day and from the smell of his breath, he'd stopped to have a beer or two.

"What happened to the money I gave you two weeks ago to pay this charge off? Or did you use it to get those damn curtains?" Stanley asked.

"I paid off the bill, but I ended up using the card again to purchase the curtains," Rachel said. She tried to ignore his angry face.

"Rachel, have you lost your damn mind? How in the world do you expect to keep money in this house if you continue going off on these ridiculous shopping binges? We're not rich, or haven't you noticed?"

"Ridiculous? How many times have you heard me say that we needed new curtains for that room? You always say the same thing, day in and day out, 'Let's hold off until we get some of these bills down.' Well, to me, they're as low as they're ever going to get. Besides, you act like the new bill isn't going to get paid."

"Oh, you're damn right it's gonna get paid. You are gonna pay off this damn bill with your own money. I'm sick and tired of paying for things around here and not knowing what the hell I'm paying for half the time. There's probably more stuff you're hiding around here. I bet this whole house has more crap hidden all through it," he said furiously.

Rachel placed the basket on the table and began to fold the clothes.

"Stanley, stop talking stupid. Why in the hell would I hide anything from you? That's crazy."

"What's crazy is you buying those expensive curtains. Where are they anyway? At the price you paid, you should be wearing them."

"Oh, shut up. It's not like you haven't gone out and splurged on something for yourself or your mother. I can think of a few things you've bought your mother that were well over a thousand and some dollars."

"Like what? Oh, I know. You're still upset over the fact that I gave my mother a grand to get a new car. Woman, please. You know damn well that her car had more problems than I care to remember. Every morning I had to pick her up and take her to work. Not to mention all the times I had to give her my car to get around. How can you possibly hold that against me?"

"If it were up to me, your mother would take the bus." Rachel and Stanley's mother were not the best of friends. In fact, they had very little to say to each other. Rachel still believed that Gertrude, her mother-in-law, had tried to ruin their marriage.

"No, if it were up to you, my mother would be walking. I know you don't like her, Rachel. Go ahead, you can say it. I'm not gonna get mad."

"Stanley, that's not true, and you know it."

"I know you've never liked my mama."

"Your mother has never liked me to this very day."

"Ever since she moved in, that time she got out of the hospital, you wished she had never stepped foot into our home," Stanley said.

"Well, it was you who tried to put your own mother on your brother because you didn't want to put up with her. I could have cared less where she stayed," Rachel said.

"Yeah, right. I bet if it were some member of your family who needed a place to stay, you'd probably put me on the street so your family would have a place to stay."

"You're damn right. Because to this very day, your mother still curses the day we got married. She wanted you to marry that slut Benita Reed. Who knows? She may still get her wish. I heard that boy of hers looks just like you. Let me find out he's your son, and your mother will really get her wish. You'll need Mrs. Benita Reed, Attorney at Law, to defend your butt when I take you to court."

"Woman, you crazy," Stanley said with a laugh.

"Your mama's crazy."

"I told you about talking about my mama," he said.

"Stanley, get out of my face. You always act crazy when you've been drinking," Rachel said as she started to take the basketful of clothes upstairs.

Stanley was still standing in the kitchen. "You want to see crazy? I'll show you crazy," he said as he stormed into the living room.

"Stanley, what are you doing?" Rachel shrieked.

"No, I'm gonna show you how crazy I am!"

"Stanley, what are you doing?" Rachel dropped the basket and raced back down the stairs. But by the time she reached Stanley at the bay window, he had already ripped down one curtain and reached over for the other one. As bits and pieces of the fabric dangled from the gold rod, Rachel knew they were beyond repair. Stanley was like a man gone mad. The running vines she had in the window were now nothing but broken leaves and dangling roots as dirt covered the floor and windowsill. The coffee table was covered with soil, and pictures were turned upside down.

"Stanley, stop it! Stop it!" Rachel cried out.

"Move!" he yelled as he smacked her to the floor in a rage. "Maybe you'll think twice the next time you go spending money you're not supposed to," Stanley shouted as he destroyed what was left of the four-hundred-dollar curtains.

Rachel was crawling on the floor in tears as she picked up pieces of cloth that were torn to shreds. She couldn't move. The anger she felt was unspeakable. Stanley's large footprints made a permanent impression in the beige carpet as he walked away.

"You need help! You're freaking crazy!" Rachel yelled out.

"Don't press your luck," Stanley said with tight lips before he disappeared upstairs.

Rachel remained on her knees, crying into her hands.

After Stacy called and talked to her children, she finished for the day and went down to the lobby, planning to catch a cab across town to meet Chauncy. As usual, there was a wait. Standing just inside the lobby doors, Stacy had the peculiar sensation of being watched. Nervously, she turned and surveyed the lobby. Everybody seemed to be about their own business and nobody seemed interested in her. Still, something seemed unsettling. Looking through the lobby doors, she examined the sidewalk. Nothing. Long shadows cast by the building made it impossible to see into the doorways across the street, but there seemed to be some kind of quick movement in the doorway directly opposite. Girl, you're letting your imagination run away with you just 'cause you're anxious about this new job, Stacy told herself. Nevertheless, she was glad to see one of the building guards come to the doorway and motion that he had a cab for her.

"I took the liberty of assigning a couple of names on your card," Chauncy said as he welcomed Stacy to sit down.

"I'd just like to know what it is you do here, and what it is I have to do, before I agree to anything," Stacy said. She tried not to stare at the lively and colorful person across from her.

Chauncy was in his late twenties. He looked more like a woman than a man with his wild, funky hairstyle, tight straight-leg blue jeans, and white bodysuit with black ankle boots. It was difficult for her to keep a straight face as she stared at the neatly applied makeup on his smooth face.

"Now, what is it that you're selling to these people?" Stacy asked as she looked over the list of names in front of her.

"Nuthin' honey. You're the one who will be doing the selling."

"Well, what is it?"

"You have no idea what we do, do you?"

"No," Stacy said with a giggle. At that moment the phone rang.

"Well, you're about to find out," he said before he pressed the flashing light on his private line.

"Hello," he said with a feminine voice. "Yes, this is Peaches. Whom am I speaking with?" he asked as he gave Stacy a sly wink.

Stacy was shocked as her mouth hung open.

"Mmm. Bill, you sweet talker you. You're makin' me hot all over," he said. Chauncy touched the tip of his tongue with his finger. "Sss! You got me steamin', baby."

Stacy was speechless. She had no idea that the job she thought was the ideal part-time work was phone sex, talking trash over the telephone to a bunch of perverts.

"What the hell is this?" Stacy asked in a loud whisper.

"Could you hold on for one minute, baby? I promise I won't be more than a minute," Chauncy said. He put the caller on hold.

"What's the matter, Stacy?"

"I thought you said this was a telemarketing job," Stacy said, surprised.

"Honey, it is. But you can call it whatever you want. I call it getting the bills paid."

"Look, Chauncy. I don't know about all this. I perceived a whole different thing. I'm not down with all this freaky stuff."

"Well, look, if you change your mind, take this list of

names. Lesa said that you were pretty desperate, and I did you a favor. Besides, a number for you has already been placed and activated into our system. All you have to do is wait for the telephone to ring. And who knows, once you talk to a few of them, you might see it's easier than you think," he said. Chauncy handed Stacy the list of clients.

"I don't think I'll ever get used to that," Stacy said as she took the sheet anyway.

"If I can't change your mind, maybe the three hundred a week will," he said. Chauncy resumed his private conversation while Stacy quietly walked out of the office.

It was after nine, and Lesa was on her way out to walk to the market two blocks from her condo residence.

"Hey, what's up, Lesa?" a neighbor asked her as she placed her key in the front door of her house.

"Ain't nuthin' happenin', Sherry. How's the post office treating you?"

"I can't complain. We're overworked and underpaid. I had to work a double today, and most likely I have to do the same thing tomorrow."

"Well, it's better than not having a job to complain about. Right?"

Sherry nodded her head and then disappeared behind the burgundy door.

Lesa pranced down the street, throwing her firm hips from side to side, turning heads as she went. Not too far behind was a patrol car. The police cruiser slowly tailed her as she sashayed along.

Seeing a police car cruising Imperial Beach, on the south side of San Diego, was not unusual. The increase of drugs on the streets and black-on-black crime caused the police force to increase its street patrol.

Lesa walked across the street as the patrol car turned at the next corner. When she approached the marketplace, the driver of a red 300ZX with tinted windows and two

LOVE'S DECEPTIONS 27

telephone antennas on the side panels, sounded the car's horn, attempting to get Lesa's attention.

"Excuse me, Miss Lady! Is it possible to talk to you for a minute?" the guy asked with his head out the window.

"Nope," Lesa said abruptly.

The music screamed out of every part of the car. Lesa whipped her long hair in the wind and walked through the electronic doors of the supermarket.

"Oh, I guess you think you all dat', huh?" he yelled.

"Yep," Lesa yelled back as she allowed her body to do the rest of the talking for her. With her white Daisy Duke shorts and matching top, Lesa didn't have to say much of anything. Her perfect body said it all.

When she disappeared behind the glass doors, the souped-up car sat as the loud music continued to spew out. A police cruiser pulled up next to it. The two officers looked over at the too-slick, too-cool brother just as the automatic windows began to roll up simultaneously. But not before the hip brother smiled a wide grin, exposing all thirty-two gold-capped teeth.

In the store, Lesa walked around with a handbasket and a shopping list. She was halfway down her third aisle when a voice came from behind.

"Excuse me, Miss. Could you tell me the difference between Betty Crocker cake mix and Duncan Hines?" the stranger asked.

Lesa turned around and saw the face of the most gorgeous man she had ever seen. This guy was a cross between Michael Jordan and Bo Jackson. He had Mike's smile but definitely Bo's physique. And when it came to checking a man out from head to toe, Lesa knew men.

She looked at the stranger with sultry eyes and stood silently examining the brother from the top of his coarse hair to the thick muscles on his athletic legs. His hands were so big that they palmed each box of cake mix. That was another advantage the handsome brother had going on. Lesa could always tell how big a man's penis was just by looking at his feet and hands. And from looking at him, it was obvious that this guy wasn't lacking a single thing, she thought to herself.

"I can't see the difference," he said.

"Well, it's obvious who makes a better cake," Lesa said, just off the top of her head.

"Oh, yeah? Which one?" he asked.

"This one." She tapped the Duncan Hines box with her gold and cream painted fingernail.

"Why Duncan Hines?" he asked, following Lesa down the baking aisle.

"You mean to tell me, the nineties man as I'm sure you are, doesn't know who Duncan Hines is?" Lesa said, as she left an aroma of jasmine to linger in his nostrils.

"No, I don't know who he is."

"Duncan Hines is Gregory Hines's brother. You know, the famous dancer and singer," Lesa said as she left the aisle and went to another.

For a minute he stood there in the middle of the aisle. He tried to connect the two, when he realized that this girl was joking.

"Well, who the hell is Betty Crocker? No, wait. Let me guess, she must be Joe Crocker's mother. You know, the famous singer." He laughed at his own silliness because he knew the two names sounded alike, but were spelled differently.

Well, this is going to be a lot easier than I expected, he thought. My simplest scheme worked. She thinks I'm just another bro' hittin' on her. Maybe I overestimated her street smarts. Her crazy sense of humor's gonna be a nice little bonus for this job. That's hard to find in any woman nowadays, especially the ones whose only concern is how much a brother makes or if he has a car and a house. Whatever happened to the old-fashioned, wholesome type? Guess they've all been replaced by the mouthy, independent, no-nonsense type like this one, he thought.

"You thought I didn't know that, did you?" he asked her, enjoying his role-playing.

"See, you do know something," she said. Lesa tried to

LOVE'S DECEPTIONS

act like she wasn't interested in his cute but wacky approach.

"You almost got me back there. You know that, don't you?" he asked.

"Well, I didn't know you were so gullible. You did look pretty stupid back there," Lesa said, still a couple of steps ahead of him.

"True. By the way, I'm Kris." He reached out his hand to shake hers. She looked at him and proceeded to walk on by. The last place she thought she would ever meet a man would be the supermarket.

"You are a strange one, you know that?" he said, still in pursuit.

"No stranger than you are walking in the feminine hygiene section with a box of mini-pads in your cart," Lesa said. She tried to hold back a smile.

Kris quickly reached down and placed the box neatly back on the shelf before anyone else saw him.

"Do you do this every time you go to the market?" asked Lesa.

"Do what?" Kris asked.

"Try to pick up women. That is what you're trying to do, isn't it?" Lesa asked. She made sure she didn't pick up anything that would indicate to Kris that she was shopping for two.

Kris couldn't help but be a bit intrigued by her cool and direct personality. Yes, he was definitely going to enjoy this assignment. This was the first time he had met a woman who wasn't turned on by his hard body and good looks. As strange as it was, in real life Kris had a hard time getting dates. Yet, he still preferred the sweet smell and soft touch of a woman over a sweaty, smelly gym any day.

"I'm not doing a good job of it, am I?"

"No, you're not. I'm Lesa." She extended her hand out to him.

Kris looked at her small, perfectly manicured hand. He

was unsure if he should accept it or not, seeing that this woman was unpredictable.

"Oh, please. You think I would do that to you?" Lesa said with her hand out.

Kris looked at her hesitantly. "Okay, if you say so." He reached out to shake her hand.

"Gotcha!" Lesa snatched her hand back and began to laugh as Kris stood looking like a total jerk. He met up with her in the checkout line.

"You know the average brother wouldn't take your little jokes too lightly," he said in her ear as he stood behind her in the express lane.

"The question is, how are you going to take it?" Lesa said as she placed her items on the belt.

"The only way a real man should. One good turn deserves another," he said with a devious smile.

Mmm. This one could have possibilities, she thought as she left the store.

Chapter Four

Stacy placed the baby down in his crib. He was teething and she had been up with him most of the night. Exhausted, she was just about to go into the bathroom to take a long, hot shower when the telephone rang. This was no ordinary ring. This was the ring of her first client.

"Hello," she said with a slight attitude.

"Hello. Is this Sheila?" a man's voice asked.

Stacy didn't recognize the voice, nor did she know anyone named Sheila.

"Who?" Stacy said strangely.

"Ah, maybe I got the wrong number. I was told that this was a special number. I'm sorry, I . . ."

"Wait! Ah, are you calling for Sheila?" Stacy asked quickly, the three hundred dollars suddenly flashing in her head.

"Yes, I am. Is this she?" the stranger asked with an important tone. Stacy hesitated for a second then she answered.

"Yes, this is Sheila. Whom am I speaking with?" she asked, closing her eyes as if to shield herself from what she was about to do.

"John. For a minute there I thought I had the wrong number. This is my first time. I suppose you've guessed now," he said, as the calmness returned to his voice.

"Is that right, John?" Stacy deepened her voice as if she wanted to disguise it.

"You have an accent. Where are you from originally?" he asked.

Stacy stood in her living room buck naked as the television flashed a commercial about Jamaica.

"Jamaica," she said quickly. "Have you been there?"

"Sure. Many times," he answered.

Stacy wished she was somewhere other than her apartment at that moment. She felt her stomach knot up and her heart beat very fast.

"So I take it you're African-American?" John asked. All of a sudden Stacy's eyes widened. What in the hell does that have to do with anything? she thought. Does everything in this world have to be distinguished between black and white? She knew that the man on the other end of the phone was obviously white. Why didn't I just hang up when I had the chance? Stacy thought.

"Do you have a problem with that?" From disgust, Stacy lost her Jamaican accent for a minute. She sounded more like a sistah with an attitude.

"Heck no! I'm all for interracial relationships. As a matter of fact, I find black women to be very mysterious and unique. Some of my closest colleagues are African-American," John said honestly. "I hope I didn't offend you, Sheila."

"No, mon. I find your honesty refreshing," Stacy said as she took a couple of deep breaths to keep from throwing up.

"Sheila, could I ask you a question?" he asked.

Oh, hell. Here we go. I knew this was too good to be true. I thought for sure he didn't want to talk about anything but my accent and culture. But he didn't call for small talk.

"Have you done it with a white guy before?"

I knew it! Stacy screamed silently in her head. What in the hell does he expect me to say? Yes! He must be trippin', Stacy thought. She could never, ever see herself

LOVE'S DECEPTIONS

with a white man. Unless it was that white rapper who did the commercial for Calvin Klein underwear. Maybe then she would make an exception.

"Does it matter, John?" she asked falsely. "I can't touch you and you can't touch me," Stacy said. Thank God, she thought.

"No, but I'm sure you've heard that white men are not so well-endowed as others." Stacy tried desperately not to burst out laughing in his ear. She didn't care one way or the other. At the present time she wasn't about to start swirling now, not with all the remaining brothers around her. If push came to shove, Stacy would find a pen pal to write to before she turned her back on her own kind.

"You shouldn't listen to gossip. What you have was obviously meant for you, John. Sexual pleasure is supposed to be a gift, not a goal, unless you have some serious cash. Then you may have a chance. Are you rich, John?" Stacy asked.

"No, not really. But I do have some pretty good investments here and there that one day may bring me a fortune. But enough about me. What about you, Sheila? What are you looking for in a man? If you don't mind me asking?"

"Well..."

"Bet I know what you want," John said.

"And what is that?" Stacy asked.

Stacy slammed the phone down after she heard his response and ran into the bathroom to throw up.

For the next couple of weeks the Medical Insurance Center was hectic. It was as if the whole building was under attack. The workload was the heaviest in months because a sister company had shut down due to cutbacks, and all their records and client reports had to be transferred. All the hubbub made it impossible to determine whether strange faces belonged to legitimate transporters of files and equipment or to outsiders who saw the activity as an opportunity to perpetrate whatever mischief they wished. Conscientious supervisors like Fred Wilson cautioned female workers to be extra careful and to seek escorts when they left late.

"Damn!" Lesa exclaimed as she wiped her forehead with a handkerchief. "They got us working like a bunch of real nervous racehorses around here."

"Girl, tell me about it. I'm so tired, I could pass out right here on the spot if I wasn't so edgy," Stacy said. She attached rows and rows of labels of new clients to folders while Lesa sorted and filed.

"I gotta good mind to fall out just so that I can go home. They ain't paying me nearly enough to make me sweat like this." Lesa unbuttoned three buttons on her blouse, just barely enough to reveal her beige cleavage underneath. "Stacy, did you ever take that job I told you about a week ago?" Lesa asked.

"What?" Stacy asked. She was searching her desk for the small desk fan she had bought at a yard sale.

"That job. Remember? You know, the one you had an interview for."

Stacy found the fan, attached it to the corner of her desk, and turned it on high.

"Girl, don't mention it," Stacy said, as she continued to stick labels on manila file folders.

"So, you didn't take it, huh?" Lesa asked.

"Let me tell you about that job," Stacy said, with a strange look on her face.

"What happened?" Lesa asked.

"That job," Stacy lowered her voice. "That job was nothing more than a telemarketing job for 1-900-HOT-SEXX!" she said with her hand up against the side of her mouth as she whispered.

"1-900-HOT-SEXX!" Lesa said loudly.

"Sheww. Don't tell the whole damn office," Stacy said. She smacked Lesa on her arm.

"Sorry. Are you telling me they offered you a job as a telephone sex operator?" Lesa laughed.

"Girl, you should have heard some of the things these

men were saying on the phone. The first caller made me throw up," Stacy explained. "They really can talk some crap."

"But I thought the idea was for you to get them heated up?" Lesa asked.

"Well, it went both ways. But after throwing up a couple of times I finally got it under control," Stacy said.

"So, are you going to quit?" Lesa asked.

"Are you crazy? I got my first check already, and it's not bad."

"Tell me some of the stuff you'd be saying," Lesa said.

"Hell no!" Stacy walked back to her desk. "It's bad enough I gotta talk that mess on the phone. After a while you get a horrendous headache. And besides, I get paid to talk like that. Are you gonna pay me?" Stacy said to Lesa seriously.

"Who? Shucks. Sometimes I feel like asking somebody to talk trash to me. Having sex with Tony is like not having any at all. He's zigging when he should be zagging," Lesa confessed.

"I can't believe it. You're complaining? Not you. I thought sex was your strong suit. But I suppose everybody has problems in the bedroom," Stacy replied.

"Sometimes when Tony and I make love, he doesn't know how to. He gets in it and starts pumping all fast and wild." Lesa simulated Tony's movements. "Girl, I'm serious. There have been a couple of times I had to tell him to just stop."

"Maybe he's just trying to get it over with so he can go to sleep," Stacy said.

"Sleep! I'm the one he's putting to sleep. I make sure he gets his, for whatever it's worth. I hate to be cheated out of a nut. That'll only make me start looking elsewhere," Lesa said as she put away several files.

"Well, you can bet one thing; I'm only doing this phone thing until I can save up enough money to move my babies into a better place and get away from those junkies around my way. I refuse to raise my kids in a neighborhood where we're killing each other on a daily basis," Stacy said adamantly.

"Well, I tell you this. I just may check this one guy out I met at the market the other day. He looks like he can really rock this thang right," Lesa said with a sly grin.

"What about Tony?" Stacy asked.

"Please. He has really been showing his ass here lately. Coming in later and later every night. But that's all right. Sooner or later he's gonna come home to an empty house."

"Just be careful, girl. Don't let what Tony's doing out there in the streets pull you down with him," Stacy said to her friend.

"So, Rachel, you never said how Stanley liked the new curtains you bought," Mattie said. Rachel sat silently as she proceeded to calculate insurance figures on the PC.

"Rachel," Mattie called out.

Rachel jerked her head as she turned in Mattie's direction.

"I'm sorry, Mattie. Did you say something?" Her mind was definitely preoccupied.

"What's the matter? You seem out of it today. Is there anything bothering you?" Mattie asked.

"No, I'm fine. I can't seem to get from under all these forms, that's all." The entire morning Rachel threw herself into her work.

"How did Stanley like the curtains? Did you put them up when you got home?"

"No, I didn't. I thought I would wait until the weekend to put them up," Rachel said with her eyes cast down.

"Don't try to do 'em all in one day. Save some for the next day and the next," Mattie said. She tried to get a smile out of Rachel, but to no avail. Her little humor did not work. All Rachel did was excuse herself to go to the ladies' room.

Mattie wasn't sure what was going on, but she knew Rachel had more than a heavy workload on her mind. Maybe the unsolved rape and the odd happenings were getting to her, now that she was working later hours.

Chapter Five

Later that evening at her apartment, Lesa was in the kitchen preparing a little something for dinner. Although she had a flair for cooking, she never went beyond frozen dinners because there was no one there to eat her meals. For the last couple of months, Lesa had been eating alone. She couldn't remember the last time she and Tony sat down at the table together and had a decent meal. With him, his business always came first. So it was dinner alone as usual.

Lesa went to sit down just as her doorbell rang. She went to the door in a pair of peach-colored cut-off shorts and a black bralike top that barely harnessed her medium-sized breasts. She opened the door and found Kris standing at the threshold.

"How did you find me?" she asked while placing one hand on her hip and the other across the doorway.

"Does it matter? You're here, aren't you?" Kris said, not taking his eyes off her. To him, Lesa had already become more than just an assignment. He found her very intriguing. She had a gentleness about her that she tried very hard to hide. He suspected the hard exterior Lesa tried to portray was just a facade.

"Aren't you going to invite me in?" he asked.

"Why should I? I make it a rule never to let uninvited guests into my house." Lesa refused to budge. But he did look good in his Guess jeans and tight white T-shirt, she thought.

"Will this get me in?" Kris whipped a bouquet of long-stemmed roses and a bottle of wine from behind his back.

In her mind, Lesa couldn't turn him away now. No sense in wasting a good bottle of wine, she thought. "Come in," she said as she moved aside.

Kris walked in and nonchalantly scoped out the two-bedroom condo.

"You definitely have excellent taste," he said as he stood in the roomy living room observing the African art collection and paintings of African ancestors on the beige walls. Lesa was in style from the clothes she wore to the decor of her house. It was evident that she knew how to spend money and where. Her taste was very expensive. She even had an eye for men.

"Wow! This place is sharp. I bet you've spent a lot of time and money for this art." Kris looked on in awe. The closest he'd ever come to Italian and high-priced art was in a magazine. He was curious to know how Lesa would explain such luxuries.

"I try to catch a sale when I can," she said from the kitchen.

There were family pictures sitting on top of the fireplace mantel.

"Is this your family?" he asked as he got a closer look. Lesa was in the kitchen. She wrapped up her dinner so it would not get cold sitting out. She then returned to the living room with two wineglasses.

"Yeah. That's the whole Gains crew." She sat down beside Kris on her ivory leather sofa.

"I can see where you get your good looks from. Your mother is very beautiful," he complimented.

"Yeah, well, some people see it as a blessing, but I see it as a curse at times," Lesa said bitterly.

"Sounds like you know from experience," he said. Lesa handed him the corkscrew and wine bottle.

"Boy, do I. My mother let her good looks control her

LOVE'S DECEPTIONS

life. After she and my father got married, mommy dearest found it difficult to be committed to just one man," she said, painfully reminiscing about the past. "I can remember like it was yesterday. Mommy would always call to my father's job to check up on him, to see what time he was getting off or if he had to work at another job at night. And when she found out that he wouldn't be home until midnight or early the next morning, she would meet her other men friends at some motel," Lesa said, as a knot suddenly lodged in her throat.

"Are your parents still together?" Kris asked.

"Please. With my father's one-hundred-and-one jobs, my mother was in heaven. She not only drained him dry, but when she couldn't get any more money out of the old man, she packed and split." Lesa sipped the red wine.

"How did that make you feel?" Kris asked, seeing the old emotional wounds of Lesa's childhood painfully surface.

"I was mad at first at my father. But I soon realized that it wasn't my father's fault for my mother leaving us. But it was a fact that no matter how many jobs Daddy had, Mommy was never satisfied. Not with him, not with herself. I guess she couldn't face the reality that somebody could love her so much that he would sacrifice his own freedom and needs to keep her happy," Lesa said, as tears formed in her cool green eyes. Lesa usually lived only in the present because thinking about her girlhood was a real downer and she left the future to take care of itself. In those rare moments when she was introspective, she knew that the kind of relationships that she chose probably grew out of her feelings about her parents' marriage. The only kind of "permanent" relationship she had seen up close hadn't worked, and her solution so far had been to avoid real commitment, simply "to go along for the ride."

"Have you seen your mother since then?"

"No. And I don't care to, either. She left us. It should

be her who should be wanting to see her family," she said angrily.

"Do you miss her?" Kris continued to ask.

Lesa took in a big whiff of air. "Of course I do. She's still my mother," she said. "But enough about my depressing past. You still haven't answered my question. How did you find me?" she asked.

Kris sat back on the sofa and gazed into her eyes.

"You wouldn't believe me if I told you," he said with a mysterious smile.

"Try me."

"What if I said I followed you home one day?"

"I don't believe you." Lesa laughed.

"You see, I said you wouldn't believe me," Kris said.

"Well, I'm glad you found me," Lesa said, realizing after the fact what she had said. Why did I say that? I don't want him to think that I was hoping he would find me. I certainly don't want him to think I was hard up for some company, Lesa thought.

"So you're not upset that I stopped by then?" he asked. He poured himself another glass of wine.

"I didn't say . . ." Lesa started to say.

"I know what you said. But what you say and what you feel are two different things," Kris said.

He thinks he knows everything, Lesa thought.

"I was just about to sit down and have dinner," she said, trying to get from under the spell he had cast on her. "There's enough for two. Would you care to join me?"

"Sure, if it's not too much of a problem," Kris said. He followed her.

"It's no problem at all. I hope you like seafood." She placed another plate at the dining room table. Kris pulled out a chair and sat down.

"This sure looks delicious. Do you cook like this for your man every night?" Kris asked.

"How did you know I had a man?" Lesa asked. She caught Kris off guard.

"Uh, I just assumed you had to have somebody, considering you are a good cook and as beautiful as you are. Why shouldn't you?" he asked.

Lesa refused to answer for a minute. For a brief second she felt that there was more to him than met the eye. But she wasn't about to let her feelings get in the way of such a pleasant visit.

"For your information there is somebody, but that still doesn't give you any reason to assume anything," Lesa said, as she set the record straight.

"Well, it just makes me a little crazy when I see a beautiful woman not being appreciated." He took a forkful of Mrs. Paul's Seafood Newburg.

"You really think you have the answer to everything, don't you?" Lesa asked Kris with a slight attitude.

"Well . . ."

"Well, you don't. Who are you to come off like you're God's answer to women? Oh, yeah, you may be fine and everything like that, but you're no different than the rest of those dogs out here. Always itching and looking for a place to scratch," Lesa said.

"Hold up! Hold up! You come on strong when threatened by a man, don't you think?" Kris said.

"Strong!" Lesa laughed. "You didn't find me on your doorstep, did you?" For the first time she felt threatened by Kris's demeanor and assertiveness. She felt she could not control him as she could all the others. "But since you think you have all the answers, why don't you just tell me what I'm thinking then," Lesa said. She put her fork down and sat back in her chair waiting for a response from Kris.

"I'll tell you what I think. I think you're tired of eating alone for one thing. I think you need to be loved the way a woman should be loved. Not with flowers or candy or expensive gifts. You need to be held and caressed. I believe your friend gives you these nice things because he's not here to supply you with what you really need," Kris said.

"And I guess you know what that is?" Lesa asked.

"You need a real man, Lesa Gains. A man who is going to take you into his arms," Kris got out of his chair and walked over to her, "and do this." He pulled Lesa out of her chair and kissed her passionately.

Across town a taxi pulled up in front of Hilda Carr's house. Stacy got out with an armful of shopping bags. She paid the driver and walked up the flower-trimmed sidewalk. Anxious to see the beautiful new clothes on her sons, she never noticed that a man was slouched against the light pole across the street and that he obviously had intense interest in her.

"Mommy! Mommy!" Tyron yelled happily as his mother walked through the door.

"What in the world?" Stacy's mother said as she rushed from the kitchen into the living room. Stacy could smell the aroma of fried fish, potatoes, and corn bread before she got inside the house. Friday was always fish day at her mother's house.

"Hey, Mama. I tried calling you earlier to let you know that I would be a little late. I had to pick up the kids' clothes that I had on layaway," Stacy said.

"I was just about to sit the boys down to supper. What do you have in those bags?" Hilda asked. She didn't know what sort of part-time job Stacy had, but she did know that her daughter had been spending an awful lot of money for the past several weeks.

"You sure have been spending a lot of money here lately. I bet you've not once thought about tithing some of the money, have you?" she asked Stacy, who was pulling out outfit after outfit for her kids.

"Ma, I give enough to Uncle Sam. Not this time; this time I'm spending for my kids," Stacy said, not once raising her head. She was feeling better than she had felt in a long time. It felt good to be able to spend money without worrying about an unpaid bill or skimping here and saving there. This was a long time coming, and she spared no expense.

"You never said what type of work you're doing on this part-time job," her mother said curiously.

"Yes, I did. Don't you remember?" Stacy knew she had not told her mother about anything, and she wasn't planning on telling her either. She couldn't look her in the face and tell that bald-faced lie. When I was little, I could never tell my mother a lie and get away with it. Somehow she could always tell when I was lying, Stacy thought. For the life of me, I couldn't see how she did it. But now was no time to find out.

"Well, I can't remember you saying anything to me about it. The only thing I heard you say was that you was doing it from your place." Hilda stood with her hands in her apron pockets.

"Perfect fit," Stacy said as she tried one of the outfits on Terrence. At a year old, Terrence was already in a size three and growing. "I can see it now. The doctor is going to put your little fat tail on a diet," she said, bouncing the baby on her knees as slobber ran down her arm.

"Do you hear me talking to you, girl?" Hilda asked.

"I'm sorry, Mama. What did you say?" Stacy rose to her feet and twirled Terrence around in the air, while Tyron modeled and posed in his spanking new red suspenders, blue dress pants, and white shirt.

"What sort of job you got that's making you spend money like you're some long distant relative to the Rockefellers?"

"Why are you getting an attitude? Gosh! You complained when I didn't have enough money, and now you're complaining still when I have too much money," Stacy said. She still refused to look her mother in the eye.

"I'm not complaining. I just asked you a simple question. It's you who's getting an attitude," Hilda said. She didn't want to make Stacy angry, although it didn't take much. "Maybe your father can get it out of you because

I'm tired of talking." Hilda had started to walk back into the kitchen when Stacy finally spoke up.

"It's a telemarketing job. Now, are you satisfied?"

"Now was that hard? That was all you had to say," Hilda said.

"Yeah, but you act like I should be telling you everything I do. This is my life, and these are my children. I do what I have to do to provide for them. I don't like asking you and Daddy for money all the time. Don't you think I want to stand on my own two feet for once?" Stacy asked assertively.

"I know that, Stacy. But I just worry about the children. They need someone to look after them just like you do. Is that so wrong? We only try to do what's best for you," her mother said.

"Don't worry, I'm their mother. I know what's best for them." Stacy threw the clothes back into the bags.

"Oh, sure," Hilda said under her breath. "Are you gonna wait until the kids get something hot in their stomachs?" she asked Stacy, who was preparing to leave.

"No, I can't. Just wrap something up for them and I'll take it home. I have a lot to do before it gets too late." The truth was that she didn't want to miss one call from her clients.

Hilda packed two healthy bags of hot food. She even put three slices of fresh-baked apple pie in as well. She bent down and grabbed Tyron in her soft pudgy arms and gave him a big hug and a kiss. Then she did the same to little Terrence.

Stacy grabbed the bags in one hand, held Terrence in the other, and asked Tyron to hold on to her skirt as they walked out the door.

At the Hotel Del Coronado, Tony and two of his business partners got together for a private meeting. When a knock sounded at the door of their suite, Buster, Tony's right-hand man, got up and answered it.

"Is Tony here?" a female voice asked at the front room.

"Yeah. Who wants to know?" Buster asked in a deep baritone voice. He blocked the entrance with his football-player physique.

"It's okay, Buster man. Let her in," Tony said, sitting with two of his other sidekicks playing a card game of spades.

The young woman walked straight up to Tony and laid a hot kiss on his lips.

"Hey, baby. Whatcha' got for me?" Tony palmed her full breast.

"I got two in Room 730 who want some cocaine. And I got one in 650 who wants an ounce of weed." She pulled out a roll of money stuffed inside her blue stocking underneath her uniform.

Buster looked on as the woman pulled up her dress and revealed her long white thigh. She had on a pink garter belt that secured her blue stockings in place. Tony went into the back bedroom and came out with two separate sandwich bags. He placed the drugs in brown paper bags.

"Here you go, my pet. Tell your friends it's good doing business with them, and come again." Tony gave her a sly grin. "Oh, yeah, there's a little something for you, too, baby," he said to her. Tony pulled a wad of bills from his pocket, peeled off three hundred-dollar bills and gave them to her.

"Go buy yourself something pretty," he said. He took her face into his smooth hands and kissed her tenderly.

"Will you be needing any loving tonight, baby?" The woman purred like a kitten.

"Naw, baby. Don't call me, I'll call you." Tony showed his lady friend to the door and smacked her on her butt.

Now why can't Lesa be like that, he wondered. Lesa's got a mouth and just a few too many smarts. Maybe it oughta be 'bye time, one way or 'nother. "Buster, my man, let's rap."

Chapter Six

"Mama, is there anything else you need me to do before I go home?" Stanley asked his mother. This was the weekend he spent time doing little odd jobs around his mother's house, since she had no other man in her life except for Reggie and himself. Their mother, Gertrude, was the sort of woman who believed in spoiling her sons. She always stood firm on the cliche, "Boys will be boys." It didn't matter how old they were. That's why she spoiled her sons rotten, especially Stanley. He was always her favorite because he looked more like his father. When Stanley and Reggie were young, Gertrude made sure that her boys wanted for nothing. She really made sure that Stanley had the best her money would buy. As for Reggie, he was satisfied with just about anything. Gertrude's spoiling lasted even when the boys became men. Gertrude thrived on going that extra mile for Stanley. Even today, she still tried to run his life and his affairs. Stanley would get away with murder, if his mother had anything to say about it. But there was one thing that Gertrude was not going to let him get away with, and that was Benita's son, Malcolm. There had been a rumor that Stanley was the father, and the same rumor speculated that Stanley and Benita would get back together. Gertrude would do anything to see her son together with the woman she liked.

"Baby, let your mama think now. There was something else I needed done," she said, looking like she was in deep thought. Stanley knew how much Gertrude liked to show him off to her friends. She would tell all those snooty women how brilliant and rich Stanley was, when the truth was, he hardly had two pennies to rub together. If it weren't for Rachel putting her life and future plans on hold to help support him, Stanley would lose everything.

"Well, if that's it, I'd best be getting home," Stanley said. He picked up his toolbox.

"What's the rush, son? Stay and have dinner with your poor old mother. None of you boys have any time for your mother nowadays. It's always rush, rush, rush." Gertrude knew just how to play on his feelings.

"Mama, what did I tell you about calling yourself old. You're not old; in fact, you don't look a day past forty-five," Stanley said, making his mother blush like he always did when she started talking crazy. Truth was, Stanley was hoping that she still had his name as the beneficiary for the house, if anything should happen to her. Gertrude always threatened to take his name off and put Reggie's on whenever Stanley disappointed her in some foolish way.

"You know, now, when my time comes I want to make sure you boys have everything you need. I hope the good Lord takes me in my sleep." Gertrude continued her little ploy.

"Okay, Mama, I'll stay for dinner." Stanley dropped his toolbox where he had found it.

"Good! Now go upstairs and wash your hands," she said in a happier mood.

"Just let me call Rachel to tell her I won't be home just yet. She gets upset when she cooks, and there's no one there to eat it," Stanley said, going to the phone.

"Call her later. She knows you come over here every other weekend to see me. I'm your mother," Gertrude said.

"Mama, don't start with that again," Stanley said with the phone in his hand. Just then his mother's doorbell rang.

"Oh, look, Stanley. Look who's here. What a coincidence!" Gertrude stood at the kitchen door.

Stanley heard the phone ring on the other end of the line, but hung up when he saw Benita standing in the doorway. He was stuck. There was no way his mother was going to let him go now. And in the back of his mind, Stanley wasn't sure if he wanted to go after casting his eyes upon his high-school sweetheart.

"Come in, honey, make yourself at home," Gertrude said, practically pushing Benita in Stanley's direction. "Son, look, she brought little Malcolm along. I'm gonna have to stop calling him little. He's growing up to be a very handsome young man." Gertrude pulled at Malcolm's cheeks.

"Hello, Stanley. It's good to see you," Benita said. Stanley was held by her beauty, as always. Although he saw her from time to time leaving work or just passing her as they drove by, Stanley could see his mother written all over this coincidence. He tried to figure out why he and Benita broke up in the first place. She was definitely going places; in fact as one of the top attorneys in California, Benita had arrived.

Damn! What was I thinking about when I let this woman go? I must have been out of my mind, Stanley thought, chastising himself privately.

"I've been making it. You really look good, Nita," Stanley said as his mother looked on from a distance. Nothing could make her happier than to see Stanley with the woman she thought was right for him.

"Come with me, Malcolm. I got something real exciting to show you." Gertrude took Malcolm into the den, so Stanley and Benita could rekindle what she thought was love.

Stanley and Benita were so caught up in each other's eyes that they didn't notice they were finally alone. They both looked at each other trying to read each other's thoughts and feelings.

"How is everything really, Nita?" Stanley asked.

"I'm fine," she said, shifting her eyes away from his. After all these years, he still calls me by my pet name. It always sounded good when he said it. And even after those long, hot summer nights we spent together in my bed, I could still hear Stanley's voice echoing in my head.

"I heard you say you were fine, but for some strange reason I find it hard to believe." Stanley watched her every move.

"I see you haven't lost your touch." Benita allowed a smile to escape from her face.

Stanley could always tell if she was hiding something behind those eyes of hers. They were the same eyes that captivated him the first time he saw her as she tried to hail a cab to the high school they attended. She hadn't lost her sex appeal, Stanley thought, as his eyes danced to the rhythm of her body.

"I heard that you and Fish are separated. It seems like everybody we know is going through something or another." Stanley was talking about his own marriage. He rolled his eyes up toward the ceiling, as if to hide his own discontentment.

"News travels fast when it's somebody else's business," Benita said sharply.

"I'm sorry. I just assumed," Stanley said.

"Don't apologize. It should be me apologizing. It's been hard as hell trying to keep up this front. I don't know if I can do it anymore." Benita tried to hold back the tears that had welled in her eyes.

Stanley also had to fight his own feelings. He desperately wanted to rush over and grab Nita in his arms and squeeze all the hurt away, like he used to do. But all he could see was Rachel's face in front of him.

Benita saw the longing in Stanley's eyes as he held back his feelings toward her. She was praying that he would set aside his fears and hold her until the world went away, just like he used to a long time ago.

"Did you receive the birthday gift I sent you after New Year's Day?" she asked.

"Yes, I did. Thank you. But of course you know I could not take it home with me, with Rachel being there and all," he said. Stanley shrugged his broad shoulders like a big kid.

Hell, Benita thought, I didn't even ask about his wife. He must think I'm being real inconsiderate.

"How is Rachel, by the way?" she said, literally forcing the name out of her mouth. Benita still resented the fact that Rachel ended up marrying the man she was supposed to marry.

"Well, you know. Like I said before, we all have our problems. Rachel and I are going through some tough times as well," Stanley said. "But it's not going to beat me down like some of these other brothers are allowing to happen. Some of us are getting the worst end of a relationship. Women complaining about what we're not doing, what we should be doing," he babbled on, something he did quite often when he couldn't put his feelings into words.

"I'm sorry to hear that," Benita said falsely.

"But, whatever," he said, exhausting himself.

"It's good to see you," Benita said, smiling.

"Let's go out here onto the sunporch." Stanley escorted Benita to another part of his mother's house.

Gertrude and Malcolm were in her den laughing and talking.

"Mrs. Grier," Malcolm began.

"Listen to me. Whenever you see me, I want you to call me Grandma. Okay?" she insisted.

"Does that mean I have two grandmothers?" he asked, looking up at Gertrude with innocent eyes. "Isn't my daddy's mother my grandmother, too?" he asked.

"Yes. But I feel like I'm your grandmother, too. You look so much like my son Stanley. He could pass for your father; you look so much like him." Gertrude hoped she had planted the idea in Malcolm's head that Stanley could also be his father.

"Did your mother ever tell you about her relationship

with Stanley? They were very much in love a long time ago." Gertrude took her hand and rubbed Malcolm's curly hair.

"No, ma'am," he said, unconcerned. He was too busy matching up all the different coins she had collected over the years as a hobby.

"Isn't Fish my daddy, too?" Malcolm asked. He called his father by his first name because Fish told him to.

"Sure he is, and don't you forget it. But just keep in mind that when one daddy doesn't work out, you have another daddy waiting to love you even more." Gertrude placed her hand on Malcolm's face and captured his attention. "No one must know what we talked about in here today. Okay? This means we have to shake a special handshake to seal our secret," Gertrude said as she held her hand out to Malcolm. They shook a "special" handshake and then Gertrude gave him a big hug.

Back on the sunporch Stanley and Benita were searching for the truth to their ancient love affair and their present dilemma.

"I know this is kind of late to be asking this, Nita," Stanley said as he looked out beyond the flower-filled lawn. "Is it true that there may be a possibility that Malcolm could be my son?"

Oh, Lord, I knew it was going to come out sooner or later. Why does it have to be now? Benita thought.

"What does it matter now? You're happily married with your own family." She looked away.

"But that's not what I asked you, Nita. I asked you, is Malcolm my son?" Stanley reiterated and gently grabbed her shoulders and turned her in his direction.

"Why now, Stanley? Why, after all these years do you ask now?" she said, pulling away from his grasp. If I tell him the truth, what guarantee do I have that he will want to see me again? Benita thought. She knew Fish had started the rumor. After they split, he was bitter and angry. Fish had the notion that Benita and Stanley somehow still had a thing for each other. But if she told Stanley the truth, would it change anything? Could they start where they both left off?

"Stanley, I don't see what good it would do, telling you something that should have been said a long time ago. Malcolm has a father."

"Nita, why won't you tell me the truth? I can't go on living with myself knowing I got another son to support. It's not fair to Malcolm, and it's certainly not fair to you," Stanley said, as his emotions took control.

"Look, Stanley, let's just drop it. Let's just continue to live our lives the way we have been doing. I shouldn't have come over here." She attempted to walk into the next room.

"Nita, don't do this." Stanley stopped her from walking away. "What type of man would I be if I disowned my own flesh and blood? How would that look to everybody?"

"I don't know. How would you feel if it turned out that he wasn't your son? Would that change the way we feel about each other? Or would it be a load off your mind?" she asked, staring into his eyes. She could see the relief float away from his face.

"If that was the case, I would jump for joy right here." Although he's a good-looking kid, there's no way in hell I could afford to support him, Stanley thought. "Could you handle knowing that you could possibly be the parent of a child you never knew existed? Wouldn't you want to find out if that was true?" he asked.

"What do you want me to say—no, he's not your son?" Benita was angry.

"That would be a start," Stanley replied.

"Okay, no. You only have one son, and that's Nicky," she said coldly. Stanley didn't know whether he should believe her or not. He felt no closer to the truth than when he first heard the rumor.

"Whatever happened between us, Nita?" he asked emotionally.

LOVE'S DECEPTIONS

"Maybe we loved each other too much to ruin each other's lives," Benita said before they embraced.

As the sunshine poured through the stained-glass windows, Gertrude walked through the adjoining rooms with Malcolm and found Stanley and Benita holding each other lovingly.

"It won't be long now, Malcolm. It's just a matter of time now before the truth is told." Gertrude snuggled Malcolm's body against her hip and looked on with great hope.

Chapter Seven

Mattie was in her backyard clearing out the vegetable garden. She had found out a long time ago that working in the earth was a good time for sorting out your thoughts. There was a lot from work to ponder—the police were no closer to identifying the rapist and strangers were still coming and going. And was somebody stalking Stacy? She was troubled by what Stacy had confided to her.

Stacy wasn't the sort to imagine that somebody was watching her or exaggerate the number of times callers hung up as soon as she answered the phone. Those children being so young made her especially vulnerable, an easy victim, you might say. Mattie was glad Stacy had come to her and that she had urged extra caution. And what about Fred? Even though he hadn't said anything to her, you could tell that he lacked his usual easygoing manner at work. She was on her knees rooting and digging and thinking, while her all-time favorite cassette, *The Best of Nancy Wilson,* played. Mattie had prepared for a long session in the garden by stuffing a recent cassette of her idol inside her smock top pocket. Clearing out the garden and flower beds and thinking over the previous week was a weekend ritual for Mattie, who thrived on Mother Nature's beauty. It always made her feel good when she could see something she created prosper in front of her eyes. She knew homegrown vegetables and fruits tasted better than the ones at the market. In fact, Mattie had a problem when it came to eating something when she didn't know who or where it came from. Singing above her normal voice range this morning, Mattie didn't notice the figure sneaking quietly up behind her.

"Boo!" he yelled, grabbing Mattie by her thirty-inch waist.

"Fred! I'm gonna kill you!" She turned around with her eyes bulging halfway out of her head. "Whatcha trying to do? Give me a heart attack?" Mattie asked, as her hand went up to her chest as if to slow her heart down.

Fred Wilson was enjoying the prank more than Mattie because he liked touching and feeling her. "Mattie, come on. You don't scare easy. What man could resist touching such a voluptuous woman like you?" Fred asked as his eyes sparkled brighter than the sun in the sky.

"You mean I used to not scare easy. What are you doing out this way bright and early this morning? I know you're not just coming from the office," she said as Fred helped her to her feet.

"As a matter of fact I am. But before you get on me about being a workaholic, I had to get some important papers to my attorney," Fred said as he observed the good job Mattie had done on the garden.

"Anything serious?" Mattie asked, trying to find out what he had to see his lawyer about.

"No. It's just a routine check about my will, that's all. Nothing to worry about."

"Whenever you say something is not important, it usually is," she said, taking one last look over her work. "Would you care for a tall glass of lemonade?"

"That would be very nice." Fred followed Mattie up to the house like a lost puppy. He had an undying attraction toward Mattie and he knew she liked him, but didn't dare to admit it. Mattie reminded him a lot of his late wife, Millie, an old-fashioned woman who liked to make and do things with her hands, too. The one thing Fred was more concerned with was whether Mattie could cook as well as his Millie had.

"It's nice and cold. I got up early this morning and cut up fresh lemons." Mattie reached into the cabinet and pulled down two glasses. Fred never took his eyes off her. Mattie was pleasingly plump like somebody's grandmother, with full breasts, broad hips, and hair cut in layers that sat perfectly on her head.

"Here we are." She poured the lemon-pulped drink into the glasses.

"Mattie, you sure do make a man feel welcome in your house. I can't understand why you don't have a man around to enjoy all this good stuff," Fred said between sips of lemonade.

"Fred, what are you talking about?" She waved her hand at him as if to shoo him away like an insect.

"Mattie, you're the prettiest woman I've ever seen." He caused Mattie to blush.

"Go on away from here, man. You're just saying that stuff." Mattie found it hard to keep the smile from her face. "And what about you, Fred? Why aren't you charming the pants off of some woman?"

"That's just it. I don't want just any woman at my age. I want somebody who's not afraid of growing old, and not afraid to live a little on edge," he said as Mattie got up and took their glasses to the sink and ran water into them.

"So, what you're looking for is somebody who's youthful, spontaneous, but old enough to soak their teeth in a glass of Efferdent every night as well," Mattie said jokingly.

Since the death of Charles, Fred was the only man she felt comfortable and open around. He let her feel like herself.

Fred was fifty-five years old, three years older than Mattie. But he took care to keep his weight down by working out at the gym. He had stopped smoking two years ago. One good thing about Fred that Mattie found very surprising was that he still had his own hair. Men that she met tended to go bald before they reached their fiftieth birthday. Fred still had all of his hair, even if it was gray.

"That's what I love about you, Mattie Thompson. You know when to laugh at life," Fred said, walking over to where she stood near the kitchen sink. "I want a woman who's full of life, yet comfortable with her maturity. And that's you." He pulled Mattie into his strong arms and kissed her tenderly.

"Fred!" Mattie said in shock.

"What's the matter, woman? You don't know when a man is attracted to you?" Fred asked before Mattie took it upon herself to plant a serious kiss back on him.

On Harbor Drive and Broadway, at the Harbor Pier, *Saradina,* a thirty-two-foot sailboat, sat nestled between two larger sailboats. Kris had invited Lesa aboard for brunch.

"After that little incident last week, I wasn't sure if you'd ever want to talk to me again," he said as he and Lesa sat at a small table inside the cabin. The table was garnished with lavish slices of passion fruit, honeydew melon, and other delectable fruits.

"I wasn't sure if I wanted to see you, either." Lesa looked at him as she ate the delicious array of edibles. "You tend to take a lot for granted. Not to mention all the questions you ask that are none of your business," she said as she sipped on a glass of vintage white wine.

"And for that, I apologize again. Do you accept my apology?" Kris gazed into her eyes.

"Only if I can have another glass of wine." Lesa accepted his apology with a smile. Kris refilled not only her glass, but his as well.

"You never said what it is that you do for a living. For someone who can afford such an expensive boat, you've got to be doing quite well. And where did you come up with such a sexy name for it? I suspect there is or there was a special lady in your life," Lesa said as she gave him one of her seductive glances. "Wherever she is, I'm sure she's kicking herself right now," Lesa finished as she observed her surroundings.

Kris just smiled, enthralled by her refreshing, untamed spirit and her gift for gab. He considered what response he might make that would allow his professional and personal lives to coexist.

"Didn't I tell you?" He placed the bottle of 1964 White Zinfandel back into the ice bucket.

"No, you didn't. Is it some big secret or something?" Lesa sucked on a big, red strawberry.

"What I do requires confidentiality and trust," he said very intensely. "Can I trust you, Lesa?" Kris asked. His sudden change of heart took Lesa by surprise. "I'm a . . ." he began to say.

"Wait!" Lesa shouted. "I don't wanna know. If it's something heavy, Kris, I don't wanna know."

"Are you sure? I like to lay all the cards on the table. But if it makes you uncomfortable . . ."

"Let's get something straight. If for any reason I thought you were perpetrating some scheme or if you were trying to be someone you're not," she said on a more serious note, "you wouldn't have to worry about seeing me ever again."

Disturbed by this passionate response, Kris quietly got up and went over and picked up a camera.

"Don't say that. Why talk about ending something when it's just starting?" He focused and took a picture of Lesa, who sat motionlessly at the table. "Smile." He took another, then another.

"Okay, it's my turn. Take off your shirt." Lesa got up and took the camera out of his hands.

"Why should I take off my shirt? You didn't take off anything," Kris said.

"You didn't ask." Lesa took aim and clicked.

Kris reached over and picked up the remote control to his stereo and pushed the "Play" button to his compact disc. The light flashed "Playing" and then the sounds of the legendary John Coltrane began to fill the small sleeping quarters with sultry jazz.

Lesa looked on as Kris slowly pulled his white cotton Oxford shirt over his head. The black chest hairs seemed to pop out uncontrollably. Kris tossed the shirt onto the medium-sized bed that extended out from the corner wall. She tried to slow down her excited heart as she took a deep breath.

"Is this what you want to see?" Kris stood in front of her in his jeans that seemed to be molded to his body. She tried to keep a steady hand, but just the sight of Kris's hard, bulging biceps shook her up.

"Yeah, just like that." She snapped picture after picture. Kris walked closer and closer to where she stood. When he was close enough to her, he slowly took the camera down from her face.

"I want us to take a picture together," he said in a low deep voice. He went over to the closet and pulled out the camera's tripod and attached the camera on top of it.

Oh, God. I don't think I'm ready for this, Lesa thought. Or am I? She questioned her own feelings for the first time. Kris removed her silk fuchsia jacket and revealed the spaghetti-strapped white silk blouse that accented matching fuchsia shorts. He held the remote to the camera in his hand and snapped one picture as he partially undressed Lesa in the middle of the cabin.

"Does this excite you?" Kris asked, reaching up to remove the gold barrette that secured Lesa's reddish brown French roll. What could she say? His body touching hers, Lesa could easily melt into his huge arms. But she wanted to see just how far he was going to go. She had an idea, and she wanted to give him every opportunity to get there.

"Wait." She stalled his advances in order to control him.

"I see it's going to take a little more to get you warmed up." Kris stroked Lesa's lean, slender neck with his full lips. "Warm yet?" he whispered. He snapped another picture. His lips traveled down to her bare shoulders. Lesa felt her knees buckling. Damn, she thought. This was the first man who had ever made her weak in the knees; not even Tony had that ability.

Kris had worked his hands down to the buckle of her shorts and with one hand, he managed to get the belt unbuckled and the button to her shorts unbuttoned. By this time, Lesa was not only warm, she was like a teapot ready to sound off.

Sighs of pleasure escaped her mouth as Kris's hands finally made their way between her soft, hot thighs. Lesa could feel the hardness of Kris's erection pressing low and hard against her. The camera continued to click.

"I want to make love to you, Lesa, but I want to satisfy you sensuously before I satisfy you physically," Kris whispered into her ear. Lesa gave no indication that she even heard him. She was wrapped up in the rapture he had provided through his fingers and his wet tongue.

Minutes passed. Lesa's and Kris's naked bodies merged together as they both sat in a chair. Lesa mounted his erection and slowly rocked back and forth as Kris held on to her hips with the remote pressed against her butt. The camera continued to click as they both fell captive to their lustful passions.

Hours passed and the daylight soon became night. Lesa and Kris lay entwined in each other's arms.

"What are you doing next month?" he asked.

"Next month?" Lesa raised her head from his chest. "You mean to tell me that I'm not going to see you again until next month?" she asked in a high-pitched voice.

"No, I didn't mean it that way," Kris said as he laughed at her question. "Next month is Valentine's Day," he said. He took his hand and brushed her hair from her face.

"I was wondering if you would like to go sailing with me?" he asked.

"Sailing! Wow! I have never been sailing before," Lesa said. Her eyes sparkled with excitement.

"From now on, whatever you want to do, wherever you want to go, just tell me and we'll do it." He kissed her naturally plum-colored lips. Lesa felt like this was the only place on earth she ever wanted to be. Kris had supplied in one day the love, passion, and everything she had been longing for from Tony. All the excitement and attention she craved from her relationship with Tony, she found in the arms of another man.

"What's the matter? You seem as if you just remembered something awful."

"I almost forgot. I'm already involved with someone, remember?" she reminded him.

"You could have fooled me; you didn't make love like you were involved. Seemed to me this was exactly what you needed."

"Well, I'm sorry. You knew that when you met me. I can't drop one relationship and start another just like that," Lesa said, as she got up and went into the bathroom.

"You can't get out of a bad relationship for a better one? What kind of power does this guy have over you?" Kris asked, appreciating her nakedness.

"Don't you think I tried that, many times? But he just brushes it off. And then he goes out and buys me something real expensive," Lesa yelled from the bathroom.

"Well, money can't buy you love. It can only give you a lot of worries and friends you don't need," Kris replied. And surround you with people who are dangerous to you, he thought.

"What do you know about worries? It doesn't seem that you have anything to worry about." Lesa returned to the room and began to put her clothes on. "Look at you. You're living on a yacht. How many of us do you see living on a thirty-thousand-dollar vessel?"

"There's a lot you don't know about me," Kris said, beginning to worry because she was totally in the dark about the reason he had plotted to meet her. Now that he knew he wanted this desirable woman to be a part of his life permanently, he wondered if he would be able to make things right with her when the truth finally came out.

"And I would like to know more. I already know how good you are in bed," Lesa said as she bent over and licked his lips with her tongue. "But that doesn't make the man. Tell me something I don't know." Lesa looked into his dark eyes.

"What's the use in us getting into each other, when you can't decide what you want in a relationship? I already know what you want physically, but mentally I haven't a clue," Kris said. He was hesitant to trust her with the truth when she seemed so loyal to Tony. He had to be careful that he didn't let slip that he knew her other lover's identity.

"I owe this guy a lot. I just can't up and leave. Besides, it wouldn't be right," she said.

"Is it right to throw your life away? You're a beautiful and intelligent woman, Lesa. You do have a choice. Who is he? Do you want me to talk to him for you?" Kris asked, pretending he didn't know everything there was to know about Tony.

"No! He would freak out if he knew I was even considering leaving him. He'd probably want every last penny he spent on me back. And believe me, I don't have that kind of money." Lesa put on her clothes and put her hair back up the way she had it when she first arrived.

"What does he do? I'm sure you don't owe him that much. If it's money you're worried about, I have money," Kris said, hoping Lesa would confess the truth about Tony. If she does, then I'm going to chance trusting her with the truth about me, he thought. I don't want her to get hurt and I don't want to end any chance for a future together.

Lesa laughed. "You're really sweet. But even with all of this, baby, you still couldn't afford me." She grabbed her purse off the table and left Kris where he lay.

Chapter Eight

Rachel was at home waiting for Stanley to return from his brother's house. Reggie had called early in the morning asking for Stanley's help in placing a ceiling fan in the living room of his condo. Rachel had been waiting practically half the morning for Stanley's return, so they could go to the hardware store and buy wood to replace the wood he had broken away from the windowsill when he went on the curtain rampage two weeks earlier. She was about to call Reggie's house when a knock came at the kitchen door.

"Hello, I'm Malcolm. Is Mr. Stanley here?" Malcolm stood on the welcome mat at the threshold of the door. But to Rachel, this was definitely an unwelcome surprise. Rachel was speechless to find Benita's son, and possibly Stanley's illegitimate child, standing on her doorstep. *What is he doing here, and why all of a sudden does he just pop into our lives like this?* She soon snapped out of her trancelike stare and responded to Malcolm's question.

"No, he's not at home, Malcolm. Is there something I can do for you?" Rachel asked as she looked the boy over from head to toe. There was a slight resemblance to Stanley, but it was very little. This boy could have been anybody's. Benita was trying to pin this boy on Stanley. His facial features were strong, but the child's cheekbones were higher and more defined like Fish's. On the other hand, Malcolm's skin was the same toffee brown as Stanley's; whereas Fish's and Benita's complexions were much darker. Of course he did have that fine, naturally curly hair like Stan's, but what man didn't nowadays? Half the black men Rachel saw in California had a good grade of hair, whether it was coarse, curly, or processed curls like Fish's, with that Classy Curl mess that made his hair always look wet and stringy.

"What is that you're carrying?" Rachel asked the child.

"It's Mr. Stanley's toolbox. I was told to bring it over to him," Malcolm replied.

Rachel saw that the boy had lugged the big box on his mountain bike. She noticed the small beads of sweat trickling down from his temples, the same exact way Stanley sweats, she thought.

"And where did you get it?" Rachel asked, taking the box from his hands.

"Mrs. Gertrude asked me to bring it over. She said that Mr. Stanley called for it yesterday," Malcolm said as he wiped his face with his sweaty palm. Rachel couldn't bear to see the child suffer from the heat. She swallowed her pride for the moment and invited the boy in.

"Would you like some juice?" Rachel asked as she invited Malcolm to sit down at the kitchen table. Malcolm soon found his attention diverted to the plate of chocolate chip cookies on the kitchen counter. Rachel turned just in time to see his eyes light up with delight. "Or would you rather have some milk and cookies?" She went to the refrigerator and took out a gallon of milk and a glass from the dishwasher.

"Yes, ma'am!" he said with a wide grin. That's one thing he and Nicky have in common, she thought, as a smile enveloped her face.

Rachel closely observed her little guest as he ate the cookies and drank his milk. But as much as she hated to admit it, Benita had raised a fine boy. For the life of her, Rachel couldn't see how Fish could have produced such a handsome son. He wasn't the best-looking man. But whatever the story was behind Stanley, Malcolm, and Benita, Rachel was going to get to the bottom of it. Nine times out of ten, she suspected Gertrude would be at the end of it all.

Music by Allyson Williams was booming throughout Reggie's house. Other than his white '92 Jetta that he had ordered custom-made, the two-bedroom condo was Reggie's pride and joy. With that in mind, he was a nineties kind of man in every sense of the word. With his savvy, charismatic demeanor and his open-mindedness, he could practically change a person's way of thinking just by his powers of persuasion.

Reggie had been employed at the San Diego post office for the past three years. After taking a couple of management courses at the local university, he had been trying to get his own personal endeavors off the ground. Stanley's influence on him was the real reason he never married. Although Stanley and Rachel had been married for quite some time now, Reggie knew that their marriage hadn't been stable. His sister-in-law wasn't at all what Stanley had made her out to be. In fact, Reggie couldn't understand why Rachel still put up with his brother as long as she had. Even though Reggie and Stanley didn't have that close brother-to-brother relationship, there were times when Reggie wished Stanley would confide in him. But deep down Reggie knew that his dear old mother was partly to blame. He felt it wasn't his place to butt into his brother's family life. Stanley absolutely forbade it.

Both of them had been trying to put a white and gold ceiling fan up for the past hour, without much success.

"Reggie! Hold your end up straight," Stanley yelled as he tried to twist the screws into the ceiling, while Reggie was busy dancing to the music.

"Man, doesn't she have a great voice to go with those

thick, juicy lips of hers," Reggie said with his eyes closed as Allyson Williams's voice invaded his head.

"You gonna screw this fan up if you don't hold your side up!" Stanley demanded. "Besides, I've heard better."

"Man, you gotta learn to lighten up a little. All that anxiety you store up inside will kill you!"

"Reggie, that's all you think about. 'Lighten up, take it easy.' You think that's the cure for everything. Well, sorry to disappoint you, my brother, but that crap don't work in the real world. I betcha won't be saying that when you finally get hooked. Just wait. You'll be singing a new tune after you're married," Stanley said.

"Who married? Me? Naw. That won't happen for a long time. There are definitely too many beautiful women out here to do that. Yep. Black, white, yellow, fat, skinny, short, tall, ten women to every man," Reggie said.

"Do you believe that? With those odds, it makes you wonder who is doing the researching. Yeah, right. Ten women to every man, where at? It sure ain't in this city." Stanley wiped the sweat from his brow.

"Well, I believe it. Can you imagine there are women out here who want to get laid, paid, and a man who'll stay? Some of them haven't had a real man who would treat them the way they're supposed to be treated. A woman is a special creature. She's looking for a man who can tease, please, and ignite that flame of passion that's deep inside her."

"Do you hear yourself? You sound like somebody onstage with a stuffy smoking jacket, glasses, and a pipe stuck in your mouth reading a book of poetry." Stanley laughed at Reggie's soft side. "When did you become such an expert on romance? I can remember when little Shirl Hambrick kissed you in the back of the bus, and you pissed on yourself," Stanley teased Reggie.

"But I more than made up for that on graduation night. I rocked that big girl's world," Reggie boasted triumphantly. "But what I'm saying, Stan, is that a man has to eat, sleep, and breathe romance, or else a woman won't give you no play. And with Valentine's Day coming up, man, believe it or not, between Christmas, Valentine's Day, and Mother's Day, I spend a helluva lot of money," Reggie said.

"Mother's Day!" Stanley said.

"Man, it's not what you think," Reggie said. Stanley always knew his brother was quite the player. The mere mention of children coming from Reggie's mouth was a shock to Stanley's system.

"There better not be," Stanley said to his little brother. Just then the doorbell rang.

"Doorbell!" Reggie shouted, as he jumped off the ladder, and jetted to the door.

"Damn!" Stanley yelled, grabbing the collapsing fan.

"What's up, man!" a loud voice at the front door said.

"You got it. Come in," Reggie said as he and his friend embraced and gave each other the ritual soul shake.

"Stanley, you remember Joe Styles from the basketball tournament?" Reggie reintroduced his buddy to Stanley. Stanley looked at the cool, hip-looking brother with his white Kangol cap, blue jeans, print shirt, and white Air Jordan tennis shoes.

"Yeah, I remember you, Stanley. Who can forget that pretty three-pointer you made right before the buzzer sounded a couple weeks ago," Joe said, boosting Stanley's almost deflated ego.

"Thanks, man. You weren't so bad yourself. You're looking like life has been good to you, too, since the last time I saw you," Stanley said from the top of the ladder.

"Man, this guy has hit the lottery more times than anyone I know." Reggie playfully boxed with his friend.

"What was that number, man, you hit last week for five grand?"

"2836," Joe said modestly.

"What! That's my number. I've been playing that number for the last six weeks," Stanley shouted.

"And you didn't play it? Man, I thought you always kept your lucky number in," Reggie said. The doorbell rang again.

"Hey, what's up?" Three more guys, friends of Reggie's, stopped by as well. Soon the two-man afternoon turned into a loud, festive party with a house full of rowdy men watching the basketball playoffs on a wide-screen T.V.

"Rebound, sucker!" Carl, one of the guys who worked with Reggie at the post office, screamed.

"Man, Jordan is so sweet. I wish that I could dunk like that on the court."

"Carl, man, if you even do half as good as Michael J., we might even think about putting you in one of our games next time. But you first got to learn the game. You be playing like a little punk sometimes," Dominic said as he drank down his second bottle of Löwenbräu.

"Hey, Stanley, Reggie tells me that you're an accountant. What do you charge for your services, man?" Dennis Jenkins asked.

Dennis was an up-and-coming corporate lawyer who had moved from Seattle, Washington, to go into business with his uncle in San Diego. "Being a poor black man trying to get rich is a hard road to travel on when you only have two pennies in your pocket to rub together," said Dennis. "I give my services to one of our own every chance I get. Trying to keep a small business afloat is sure enough rough on a man. My uncle has the potential to really do well in the retail business, but his location isn't all that great. We're attempting to move to a more lucrative location where everyone can benefit, especially my uncle." He wrapped his lips around the beer bottle.

"You're an attorney and your uncle is an entrepreneur?" Stanley asked, amazed.

"I don't know if I would put it that fancy. He's just a black man trying to get ahead." Reggie's reputation for friends and women exceeded Stanley's expectations. He had no idea that his brother had such good friends, ones who were working to better their lives as black men. Why couldn't I succeed in my own business? It's not hard. All these brothers stuck to their guns, no matter how hard things seemed to get. Why did I buckle under and run away like some damn scared dog when things got rough? Stanley asked himself as he looked around at all the other brothers who were doing well, like Dominic, who was in law school. Although he still lived with his mother, Dominic was standing on his own two feet. Joe, who was lucky as hell when it came to playing the numbers, had been a cop for the city of San Diego for going on four years. Wes Turner, who didn't say much but was throwing down chips and beer as if he hadn't had a meal in days, even he was a successful salesman. He ranked number two at his job last year and received a two-thousand-dollar bonus. And he still refused to buy himself a car. He'd rather save his money and drive those company cars, switching up to three or four times a week. Even Reggie had this bachelor pad that looked like some fancy interior decorator came in and did his best work. His little brother was living large. Stanley wanted to do what these fellahs were doing, whatever that was, he thought, as he sat and critiqued the lives of his peers.

"So you have your own business, right, Stanley?" Dennis asked, unaware that Stanley no longer was in business for himself.

"No, man. I didn't have any collateral," Stanley said with his eyes cast down to the floor. "Sometimes I wonder if I'm in the right business." He swallowed the last swig of his beer in one big gulp. Stanley hated to talk about his business failures. It always left a bad taste in his mouth.

"Big brother, please. You're in the right business all right. You helped me to collect close to a grand last year on my taxes," Reggie said.

"Yeah, right! I didn't get one red cent from you, either, for doing you a favor," Stanley replied.

"Look, I tried to give you a little something for your troubles, but you said forget about it. You told me to look at it as a favor from you."

"Don't you know the difference between somebody trying to be generous and somebody who's trying not to come right out and beg?" Stanley finally cracked a smile. All the men broke out in laughter before their attention was diverted back to the basketball game on T.V.

"Oooh! Man, those Laker cheerleaders are B.A.D. Bad!" Dominic shouted as he sat on the edge of the sofa. He was considered to be the skirt chaser out of the bunch.

In his late twenties, Dominic had a birthday coming up in a couple of weeks. His fantasy was being able to make love to two women at the same time, preferably a mother and daughter, if the mother looked a whole lot like the daughter. The guys always teased him because he was the only one who could never get laid on the first date, or the second, third, or fourth. He was said to be a little quick on the trigger when it came to getting intimate. Dominic said it was just a matter of relaxing and letting Mother Nature take charge, but Reggie and the rest of them said he was ashamed because he probably had a small penis and he was too afraid to let his dates see him naked.

"Yeah? How come we don't have any girls with those big butts jumping up and down for us when we play in the big tournaments?" Joe asked.

"For real," Dominic agreed.

"For what, Dominic? You spend more of your time on the court making passes at females than you do making baskets. You know how you get when you see a P.Y.T. Pretty Young Thang. You get to stuttering and trippin' over your own big feet," Reggie said, poking fun at his buddy.

"Like you got it all together, Reg. I can remember a certain lady friend who you were supposed to have had a date with one night and she ended up going out with some other guy," Dominic said.

"See. There you go with that ol' tired story again. Man, don't you get sick of sounding like a broken record?"

"Not when it's concerning you and your so-called Don Juan reputation."

"What's so strange about that?" Stanley asked.

LOVE'S DECEPTIONS

"Reggie went to pick up this girl and when he was pulling up in front of her house, she was walking out the door on the arm of another man, and she saw Reggie and told him that he was her cousin from Des Moines." Dominic nearly cracked his side laughing.

"And you fell for that, little brother?" Stanley laughed.

"What could I do? It was her cousin from out of town," Reggie said innocently.

"Her cousin moved in with her a week later. And a couple of months later they were married." The men fell out laughing.

"This is certainly one for the books," Stanley continued to tease him. Reggie got up after being embarrassed by his friends and walked into the kitchen to bring back another six-pack. He set it on the glass cocktail table in the middle of his guests.

"Speaking of babes. Reg, have you seen that new mail clerk in the basement at the job? Man, talk about hot. She's got it going on." Carl finally got into the conversation.

"Cherise?" Reggie popped the top off his third beer.

"Cherise. Her name is like music to my ears, and her body like a finely tuned guitar," Carl said as his eyes rolled around in his head.

"Well, if you touch her, you'll be hearing a different tune, the jailhouse rock," Reggie said. "That girl is young enough to be somebody's daughter."

"How come you know so much about her?" Joe asked.

"I just do, that's all. Take my word for it." He belched.

"I bet he tried to jump on it himself," Carl said, looking at Reggie sideways.

"That's what it sounds like to me, too," Stanley remarked.

"You crazy. All of you are crazy. I only fool around with full-grown women. Baby-sitting ain't my thing, fellahs, you know that." Reggie grabbed the remote control off the end table and switched to another channel and hopefully another subject.

"I'm not trying to change the subject or anything, but,

big brother, I've heard some news about a certain lady lawyer whose son could possibly be yours." Reggie turned the tables on Stanley.

"Woo!" the guys cried.

"Don't even try it, Reg. That's nothing but a hoax. Besides, I already talked to her, and she has assured me that I have nothing to worry about."

"Is Rach assured of the same thing?"

"You know Rachel." Stanley looked away briefly. The room got silent.

"She doesn't know," the rest of the men said in unison.

"Women can do some really crazy things when they find out that their marriage is in jeopardy. Look at Bobbit," Carl said, grimacing.

"For real. Mrs. Bobbit might as well hang it up if she thinks that her husband is gonna go back to her after she gets out of that asylum."

"Yeah. As far as he's concerned, their marriage is dead and stinkin'," Joe said.

"Stanley, don't let that happen to you. I hate to see anything happen to you in that way. No woman is that important to lose your livelihood, if you know what I mean." Once again, the room got quiet.

"That happened to me one time," Dennis said, participating in the male bonding. "This girl back home I was dating for a short time wanted more out of our relationship than I wanted to give. But she just wouldn't take no for an answer."

"What does this got to do with anything?" Wes asked. He was feeling pretty good since he'd drunk the most beers out of the whole group.

"Well, if you shut up, I'll get to it," Dennis said. "But anyway, I told her that I was thinking about going back to school to become a lawyer, and I told her that the relationship would suffer because I wouldn't be around like she would want me to."

"So, what happened? She tried to clip your 'jimmy'?" Wes laughed loudly.

"Man, why don't you shut up. You're drunk," Reggie said, sick of Wes's loud outbursts.

"Shh! Be quiet." Dominic elbowed Wes in the ribs.

"Ow! That hurt," Wes cried. "Punk," he said under his breath.

"Well, to make a long story short, when I came home to visit, she told me that she was pregnant with my kid and that she wanted to get married right away. And if I didn't marry her, she was going to take me to court and I would have to kiss my law career good-bye."

"What happened, man? Was she pregnant or not?" Reggie asked with bated breath.

"Yeah, she was pregnant all right. But come to find out the guy she was fooling around with in my absence hit the lottery for fifty grand. And you all know the rest. A month later they bought a big house, two cars, and blew the rest in Las Vegas." Moans and groans escaped their lips.

"So, what's the moral of this story?" Reggie asked.

"Now, they're in debt up to their necks and the worst thing about it, the guy still hasn't married her. It's never the contents of a brother's character, it's the contents of his wallet."

"That's what I'm saying, man. Some of these women are just out to get a man who's got money, a house, a good job, and is halfway decent-looking," Joe said.

"And some of them don't even care what you look like anymore. I've seen some really fine women in my time, but the fellahs they be with look like hell. But they got bacon," another said.

"I know that's right." Dominic and Joe gave each other a high-five.

The men sat silently for a minute. It was as if they all were sorting out their own personal experiences and thoughts. Suddenly, Stanley cried out, "Do you remember what number he played?"

Chapter Nine

Lesa placed the key in the front door and, as she opened it, the smell of reefer smacked her in the face. She slammed the door because she knew it was Tony and his hoodlum friends stinking up the place, including her rug, furniture, curtains, and everything else that absorbed the odor.

"Tony! I told you. Don't smoke that stuff in here, you and your stupid friends," Lesa said angrily.

"Girl, I got the central air on. You don't smell nuthin'," Tony said with his eyes barely open. He was really blitzed and so were his two gun-slinging buddies.

"How you doing, Lesa?" Buster said, stuttering terribly. He was Tony's best friend. They both grew up together and got in trouble together when they were in the old neighborhood.

"Get your feet off my cocktail table." Lesa walked over and slapped his size eleven-and-a-half Air Jordans off the glass table. That's when she saw all the large and small sandwich bags of cocaine and marijuana surrounded by stacks of twenty-, fifty-, and hundred-dollar bills.

"Hey! Hey! Don't come in here and boss my guests around like you're Five-O." Tony tried to stand on his feet.

"Tony, I can't believe you. You let anybody come in here and do anything they want. They don't live here. If you don't have any respect for yourself, have some respect for me," she said as Tony looked up at her with bloodshot eyes.

"I do. But I also respect my friends and they me, so, if I say it's all right for him to put his feet up, then he can put his feet up," Tony said. "Go ahead, man, put your feet up," he said to Buster. Buster looked up and saw Lesa's facial expression and decided to keep his feet on the floor.

"See what you did? You come in here and make my guests feel unwanted. Don't you think so, man?" he said to Hakim, who sat on the other side of him on the loveseat. Hakim remained silent as Lesa walked by the both of them and went into the kitchen. Tony reached out and smacked her on her backside.

"While you're in there, bring us a couple of beers, too." Lesa responded by sucking her teeth.

"You know what? Too many women got this idea that they can control a man. But I'm not going to let any woman control me." Tony sat on the edge of his seat. "If I ever catch my woman trying to dis' me, I'm going to show her who's the boss." He got up and staggered his way into the kitchen. He then reached behind his back.

"Here, Tony, take these." Lesa turned and was startled to find Tony standing in the middle of the floor holding a black and silver revolver.

"Tony!" she screamed. The tray of open beers fell to the floor.

"What?" he yelled back. "It's not even loaded. I just bought it today." He dropped it to his side. Lesa was shaken up as she paced back and forth in the kitchen. She knew Tony and his friends were packing, but she never thought he'd actually bring a gun into her house.

"I told you not to bring guns in here. I don't care when you bought it, I don't want it in here!" Lesa screamed. Lesa knew Tony was crazy, but she didn't know how much.

"See what you made me do?" Lesa grabbed a dish towel and sopped up the spilled beer.

"I didn't do nuthin'. You're the one who came in here screaming like some crazy woman." Tony stood over her.

"Oh, right. Seeing somebody pull out a gun all of sudden wouldn't scare you at all, I guess!" Lesa tried to get up what she could without cutting her hands on the broken glass.

"Ah, baby. I told you it ain't loaded. I don't know why you're scared of it. It's not like I'm gonna use it on you." Not this time, anyway, he thought. Tony went and placed the gun inside the black and gold coffee table that concealed a secret compartment in the center of it.

"And you better not." Lesa got up and went to the sink and rinsed the cloth out.

"See, there you go talking crazy again. Why should I use it on you? You doing something I don't know about, girl?" Tony asked. I never seen her so nervous, he thought. "You better not be cheatin' on me. 'Cause if you are and I find out, you might as well kiss him good-bye," Tony said in a threatening tone. "And yourself, too. You bettah know I ain't paying for you lovin' somebody else. Plenty other women know how to show a man real respect."

"Now who's talking crazy," Lesa said, as she kept her eyes on the water running down the drain. "Tony, I swear, you always think the worst about a person. If you don't trust me, get out then." She turned and looked directly in his face. Lesa wished deep down that he would do just that, considering she had just been with Kris on his boat.

"Girl, you so crazy. I ain't going nowhere." Tony pulled her into his arms and began to kiss her roughly. "And neither are you. You're my baby and no one else's."

If Lesa didn't know it before, she knew it now. Tony may have been high and all that, but she knew he meant every word. Now Lesa feared not only for her life, but for Kris's as well.

* * *

LOVE'S DECEPTIONS 77

On his way home from Reggie's house, Stanley felt pretty good. He didn't give a second thought about going to the hardware store as Rachel had asked him to do before he left the house that morning. He soon remembered he didn't pick up what was needed to fix the windowsill where he had snatched the curtain down, nor did he call to tell Rachel that he was at his brother's house all day, shooting the breeze and drinking beers. Stanley had the tape player in the car blasting Allyson Williams, the tape he borrowed from Reggie. Suddenly, when his turn came up to go home, Stanley drove on past it. He continued to drive on and in no time he was slowing down in front of Benita's house.

He peered up at the house and checked to see that Fish's car was not parked outside. Even though he and Benita were split up, he wanted to be sure. He saw only Benita's teal green Honda Accord parked in front. Stanley backed his car behind hers and turned off his car lights but kept his fog lights on. He hit the horn a couple of times and waited to see if anyone would come to the window. He continued to look up the walkway until he saw the shadow of a womanly figure not only in Benita's house, but in the house beside hers. Stanley's heart raced as Benita opened her front door and came walking down the sidewalk to meet him.

Why did I come here? Stanley thought. He wasn't sure if he had the answer to the question.

"Stanley, what are you doing here?" Benita stuck her head inside the passenger-side window. Stanley sat looking out beyond the windshield with one arm slung across the passenger-side seat and the other hand around the steering wheel.

"That's funny," he said as he sighed. "Honestly, Nita, I don't know. I was on my way home and here I am." Stanley shrugged his shoulders. He didn't have a clue as to why he was there, and what he wanted to do. Benita looked at him with a warm smile and inviting eyes.

"Well, since you're here, you may as well come in,"

she said. Although she didn't say it, Benita was happy to see him.

"Are you sure? I mean, I don't want to impose," Stanley said, still glued to his seat.

"I'm sure. Please, come in." She backed away from the car while Stanley got out.

"Make yourself at home. We finished dinner not too long ago. Would you care for something to eat, Stanley?" Benita stood between the living room and the dining room.

"No, thanks. But if it's not too much trouble, I could use some coffee. I'm a little buzzed right now and I need to get myself together." Stanley was more than a little blitzed. If it weren't for the wall holding him up, he would have been facedown on the floor.

He stood staring at how different she looked from the last time he saw her. Benita looked even better than before, he thought.

"Sure. Have a seat, I'll be right back." She gave Stanley a warm smile and went into the kitchen.

Stanley didn't move. He watched her until she disappeared beyond the threshold.

Not bad, he thought. Things weren't that much different since he was here a year ago. It looked larger somehow. Maybe because Fish was gone, along with his belongings, Stanley thought, as he looked around waiting for Nita to return with the coffee.

He noticed she still had that old Shakespearean book he'd given her when they'd been in college. He picked the book from the bookcase and looked inside to see the note he had written to Benita before giving it to her.

"I hope you don't mind instant," she said, startling Stanley as she walked back into the room.

"That will be fine." He slid the book back on the shelf.

"What are you looking at? Old William Shakespeare?" She pulled the book back out. "Do you remember when you gave this to me?" she asked Stanley as he stood beside her trying to keep a steady balance. He still was feeling light-headed from all the beers he had drunk at his brother's house earlier. But he was determined to at least pretend he was sober.

"Sure I do. After seeing the fantastic job I did playing Shakespearean roles in college, how can I forget. I was good."

"Yeah, right. The stage director had to coax you onto the stage because you didn't want the ladies to see you in tights," Benita said with a laugh.

God, she is beautiful when she's happy. It's been a long time since I've seen her so innocent and free, Stanley thought as he watched the Benita he knew long ago come to life.

"Come on. I'll fix you that cup of coffee," Benita said as she heard the kettle whistling. She led Stanley into the kitchen.

After their second cup, Stanley and Benita reminisced over good times and bad. It was as if they had been really good friends instead of lovers after all these years.

"Whatever happened to 'ain't-in-it' Bennett? The last time I heard he was working for the IRS," Benita said.

"I don't know. Who would have thought the one man who made it a rule never to interfere in other people's business would wind up working at a job where other people's business is his business," Stanley said as they both laughed the night away.

"That's pretty funny." Benita tried to keep her mind focused on the conversation, instead of the attraction she was feeling toward Stanley.

"Well, I guess I better be heading on home. I've wasted enough of your time tonight." Stanley got up from the table. "By the way, where's Malcolm? I was kind of hoping I would get a chance to see him."

"He's spending the night over at one of his friends' houses tonight. I try to give him as much freedom as possible, without restraining him too much," she said. "It's pretty hard not having a male figure in his life now. Fish and I haven't exactly been the best of friends here lately."

"It's pretty rough, huh? Does he visit at all?" They walked into the living room.

"Sure, when his schedule permits. But to tell you the truth, Stanley, I wouldn't care if he never came to see us. My life has been a whole lot easier since he left." Benita stood at the door.

"Are you two heading for a divorce?" Stanley asked.

"It looks that way. But I don't regret anything. I can live with the fact that I may have to live the rest of my life alone, but I couldn't live with the lie that I loved him," Benita confessed.

"I'm really sorry to hear that. But you'll never live the rest of your life alone. You're a wonderful woman and any man would be happy and blessed to have you as his wife," Stanley said.

"You really think so?" She smiled. "Will I ever get the chance to love and to be loved by someone like you?" She had finally said it. It had been pressing on her mind ever since Stanley set foot in her house.

Stanley was at a loss for words. He knew Benita reserved a place in her heart for him, but he didn't expect her to make her feelings known, not after telling him that Malcolm was not his son.

"Look, Nita, I . . ." he began.

"I'm sorry. I didn't mean to put you on the spot like that. I guess that's the lawyer in me. I just thought maybe you felt the same thing I did. I'm sorry," she repeated.

"Don't worry about it. If it gives you any comfort to hold on to something that makes you happy, then do it. But I can't say what I feel right now. Sometimes I feel like walking away and never looking back. But I know I can't do that." Stanley moved closer to her. He put his hands on her shoulders. He could feel her body tremble beneath his touch. Then he saw a tear fall from her eye.

"Nita, please don't cry. It's gonna be all right," Stanley said, as he held her in his arms.

LOVE'S DECEPTIONS 81

"I'm scared. I'm really scared," she cried into his chest.

"As long as I'm around, you'll never have to be afraid of anything." Stanley lifted her face up and slowly lowered his lips to hers.

"Stanley, wait." Benita paused. "If you're going to leave, you better do it now," she said as her reflection appeared in his eyes.

"I'll leave when I'm ready. Is that okay with you?" Benita then wrapped her arms around Stanley's neck and they both continued a long-awaited kiss.

At the stroke of midnight, Rachel lay awake as she counted the hours that had passed since the last time she saw Stanley. Where in the hell was he? Rachel thought. At times she found herself not even giving her husband a second thought. But deep down in her spirit, she was feeling something else.

Early Sunday morning the telephone in Stacy's bedroom rang.

"Hello," she said in a dry, sleepy voice.

"Sheila, good morning. Did I wake you?" the voice said. Stacy lay with her face mashed into her pillow.

"I know this is against all rules and regulations, but I want to meet you," the voice said. This request brought Stacy to full consciousness.

"Who is this?" she said with wide, tired eyes.

"It's me. Kelvin."

"Kelvin? What do you mean, you want to meet me?" Stacy wasn't nearly prepared for a call like this so early in the morning.

"Look, I'm tired of just talking on the phone with you. I want to finally meet you without a telephone receiver glued to the sides of our heads." Kelvin was adamant. Stacy was not ready for a one-on-one meeting with anybody, especially with a man she only recognized by voice through several weeks of chatting on the telephone. This was not part of her job description.

"I know but . . ."

"But what, Sheila? And that's another thing. If we're going to be honest with one another, I think you should start by dropping the phony Jamaican accent," he said bluntly. "My mother is a native woman from the islands and I know a Jamaican when I hear one. And, Sheila, you're not from Jamaica."

Stacy was so embarrassed. She didn't know whether to remain silent or hang up the phone. She really felt dumb. He thinks he's so smart, she thought.

"Now, if you like, we can start all over with a clean slate. What do you say?" he asked. "It's up to you. Or, we can stop it right here and right now. You wouldn't have to worry about ever hearing from me again." He sounded so final, Stacy thought, as she listened to the words roll so eloquently off his tongue. She didn't know what to say, or if she wanted to say anything at all. This was the first time in a long time that a man had ever been this straight-up and truthful with her. Should she open up to this stranger, who wasn't really a stranger to her anymore? All sorts of thoughts ran through her mind. She tried to think of a legitimate reason why she couldn't meet him.

Should I do it? Why am I so scared to accept his invitation? she thought, as she rolled on her back, only to find her older son cuddled in a ball beside her. There was nothing Stacy would like better than to have a decent man in her children's life and her own. It's been too long a time, she thought. But what if he doesn't like children? And what about Clyde? she thought, as she looked into the face of her child. I can't afford to put them through another dead-end relationship, she contemplated.

What is wrong with me? I can't afford to lose this job over some man. This guy could possibly be just like all the other men who are out looking for a place to lay their heads and get a free meal; not to mention a warm body to

LOVE'S DECEPTIONS

lie up against every night for their own sexual needs. Besides, what sort of man spends most of his time on the telephone with a woman he knows nothing about, Stacy thought, while Kelvin waited patiently on the other end of the phone. But what if he's straight-up about what he said? Lord, how long must I wait for Mr. Right? I know this may seem strange coming from me, seeing that I never really took the time to speak to you, except when I needed a new washer and dryer, a car, and, oh yeah, that VCR. But, Lord, I'll forget about all those material things just for a decent man.

Stacy snickered to herself. This was the first time she had spoken to God in a while.

"Kelvin, could I think about it a little longer, please?" There was a long sigh coming from the other end of the receiver. Stacy knew her answer wasn't the one he was counting on.

"Well, if that's what you need. I'll wait, but not for long. But if you change your mind, you can find me at the Minority Youth Recreation Center. I do volunteer work there every other Saturday," Kelvin said before he hung up. Suddenly there was nothing between them except the sound of a dial tone.

"Damn. I hope I didn't make the mistake of my life," Stacy said, holding the receiver close to her chest.

As the first sign of daylight slowly filtered through the gold metallic miniblinds in her bedroom, Lesa lay wide awake. She'd been lying there for some time now, just drifting in and out. She was miserable. It had been well after midnight when Kris brought her home and as it was every weekend, Lesa came home to an empty house. She had stopped worrying about Tony's whereabouts a long time ago, especially now, since meeting Kris. In fact, the more time she spent with Kris, the more Lesa despised Tony.

Just look at him, Lesa thought, as she looked at Tony's inert form beside her. He snored like some big, fat, funky drunk. He threw his heavy arm across her waist. She angrily tossed it back over on him. Tony jerked suddenly as the motion woke him up.

"Who? What?" he said, paranoid. Lesa looked over at him and sucked her teeth in disgust. She rolled her eyes.

"Girl, don't be playin' with me," he said in a growling voice.

"Ain't nobody playing. Your ass been on drugs so long you're getting paranoid," she said, upset.

"What's your problem?" he asked.

Lesa turned her back to him. "Just leave me alone," she said like a spoiled little child.

"You must want some lovin', don't you?" Tony attempted to caress her apple-sized breast.

"Get the hell off of me," Lesa snapped as she blocked his hand with her arm.

Tony's relaxed state became tense as he grabbed her.

"What the hell is wrong with you? You've been acting real funny. You got something on your chest? You got some beef with me?" Lesa snatched her arm away.

"If you don't have enough common sense to know, then I'm sure as hell not going to tell you."

"What's that suppose to mean? Are you seeing somebody else? Is that why you got this nasty attitude?" Tony's voice grew angrier.

What should I do now? He said it for me, Lesa thought nervously. I'll be damned if I'm gonna say anything about it now; he's too mad, she thought as her heart began to race.

"Lesa! Did you hear me?" he asked.

"Is that what you think?" With her back turned to him, Lesa pulled the sheet over her bare shoulder.

"I don't know, that's why I'm asking. You sure ain't telling me nuthin' else." Tony got more and more irritated. "I bust my butt out here on the streets every day for you."

"For me! How in the hell can you lay there and say you're out there selling drugs for me? That's your prerogative. I don't need you to do a damn thing for me," Lesa cried out.

"Since when have you become so damn independent? Or else, you got somebody else taking care of you. Is that what you're trying to tell me?" *Is this bitch so stupid she thinks I'm gonna roll over and play dead?* he wondered.

Lesa jumped out of bed as the argument heated up. She paced around the room.

"And what if it was? All you do is hang out with your boys from the hood and bring stuff like this home every day." Lesa ran over to Tony's dresser drawer and began tossing out bag after bag of marijuana and dope. Tony watched a week's worth of profit float in the air. Weed and white powder went everywhere.

"Bitch! What are you doing?" he screamed. Tony darted toward her and, without thinking, struck Lesa across the face.

Lesa picked up the closest thing in her reach, a black hand-crafted porcelain statue of Cleopatra and hurled it at Tony, striking him on the arm.

"I want you to take your things and get the hell out!" she screamed through her tears and fear.

"I ain't going no place," Tony shouted back. He then charged at her like a raging bull. He grabbed her by the arm and smacked her across the face. Blood started to flow from Lesa's nose. "I should kill you. You know how much money you just cost me?" Tony was furious. Portraits and expensive hand-crafted porcelain sculptures fell from the wall above Lesa's head as her body was repeatedly slammed up against the wall.

Tony's huge hands were wrapped around Lesa's slim neck as she felt her strength weaken in his grip.

"Somebody help me. He's going to kill me," she said, as she cried out for help in a strangled voice. The only image she would remember was that of Tony's cold, hateful eyes.

God, don't let me die, Lesa thought over and over

as the blood vessels in her head were on the brink of bursting.

"DEA!" Voices shouted as the door to the bedroom came crashing down.

"On the floor! Now!" a white officer screamed as he held a gun to Tony's head. Lesa sat still on the bed trying to catch what little breath she had left in her body.

"Miss, are you all right? Do you need an ambulance?" a black DEA agent asked her as he attempted to assist Lesa.

"What the hell is this?" Tony yelled as the officer pinned him to the floor facedown and handcuffed him. "Can't a man have a disagreement with his woman nowadays?"

Lesa didn't know what was happening. She just sat on the bed in silence, beaten and bruised.

"Sweep the house, see if there are any more drugs or weapons stashed anywhere," the cop said, as he gave a report through his walkie-talkie. "Operation is secured. Sweep in progress."

"I wanna call my lawyer," Tony cried out.

"You can call whoever you want, but in the meantime, you have the right to remain silent." The blue-eyed, sunburnt officer read Tony his rights.

Tony looked up at Lesa with deranged eyes. He was hotter than a pig roasting on the Fourth of July.

I knew it. I knew it was going to happen sooner or later, she thought. But she didn't think that she would be anywhere in the vicinity. Lesa couldn't move, speak, or even blink.

"Did the lieutenant get here yet?" the cop in charge asked a fellow officer.

"Yes, sir. Lieutenant Coles is on his way up."

Oh God, don't let me be on the evening news, Lesa thought. She sat motionless and afraid. What could be worse than to see her face being flashed on every news channel in the city of San Diego, looking like a common criminal. There goes the neighborhood, my job, my personal life, my reputation, and God knows what else.

LOVE'S DECEPTIONS

What's next? Lesa thought angrily. Suddenly her attention was diverted to the doorway as the commander-in-chief of the operation walked through the door.

"Good morning, sir. Everything is under control. We have the suspect and the girlfriend in custody," the officer said.

"Is the young lady okay?"

Lesa felt faint as she looked into his face. It felt almost like a dream. There, big as life, stood Kris. Lesa's body trembled like a dove lost in a storm as Kris looked in her direction. If his colleagues had not been there in the same room, all the rules and regulations in the government's handbook would not have kept him from holding Lesa in his arms. But there were rules and regulations even though they didn't apply when he was making love to her. His job was to apprehend the prisoner and arrest him. Yet all that didn't amount to anything when it came to his feelings for Lesa.

Kris could see the pain in her tear-stained eyes.

"Get him out of here," Kris ordered.

Tony pleaded with Lesa as he was dragged out of the room. "Baby, tell 'em I wasn't gonna hurt you," he shouted.

Lesa turned her eyes away from Tony. The truth about Kris had put enough strain on her heart already. The bedroom door was shut behind them.

"I guess this is why you really couldn't tell me that you loved me," Lesa said bitterly.

"Lesa, I didn't want it to turn out like this. I swear I did not." Oh, that's really apologetic, Kris, he chided himself. I can't even believe what I just said, so why should she? "Look. It's not like I could have told you the truth. I had a job to do," he said.

"Did your job include using me? Because that's exactly how it looks to me. I can't believe I trusted you," Lesa cried out. "You didn't even have the balls to tell me the truth. Tell me somethin'—was it your job to screw me, too? That was the best part of your job, wasn't it?"

Lesa was so mad that she could have shot him with his own gun.

"Lesa, don't do this. I feel just as bad as you do."

"Somehow that's hard to believe. You have no feelings because if you did, none of this would be happening to me." She attempted to find something to put on her partially naked body. Kris saw the agony she was in and tried to help.

"Get the hell away from me. I don't need your help," she snapped viciously. Kris kept his distance as he watched her slowly move around the once orderly room. His sighs went unnoticed. He tried on several accounts to talk to Lesa, but she just accused him of hiding behind that piece of metal secured to his chest. She was right, Kris thought. He knew that his relationship with her would be more dangerous than any crime. He had fallen in love with her.

Lesa requested more information about the raid, but Kris refused to comment. He did tell her that Tony had been under regular surveillance at a local hotel he operated out of. Kris even told her about the undercover cop who posed as one of the cleaning staff in order to get the goods on Tony. But Kris didn't mention that Tony's relationship with the cop went further than they anticipated. Tony's arrest was one of many drug busts in the past six months.

"You know, I told Tony that I was leaving him because I was in love with someone else. Someone who didn't lead a life of deception and corruption, somebody I could trust. That's a laugh. That somebody turned out to be nothing but a big phony," she said, as tears ran uncontrollably down her red face.

"Lesa, I am so sorry." Out of sympathy, Kris's eyes began to fill with tears.

"You have no idea how I'm feeling right now. I've just put away probably the only man who ever gave a damn about me, and for what?" she said furiously.

"Lesa." Kris tried to approach her.

"Please. Just go." He didn't want to. It would have taken the entire police force to remove him from that room. But what was left for him to say or do? The only woman he ever really cared enough about to jeopardize his job for was kicking him out of her house and possibly out of her life.

Before Kris left, he reached into his pocket and pulled out a small black box and sat it on the stand near the bedroom door. It was a token from him to her for all the trouble he knew he was going to cause. But his feelings went much deeper than he cared to admit.

"I know this may be the worst time to say this, but happy Valentine's Day, Lesa." Lesa never thought that those three little words could hurt so much.

Kris walked out of the house into the street. He ordered his men to break up the small crowd and send the people home. The officers that remained soon got into their police cruisers as Kris got into his.

Lesa watched from her bedroom window. Kris stretched his eyes up toward her. He looked up with saddened eyes as if to send a silent message to her heart. Lesa watched him through tear-filled eyes as she slowly closed the shades between them.

"Happy Valentine's Day, Kris."

Chapter Ten

Early Monday morning Stanley rolled over in hopes that Rachel's warm body was lying beside his. He reached over to the side of the bed, but the only thing he felt between him and the cold sheets was emptiness.

"No!" he shouted in a state of panic, and darted to the bedroom window.

"Damn. Rachel took my car!" He placed his hand on his naked hip and the other hand up to his face.

At the City Tree Day-Care Center, Rachel had just pulled up to the curb with Nicky. She got out of the car and walked around to the passenger-side door and unlocked it from the outside. Nicky was strapped in by the seat belt, half asleep.

"Nicky, honey, wake up. We're at the day-care center." She unlocked the child safety belt. Today Nicky wasn't his happy self. "Come on, Nicky, what's the matter with you this morning? You move like your daddy," Rachel said in a calm voice. She was still upset with Stanley for not coming home a couple of days ago, and she didn't want to take her anger out on her son. The other children and their parents walked up the sidewalk to the school while Rachel struggled to get Nicky's feet on the pavement.

"I don't want to go to school today," Nicky said, as he continued to sit in the seat with his miniature legs and arms crossed.

"Now, look. We don't have time for this foolishness this morning. We're here now, and you're going to school, you hear me?" Rachel said with a stern voice. "You're only four years old; you're not old enough to tell me what you want. I'm the grown up here, not you." Rachel took him out of the car. "I swear. More and more every day, you're getting just like your father. Thank God I can break you while you're still young. But as for your father, he can go to hell." Rachel tucked Nicky's shirttail inside his pants just as hard as she fussed about Stanley, as if Nicky understood what she was talking about.

"Come on. I want to get to work a half an hour early this morning. I have to make a few phone calls." Rachel whisked him by the arm and hurried him into the building.

As the first sign of morning peeked through the white miniblinds, the chirping of the robins, accompanied by the flushing of the toilet, were all the sounds of a wonderful morning for Mattie.

"I wish we could stay curled up like this all day," Fred said from the bathroom before crawling back into bed beside Mattie, who was lying on her naked back with a big smile on her face.

"But we can't, can we?" she said as she opened her arms and embraced Fred lovingly.

"I can't see why not. I'm the boss, remember?" He kissed Mattie's eyelids, cheek, and then her lips.

"But you're black. Only big-shot corporate men can lie in bed all day and fool around with their wives or the ones they claim to be their wives; they write their own checks," Mattie said playfully. "You're a black man in a high position to someone, and there is always someone just waiting for you to mess up so they can take over your job," Mattie said as Fred's lips found their way to her breasts underneath the sheet. "And who knows, this could be some young go-getter's opportunity, because you, Fred Wilson, decided to stay in bed and fool around instead of doing what you do best," Mattie said.

Fred abruptly stopped his fondling.

"You could be right," he said. "Let's get dressed." Fred jumped out of the bed like a young man with vigor, while Mattie lay thrilled and still dazed. It felt good to have a man share her life and her bed after all these years. To her, it had been a year since she felt whole. Mattie was as giddy as a schoolgirl. Fred had brought feelings of joy and fear back into her life. Joy, because it felt good to have a man share her deepest feelings and thoughts. And fear, because Mattie wasn't sure whether the happiness would last. But either way, that morning was the first morning in a long time that she woke up with a smile on her face and in her heart.

"Come on now. Shake your tail," Fred said as he poked his head from around the bathroom door.

"I thought I did last night," Mattie said in a playful voice.

At an off-street underground parking garage, Rachel drove up, punched the large red button, and retrieved her parking slip. She turned the corner in Stanley's champagne-colored Legend. She parked the car and reached over across the driver's seat to get her briefcase and dropped the car keys on the floor of the front seat.

"I don't have time for this," she mumbled. She stretched her arm and found more than keys under there. She pulled out a small square box that was partially wrapped in red shiny paper. She took the contents out and found a very expensive bottle of Eternity for Men by Calvin Klein.

"I know damn well he didn't buy this," Rachel said, as the anger slowly crept back. "What else is he hiding in this damn car?" Rachel reached back underneath the seat. She felt something else and she pulled it out. It was an envelope addressed to Stanley. Rachel's heart began to race as she read the Valentine card from Benita.

"So this is the reason he couldn't bring his black ass home. Okay, Stanley, if this is how you wanna play,

LOVE'S DECEPTIONS 93

that's fine with me," Rachel said with clenched teeth. She slammed the car door shut and went to work. Because she was so agitated, Rachel completely forgot Mr. Wilson's instructions to always spot a security guard before getting out of a locked and safe car. Otherwise, she would have noticed someone at the far end of the garage who ducked into the shadows as the elevator opened and a security guard emerged.

After Rachel was in the office, she sat down, pulled out her telephone book, and called her good friend Faith Nelson. Faith and Rachel had been good friends for a long time and Rachel considered her to be her best friend in the whole world. Faith was not only Rachel's best friend, she was her psychotherapist.

"Good morning, is Dr. Nelson in please?" Rachel asked.

"Yes, could you hold on, please?" asked the receptionist on the other end of the phone. Rachel waited as an old song by the Fifth Dimension played in her ear: "One less bell to answer, one less egg to fry, one less man to pick up after, but now that he's gone all I do is cry . . ." Just the thought of Stanley in the arms of another woman made Rachel sick to her stomach.

"Dr. Nelson speaking." The clear professional voice interrupted the song.

"Faith, it's Rachel. I think I'm headed for a nervous breakdown," Rachel said as she broke down in tears.

"Girl, what's the matter?" Faith said, as her doctor's instinct fell by the wayside and her sister-to-sister instinct rushed to the forefront.

"Rachel, stop crying. Tell me what happened." Faith considered Rachel to be more like a sister than a patient. They had become very attached to each other ever since their mothers had shared the same delivery room when the two girls were born. The two learned to depend on each other and share their most intimate secrets. Even though Faith's profession took her from city to city, she finally made her home in San Diego. She and Rachel still remained as close as ever.

"Faith, I need to get away from him for a while. I can't take it anymore," Rachel cried into the telephone.

"Have you and Stanley been fighting again, Rachel? Where is Nicky?" Faith asked.

"Since the last time we talked, things have gotten worse. Now I think—no, I know he's seeing another woman," she confessed.

"Rachel, are you sure? I don't want to sound uncaring or anything, but do you have proof?"

"Does coming home practically the next day and finding a bottle of expensive cologne that I didn't buy stuffed under the seat of his car make enough evidence for you?" Rachel asked. She continued to pat her eyes to keep her mascara from running and leaving a black skid down her face. "Faith, please. I need to talk to someone before I lose my mind." Faith had been aware of Rachel and Stanley's deteriorating marital situation for a long time, even before Stanley's incidental abuse flared up. Rachel had become just a shell of a woman and everything she'd had before her marriage—the life, the ambition, and the love that flowed from inward, out—was gone. Earlier Rachel had approached Faith in a seriously depressed state. Faith had prescribed antidepressants for Rachel just so she could get a grip for Nicky's sake.

"Everything is happening all over again. He's really done it now. He's actually seeing his old high-school sweetheart behind my back. And now he's even accepting her gifts."

"Okay, Rachel, I tell you what. I have some business to take care of down there for the next several days. Why don't I meet you at my condo in town after work, and we'll sit down and talk more," Faith suggested. "You haven't resorted to taking the pills again, have you?"

"No, I haven't. I don't need any more pills; I need to get away, from him and everything else."

"Go into the bathroom and clean yourself up, and I'll

see you later on this evening," Faith said, as she heard the calmness return to Rachel's voice.

"All right. But don't forget me, Faith. I really need to see you," Rachel begged.

"I won't, my sister." Faith hung up the phone.

Rachel got up from her desk and hurried into the bathroom. The doors to the office would soon be overflowing with people.

Chapter Eleven

The seventh floor was buzzing with laughter and excitement as delayed Valentine's gifts—oversized cards, candy, roses, and flowers in all colors arrived for men and women. Stacy was at her desk on the phone talking with a client about his company's health insurance policy.

"Yes, sir. I understand, but I need to know the previous medical history of your spouse before I can add her name to the policy." Stacy tried to abstain from getting an attitude.

"If you like, I can mail you a form that you can complete and mail back in to us," she continued to say.

"Sure, sir. I'll look for that in the mail in the next couple of days, then," Stacy said before she slammed the receiver down.

"His damn wife is probably in and out of the damn nut house anyway."

"Hey, Lesa. What's got your tongue this morning? This is the first time you're not running your mouth about the weekend," Stacy said to Lesa, who was in her own world. "Lesa!"

"Huh? What?" She quickly snapped back to reality.

"What's the matter? You've been staring into space all morning. What's going on? You had too much fun this weekend?" Stacy said. But Lesa wasn't in a talkative mood. "I thought at least you would be running off at the mouth."

Lesa realized that Stacy was unaware of Lesa's dilemma. In fact, she was surprised that no one else questioned her about the drug bust and her housing complex being on the television news. She hadn't been able to think of anything else.

"Come on. Tell me all the steamy, erotic, graphic details," Stacy continued. "You know I depend on you for all of my sexual interludes."

"There's nothing to tell," Lesa said in a low, scratchy voice.

"Well, this is a first," Stacy said sarcastically. "I can't believe we've finally got something in common."

"Could you just drop it? I don't want to talk about anything. I just want to do my work."

Now Stacy was really curious about Lesa's weekend. This was a first-ever for Lesa. Her mind obviously was on Kris. That was probably all she could think about.

Mattie and Fred waltzed into the office together. Heads turned in their direction. Everyone knew the love bug had smitten the both of them.

"See you at lunch, Ms.Thompson," Fred said, as he acknowledged those around him with a nod of his head. As for Mattie, she settled down to a full eight hours that weren't going to be easy, considering all eyes secretly fell upon her. "What's the matter? Are your eyeballs stuck or something?" she said aloud. They turned their heads with smirks and grins on their faces. Mattie found it hard to keep a smile off her face, as well.

"Mrs. Grier, you have a call on line one." The receptionist's voice came over the speakerphone on Rachel's desk.

Rachel picked up the handset. "Thanks, Louise," she said, as she took off her earring and placed it on the desk. "This is Rachel Grier. How can I help you?" she said in a low, clear voice.

"Rach, it's me, Stanley." Just the sound of his voice caused Rachel's heart to beat wildly. She looked around and searched the faces of her peers and thought they could hear her heart beating in fear. He was the last person she wanted to talk to.

"Stanley, what do you want?" she said in a rigid voice. He's really got some damn nerve. He didn't bring his black ass home until sometime this morning, and he didn't say two words to her as to where he was, Rachel thought, as she felt her anger starting to boil inside her chest. He did not even have the courtesy to wish me a happy Valentine's Day. But why should he? He got his chocolate last night!

"Is that the way you talk to me after I spent half the morning in a greasy, noisy garage while they worked on your car?" he asked in a calm voice. He didn't want to get into an argument with her.

"I'll talk to you any way I want to. And speaking of spending half the morning somewhere, where the hell were you last night? And don't tell me you spent all that time at Reggie's because I called, okay?" Rachel tried not to raise her voice. She didn't want the whole office to know her business.

Well, I might as well forget about that excuse, Stanley thought. He had hoped Rachel would just stay mad and not even want an excuse because he didn't have one.

"I know you're not mad about that. Rachel, there isn't a day you don't wake up with an attitude," he said, trying to turn the subject around. "A man can't go out and hang with his friends and family without being treated like some damn criminal."

"Don't you dare try to change the subject, you, you liar. You know damn well you were with Benita. What, you thought I wouldn't find out?"

Stanley tried to laugh it off. "I took the day off to get your car fixed. And all you can do is accuse me of cheating? You must be nuts, woman."

"If anyone is crazy, it's you. If you think I'm just

gonna stand by while you try to make a fool out of me, you're sadly mistaken."

"See? That's exactly what I'm talking about. You're always thinking the worst about things. Why can't you listen to what I have to say, what I'm feeling? Why can't you do that for once, huh? How do you expect this marriage to continue if you keep making up these ridiculous accusations?" Stanley argued.

"You know what? You are as guilty as hell and you can't even admit it. I hope you enjoyed yourself because this is it. If you want to end this marriage, you can go right ahead because I'm through!" Rachel slammed the phone down in his ear.

Those around her looked up and stared for a moment but soon resumed their work. Rachel managed to restore her composure and keep from screaming out in anger. Her teeth rested on her bottom lip so tightly that they broke the skin. As a child, Rachel always sucked in her lips to hold back her tears. But this time tears couldn't be avoided. She removed herself from her desk and went into the ladies' room where she broke down and wept.

At home, Stanley tried to reach Benita in court, but to no avail. He was unsuccessful. "Arrr!" he said, as he slammed the phone back into its cradle.

Chapter Twelve

At the corner of La Jolla Drive, at the office of 1-900-HOT-SEXX, Chauncy was on the telephone. He ordered a party tray for the entire office. There was a celebration taking place there after work to congratulate all staff personnel and operators for ranking number one in sales and customer satisfaction for the month of February.

"Yes. The works," Chauncy said with a very noticeable lisp in his voice as he spoke to the catering service on the phone. "Thank you, dearie," he said, as he hung up the gold metallic receiver.

The office had a reputation for originality, style, and a whole lot of chic. When the glass door opened, musical chimes were heard. The office's interior decor was chic and funky with a crystal chandelier hanging from the mauve ceiling, plush emerald green carpet, and white skylights that traced along every corner of the four walls. The first impression was a lasting one.

While Chauncy talked, he did not hear the door chimes sound as they did every time someone opened the diamond-cut double doors. He had his back turned and did not realize that there was a visitor waiting. Everyone else in the office was in the main conference room decorating for the party later on that evening. The brief silence was broken when the visitor cleared his throat. Chauncy twirled around in the paisley pink, black, and green chair and was left speechless. Although Chauncy was white and had a boyfriend, he had a secret attraction for handsome black men, especially when they looked like the cocoa brown brother standing before him. Chauncy had to be careful when it came to his job and meeting new people because his boyfriend was very jealous. As it was, Chauncy's white smooth skin, tall slender physique, and his ability to look like a woman really blew a lot of people's minds.

"And what can I do for you?" Chauncy asked, as he arched his eyebrows. And why shouldn't he be a little intrigued, considering the stranger was very handsome and every bit of five eight. He wasn't a towering giant the way Chauncy preferred his men, but as fine and masculine as this brother was, he was ready to make an exception.

"Excuse me. This may sound stupid, but for the last couple of days I have been going from one telephone service to the next, looking for someone," he said. There was no doubt in the stranger's mind that Chauncy was obviously homosexual. Besides the crimped-wavy hairdo, the neat French manicure and shiny lip gloss, there was no mistaking the high-pitched feminine voice.

"I'm not sure if I'm even close, but I'm looking for a certain young woman," the stranger continued to say.

"Whatever and whomever you're looking for, honey, I'm sure you've got the right place. We can accommodate anything you're looking for." Chauncy gave the handsome brother a subtle glance.

"Ah—I don't think you understand," he said.

"Sure I do." Chauncy got up and walked around to where he stood. He examined the surprise guest from head to toe, inspecting him like he was a hot buttery biscuit.

"Oh, yes, darling, I know exactly what you're looking for." Chauncy also admired his taste in clothes since he, too, spent most of his off time shopping and throwing elaborate parties. He could spot a fashion-conscious man anywhere; to Chauncy, that was a big turn-on.

"I'm Chauncy Parker, and you are?" He held out his hand.

"Pardon me. My name is Kelvin Baker." He slowly took off his Ray-Ban sunglasses and stuffed them inside the breast pocket of his linen blazer. Kelvin firmly shook Chauncy's fragile hand. Chauncy squinted as he felt the strength of Kelvin's grip. He quivered shamelessly as if an electrical charge raced up his arm and descended through the lower regions of his soul.

"What a grip!" Chauncy exhaled and threw his other hand up to his narrow chest.

"I need to know if there is a Sheila working here. She may be using an alias to deter any weirdos," Kelvin said with an ultrabright smile.

"And why are you looking for this person, if she exists?" Chauncy asked.

"I just want to meet her. I believe she's sort of new to this kind of thing, and from talking to her, I know she is a really nice person," he said.

"Giving out names of our operators is against company rules. And why should I believe you? She might not even know you from Adam. You could be just another weirdo," Chauncy said. "Besides, what's in it for me? Getting the 4-1-1 on not just any Sheila would require a certain something to jog my memory," Chauncy said, as his eyes gazed toward the ceiling.

"Ahhh. Well, will this help?" Kelvin slipped a crisp fifty-dollar bill in front of Chauncy's eyes, which began to dance.

"That will get you a first and last name." He snatched the money from Kelvin's fingertips.

"And what will it take to jog an address out of you?"

"What do you have to offer? A night on the town, perhaps?" Chauncy said with a devilish grin.

"There could be another fifty in it for you."

"Hell, money can do a lot of things, but it can't keep a body warm at night. What I was thinking about was more along the lines of me and you," he said as he licked his glossy lips. "And afterward I personally drop you off at Sheila's back door."

"Thanks, but no thanks. I always enter from the front, in any given situation," Kelvin said firmly.

"Oh, well, your loss," Chauncy said as he thumbed through the employee files inside the desk drawer. He soon pulled out a card with Stacy's name and her mother's address listed on it, made a copy, and gave it to Kelvin. "Keep in mind now that this is against all rules and regulations," Chauncy said, as Kelvin took the slip of paper and folded it up.

"So is a bribe. But we both got what we wanted, didn't we?" Kelvin said as he placed his sunglasses back on and nonchalantly walked out the door.

"Not exactly," Chauncy mumbled after Kelvin left the office.

Chapter Thirteen

The aroma of buttered popcorn floated through the hallways and offices. Stacy was hunched over her desk rushing through her daily chores. She popped yellow and white kernels between her cinnamon-painted lips.

"Stacy, you're not going out for lunch today, as pretty as it is?" her boss asked, as he placed another long list of client names in her in basket. There was no way she had time to take a minute to stretch from her curved posture, let alone take a lunch break. Stacy was fed up with her job as a customer service rep. She kept debating whether or not to take some college courses to continue pursuing her child development degree. She knew there was no way that she would get an opportunity to advance in her present job unless she had a college degree, or skin so light that she was damn near white.

"How can I, if you keep giving me more work to do?" she said with an artificial smile.

"We'll call it an equal exchange for all the days you've been late," he said without any concern regarding her family life or growling stomach.

"Yeah, right. Jackass," Stacy said in a whisper. As far as she was concerned, he was no better than those pain-in-the-neck bill collectors who made it a point to call her on a regular basis to harass her about money she didn't have. Her wrath was soon interrupted by the sound of the telephone.

"Hello," she said in a less-than-friendly voice.

"My goodness. Who cheated you out of a nut today?" The familiar voice brought a smile to her glum face.

"Chauncy, if you're calling to tell me that the checks did not come in, I'm liable to hurt somebody," Stacy said, as her dark mood slightly lifted.

"Calm down, Evil Lena. Checks are in. I just called to give you some good news, I think. So what's the 4-1-1 on this gorgeous hunk of a man you've been keeping all to yourself?"

"What are you talking about? What man? The only gorgeous man I've seen is the one plastered on the billboards when I'm riding home on the bus every day, and I doubt it very much that he even notices me."

"Well, honey, don't join the convent just yet. I think someone noticed. In fact, he got my undivided attention," Chauncy said.

"Will you tell me what the hell you are talking about?"

"I'm talking about this man who came into the office looking for you not too long ago. He sure was interested in finding you."

Stacy didn't respond. She was shaken by this bit of news. She thought of the phone calls when only the sound of an open line greeted her hello and the times she had felt herself being watched. She had no idea who or why anyone would be looking for her; that is, anyone who would mean good news. Except: no. Couldn't have been, she thought. Chauncy's news made it impossible to think that her imagination had been running away with her. Why would anybody stalk me, she wondered. Except there's no rhyme or reason to what crazies do!

"What did you tell him?" she asked, apprehensively.

"Nothing. I told him that it was against all rules and regulations to give out employee info."

"You never struck me as being the type who conforms

to rules and regulations." Except the rules and regulations that put money in your pocket, she said to herself.

"I'm not. I do just enough to get what I want, when I want it, and how I want it."

Just as I figured. Stacy sighed. At least he admits it. But I'm making a lot of money for Chauncy. Would he give my personal info out to an obvious weirdo? But who knows what anybody will do if the price is right?

"I wish I thought like you. Maybe then I wouldn't be in this dead-end job. Haven't you ever wanted to do something other than what you're doing now?" Stacy asked.

"Oh, yeah. Plenty of times. My original plan was to finish college and open my own hair salon. But I later found out that I was allergic to the chemicals. Then I tried to pursue a career in marketing, my major in college, but it seemed that no reliable business wanted to hire a homosexual. So here I am!"

"I'm sorry," Stacy said.

"Please, I'm not. I'm glad things turned out the way they did. Or else I wouldn't have met you, Stacy. You're a good person and a caring woman; it doesn't take a rocket scientist to figure that out. You won't be doing what you're doing forever. Just think of it as a minor detour. Before you know it, you'll be on the right road to success." He was right, Stacy thought, and listened to Chauncy tell her something she already knew deep down; she just needed someone to confirm it for her.

"Thanks, Chauncy. I needed to hear that."

"My pleasure. And if anyone tries to tell you otherwise, don't listen because they obviously don't know what they're talking about." Stacy laughed at his silliness and took the free advice to heart.

"So in conclusion, I suspect that you will get another surprise before the day is over with."

"I wonder what?" Stacy asked, as she hung up the telephone. Please, God, don't send me any more bad news.

"Psst!" The sound came from outside in the hallway.

Stacy looked up toward the entranceway and got up. She heard the noise again, and then the sound of scuffling and loud, angry voices.

She turned the corner from where she sat and before she could take another step, the doorway was filled with three people—a security guard, a young woman hiding behind the guard and shouting "That's him! He's the one!" and, incredibly, Clyde, who was clutching a bouquet of flowers as if his life depended on it.

"Stacy," Clyde pleaded, "please tell them I'm okay! They think I'm some dude that's been scaring women."

"What do you mean, *think*?" said the young woman in a shrill voice. " I *know* you're the dude who scared me to death by waitin' till all the lights were out and then wantin' to know if I was by myself!"

"I didn't mean no harm—I was lookin' for my lady here. Come on, Stacy, tell 'em I'm harmless."

"Harmless?" Stacy laughed sarcastically. "I'm to look at my life and tell them you're harmless?"

"Come on, Stace, I know you're mad at me, but you know I'm not no rapist!"

"What *are* you doing here, Clyde?" She suddenly felt as if someone had run past her and struck her in the stomach. She felt nauseated and overheated just from seeing him in the flesh. She hadn't been sure if he was alive or dead. He never once called to see how his kids were; he never sent them anything for their birthdays or holidays. It wasn't like she had an unlisted number; maybe it was cut off a few times, but still it wasn't like he didn't have the address either.

Clyde anxiously studied the woman he had left behind, broke, hurt, and alone. Has she forgiven me for skipping out on her? he wondered. "I stopped by to see how you're doin'. You've been on my mind a long time now, and I had to get the courage to come 'n' see you. That's all. I tried to call you, but every time you answered I chickened out. I even hung 'round your mama's house. Lately, I been hangin' around this building. I thought for sure you'd spotted me the other day when you was catchin' that cab. I didn't mean to scare nobody. I was just tryin' to find you and surprise you. These are for you!" He extended the bouquet of assorted flowers.

"What do you really want, Clyde? You have some nerve showing up here," Stacy managed to say without lunging forward and landing a Mike Tyson knockout punch to his jaw.

The security guard and the young woman listened to this exchange with puzzled looks. "Then you do know who this man is?" the guard asked Stacy.

After a few more questions the situation was sorted out and the guard and young woman departed, leaving Stacy and Clyde to confront each other. "It's good to see you, Stace," Clyde said. He had noticed the dramatic change in her right away. She was no longer the old-fashioned, daddy's little girl he knew. She used to be somewhat homey and quiet, even naive. And that was what Clyde liked the most. He told Stacy a lie and she believed him. She was satisfied if she only saw him at least twice a day. He always told Stacy that he had late practice, or the coach wanted him to review the playbook, when, in fact, he was making a couple of plays of his own in a cheerleader's upstairs bedroom.

But Stacy continued to believe him until her best friend opened her eyes to how he really was. But she still wanted to hear it from him, the one she had given her virginity to. The one who knocked her up and then left her behind.

Stacy definitely was a different woman now. In ways he couldn't have imagined.

"Aren't you gonna take these?" he asked, producing that little boy, shy smile that always charmed her, while practically pushing the flowers in her face. Clyde was used to women giving him flowers and little gifts. For him to return the favor was out of character. Clyde always thought of himself first.

Stacy was not amused. He still didn't care about anything or anyone in his life, but he did care greatly about his looks. That was one thing he could always depend on when it came to faking his way into a woman's heart and pants. It was true then, and for Stacy, it still remained true. She still remembered the day she met him at San Diego University. She was there to get a bachelor's degree in child development, while Clyde made it there on a football scholarship. But Clyde needed more than fast feet and a good arm to pass some critical courses in order to stay in school. Considering his chances in professional football and his chances of passing college-level math, the pass was incomplete. But as fate would have it, Clyde teamed up with the smartest girl in his class at the time, Stacy Carr. But like any fairy tale, her dream man turned out to be nothing but a horny toad.

Like a lot of promising black athletes, becoming a big star was the only thing he could see. Maybe that's why he didn't see that car when he and a bunch of his buddies were playing flag football one afternoon and he was hit. That was the end of his big dreams as a professional football player and Stacy's big dreams of becoming a football star's wife.

In spite of herself, Stacy responded to his smile and reflexively accepted the bouquet. "You didn't answer me, Clyde. What do you really want?" It was hard to believe she had not seen him in a year, probably more—she'd lost count. "If you came to get any sympathy from me, you're crazy. You walked out on me and your kids." She caught an attitude right away. "If you think these pathetic little flowers are going to make up for all the times you weren't around—" Stacy's voice rose an octave higher than normal.

Clyde took very careful and precise steps as he walked closer to the woman he had left behind. Could she be married already? The thought caused Clyde's insides to turn upside down. Naw. Knowing Stacy, the girl loved me; she'd never do that. But like they say, time heals all wounds, he thought as he reached her.

"You don't have to let the whole damn place know our problems," Clyde said.

"I don't have a problem. If I'm not mistaken, you're the one who couldn't handle the responsibility of being a real man, a father." Stacy went off.

Clyde grabbed her by the arm and marched her out of the office into the hallway, as an audience of eyes and whispers accompanied their exit.

"You haven't changed. Everything has to be so perfect, so right with you. A man can't make a mistake once in his life without you condemning him to the electric chair," Clyde argued back.

"You damn right. If the shoe fits, then put it on. Day after day I waited to hear from you. I didn't know if you were coming back. I didn't know if you were somewhere in a dark alley, dead, or in jail. If you would have just told me that you needed some time to think things out, then maybe I would have understood. But you didn't even try to contact me," Stacy screamed.

"You didn't give me a chance to say anything. It was always we this and we that. Whatever happened to me? I had a part in the relationship, too. You always had to call the shots, play by your rules," Clyde said.

"Oh, right, make me out to be the villain. If you felt shut in or trapped by the responsibilities that were rightfully yours, why didn't you say something? I could have met some other man who could have filled the bill for you." Stacy gave him an intimidating stare.

"I knew this wouldn't work," he said as he paced in a circle. "I thought we could at least talk sensibly about this. I thought maybe, just maybe, we could pick up where we left off."

"Pick up where we left off! Ha! As I recall, where you left off was when the rent was due, the telephone bill was due, the electric bill was due. Shall I go on?" Stacy said relentlessly. "Clyde, there is nothing you can say that's going to make me ever trust in you again. You walk in here like Mr. All of That, and want to come to me with some chitchat. You don't know what it's like to have to stay up practically every night with a feverish baby who can't sleep because he's too sick to sleep. You don't know what it's like to scrape and scrounge for money you don't have," Stacy said.

"But I want to be there for you and my kids now. Please give me another chance," Clyde said with sad eyes. "Are you seeing anybody else, Stace?"

Stacy sucked her teeth in disgust and turned away from him.

"Come on, girl, you know as well as I do that if you were seeing someone, you wouldn't be out here talking to me now. That should at least tell you something." He tried to read Stacy's demeanor.

"Oh, really? Like what?" She crossed her arms in front of her chest and stood expectantly.

"That maybe you're really glad to see me and that you missed me just as much as I missed you," Clyde said. He took a chance and reached out to touch her.

Stacy was undecided about how she felt. Was he right? Did she really miss him? He sure kept in shape all this time. Of course, Clyde did have the best body on the playing field. But where was that body when I needed him to help me raise not one son, but two, and when he walked out on us for the second time? Where was he when I needed him the most? Stacy thought. God, why did you have to bring him back into my life now? Just when I was about to put my life back together, she thought.

"Stace, I'm sorry for leaving you like I did. I realize now that there was no excuse for it. But I'm back now, and I want to make up for all the mistakes I've made and the hell I put you through. Will you forgive me? If not, I'll turn around and walk right back out the door."

Stacy's gaze fell to the floor to shield the tears that had formed in her eyes. Clyde was not only the first but also the only man she had ever given herself to. And that was a connection that would always make a claim on her heart until she fell in love with someone else. I know I'm going to regret this for some reason, she thought, as she forgave him.

"Oh, Stace." Clyde grabbed her in his python-sized arms and swung Stacy in the air.

"Hold it! I said I'd forgive you, not go to bed with you."

"Okay, if you want, you can hit me or slap me or something to get out all that pent-up anger you have inside." Clyde gave Stacy his best profile so that she could strike him. Stacy looked away to keep from laughing.

"Look, I'm not going to hit you. You know that I'm not the violent type," she said with a smile. She knew he was crazy but she just didn't realize how much. "But if I was, your ass would be picking your teeth up off the floor."

"It might make you feel better if you did," he said.

"I'm still mad at you, but I'm not that mad. We'll just let bygones be bygones." She held out her hand for a shake of friendship, but Clyde had another thought. He took Stacy's hand into his and yanked her into his chest and planted a kiss on her lips.

Fred and Mattie were enjoying a nice quiet lunch together in his office.

"This is really nice, taking time out during a busy day to have lunch with a beautiful woman. This is better than heaven," Fred said as he poured some of Mattie's famous lemonade from a large Thermos.

"Fred, you should have been a dentist. With all of those sweet words you could make a fortune," Mattie said, as she blushed shamelessly at his flirtatious remarks.

"Mattie, if I haven't said it yet, spending this time with you now and in the last couple of weeks has been the most exciting thing in my life in a long time. Since my wife died, I can honestly say that missing her has been replaced by just having you in my life. And I don't mind saying that it would please me greatly if you would consider sharing the rest of your life with me."

"Fred, if I didn't know any better, I'd swear you just proposed to me."

"And what if I did?" he said, as he nonchalantly reached over and took a biscuit from the small bread basket.

Mattie sat with a blank stare on her face. She watched Fred stuff his face with food he had ordered from Nyammins, a local Karibi Kafe.

"What? Are you sure of what you're saying?" Mattie asked, surprised and almost speechless. "We're not a couple of insouciant individuals anymore."

"What are you worried about, Mattie? Look, we're not getting any younger. We're on that big roller coaster of life. We've already traveled down one hill and this roller coaster is constantly picking up speed. Now, you're either going to accept my proposal or—"

"Or what?" Mattie asked with raised eyebrows.

"Or else, I may have to take drastic measures in getting you to say yes." With a smile Fred reached over to pick up the telephone, which rang at that moment. "What!" he exclaimed. Fred then slammed the telephone down and burst out of his office, heading for the stairwell.

"What's the matter?" Mattie cried as she chased after him. But the stairwell door was already closing after Fred. Mattie stood in the hallway feeling anxious, but not knowing what to be anxious about.

Only moments later, Mattie felt a hand on her arm and turned to face Rachel, who was looking very frightened. "I got a call right after Mr. Wilson. They think they've got the rapist trapped on the stairwell between our floor and two floors down!"

"Please, tell me that fool is not chasing after the rapist, that that's not what he's doing," Mattie pleaded.

Holding on to each other, Mattie and Rachel could hear shouts and footsteps pounding in the stairwell. Suddenly, in Fred's triumphant voice, they heard, "I got him!" followed by scuffling sounds. In what could not have been more than a minute even though it seemed an hour, the stairwell door was kicked back and out came Fred and a security guard dragging between them a struggling figure whose face was hidden by a stocking. Obviously winded from their sprints up and down the staircase, both Fred and the guard were panting. Fred ripped the stocking from the figure's face as soon as they pulled him into the hallway.

"Terry!" both Mattie and Rachel shouted simultaneously. Ashen-faced, Mattie declared, "But we trusted Terry. He had the run of the whole place!"

"Right," said the guard. "That's why we decided to tail him. Who'd notice Terry anywhere in the building since people were used to seeing him come and go? So we set up a little bait to see if we could catch us a rat. And did we ever!"

During this exchange Terry had kept his head down, apparently in shame. Now he defiantly met the gazes of Mattie and Rachel.

"Why?" they chorused.

"Why not?" He smirked. "What did this company ever do for me except keep me down? Too bad you bitches didn't get the chance to feel a real man!" Even though he was held, he managed to grab his crotch obscenely.

Outraged, Fred shouted, "You little punk. I'm goin' to show you—" Suddenly Fred's body seemed to spasm and he fell to the floor, clutching his chest.

"Fred, what is it?" Mattie stared at him. She was scared to death. That was a poor choice of words, Mattie thought. Death was the last thing she thought she would be faced with again.

"Help! Help!" Mattie was hysterical.

In a matter of seconds, people from the office rushed out to see what had happened. Rachel knelt down beside Mattie. She saw that Fred was unconscious.

"Mattie, what's happened?" Rachel asked. Mattie was in shock; she couldn't say a word. Her eyes were locked on Fred's glassy, fixed stare. Someone called for an ambulance; another person ran over to Fred, whose skin color had now turned to an ashy gray. He lay there seemingly helpless with his eyes wide open and his breathing erratic.

"I think he's had a heart attack," a man said.

"Mattie, everything is going to be all right," Rachel said. She placed her arm around Mattie's shoulders to comfort her.

In minutes the paramedics were there and performing CPR on him, hoisting his unconscious body onto the stretcher, and propelling it through the crowd of people who blocked the elevator.

"How could this happen? One minute we were just sitting in there talking, and life was wonderful again and then the phone rang," Mattie mumbled. I'd rather die than to have to lose another, Mattie thought as she and Rachel accompanied the paramedics to the ambulance.

As they reached the lower level, Stacy and Clyde were in the lobby. When Stacy saw Mr. Wilson lying on the stretcher with his shirt ripped open and tubes to an I.V. stuck in his arm, she gasped deeply and placed her hands to her mouth.

"What happened?" Stacy asked, but no one gave her an answer. Rachel and Mattie hurried down the front steps, headed for Sharp Memorial Hospital.

At the hospital, Mattie paced the floor of the waiting room while Fred went directly into surgery.

"Mattie, please come and sit down." Rachel watched Mattie pivot back and forth like a ball on a chain.

"It's not going to do him any good if you're out here worrying."

"What else can I do? I can't very well go in there and push the doctor out of the way and perform the operation myself," she said. She realized the sort of tone she had taken, and Rachel acknowledged Mattie's quick apology.

"Oh, Rachel, I should have known something was wrong when he said that he had to see his lawyer. How was I supposed to know that he was sick?" Rachel got up and walked toward Mattie as she stood at the large hospital window in the waiting area.

"It isn't your fault. You had no idea that Fred was going to have a heart attack. Nobody did." She attempted to soothe Mattie's broken heart.

"That's just it, Rachel. He wasn't sick. At least not when we woke up this morning," Mattie said with sad eyes.

"Mattie, are you and Fred . . ."

Mattie realized her secret was out. She hadn't wanted anyone to know that their friendly acquaintance had grown into something much more. "Oh, Rachel, he had just asked me to marry him and like a fool I was teasing him instead of shouting out yes as fast as I could. What's going to happen now? If he dies without even knowing how I feel . . . ," Mattie said with tear-filled eyes.

"Shh. Come on now. Don't think that way. Fred is going to come out of this." Rachel wrapped her arm around Mattie's shoulders and held her tight.

"Rachel, I can't bear to live the rest of my life alone! I never thought at my age I could feel the way he made me feel. I don't think I can live with myself if he dies." Mattie broke down in tears and Rachel could no longer hold back tears and fears as she thought about her own life.

"Mattie, don't worry. Everything is going to be all right," Rachel said. Her voice quivered. Behind them the doctor stood and he cleared his throat.

"Excuse me. I'm Dr. Miles Jordan. Are you the family members of Mr. Wilson?" the tall young brother asked as he pulled off his operating cap and mask.

"Yes, we are," Mattie said quickly. "How is he, Doctor?"

"Well, he's suffered a massive heart attack, and all we can do now is wait," the prominent surgeon said, as he stuffed the head wrap and mask inside the pocket of his lab coat.

"How much time are you talking about, Doctor?" Rachel asked, not wanting to make Mattie any more discouraged than she already was.

"Well, from his past medical history, this would be his second heart attack."

"What!" Mattie exclaimed. She had no idea that Fred had been a victim of a previous attack. Gasping for breath, Mattie wandered away from the two.

"Doctor, what are his chances of making a full recovery?" Rachel asked as she looked at Miles, who was young enough to be her brother, if she had one.

"Please," Miles said as he directed Rachel a few feet away from the waiting area. "Well, for right now, time is the only thing we have on our side. I had to remove a clot that had blocked his coronary artery. There is a risk that Mr. Wilson may suffer from brain damage caused by a lack of oxygen to the brain." Rachel's hand rested on her forehead. This was all Mattie needed to hear, she thought. What hope she did have just turned out to be no hope at all.

"Now, there is a chance that he will make a full recovery. But like I said, only time will tell." Miles tried to be optimistic.

"Could you let me tell her? I think it would be less painful if it came from a friendly face," Rachel explained as she gazed up at Miles towering over her.

"Sure, I understand. If you want, you can see him." Rachel thanked him and gave Mattie the news. While she went in to see Fred, Rachel stayed behind. She walked over to the coffee machine in the corner of the room. She just stared blindly at the coffee bean advertisement on the front of the vending machine. What was she going to do and say when she got home? There was no doubt in her mind that Stanley was going to be in rare form.

"I find it hard to cut back on the caffeine, myself," Miles said as he came up behind her.

"What?"

"I'm sorry. Did I startle you?"

"No," Rachel said, as the scent of his cologne aroused her senses. The smell of it was all too familiar. It was the same cologne she had found underneath the seat in Stanley's car.

"Are you okay?" he asked. Rachel tried to shake off the depression.

"Yes, thank you. I'm sorry. I didn't even introduce myself. I'm Rachel Grier." Miles reached out and took her hand into his. His hands are so soft, Rachel thought. This man must have been a doctor for a long time. Even his nails are perfectly cut and manicured. Stanley doesn't lift a finger around the house unless I beg him and even then, his hands stay rough.

"You know, I've been Fred's doctor for a couple of years now and not once has he told me about having such a beautiful niece," Miles said, obviously admiring Rachel's beauty.

"Niece? I'm not his niece." She blushed.

"Well, you must be a long-lost daughter then." Rachel was tickled.

"No. We're not related." She could see the sudden change in his face.

"So it's safe to assume that woman in there is not related either?" Miles asked.

"Would it matter? They're in love. Or doesn't that count?"

"It's hospital policy that only family members and close relatives are allowed into the patient's room after an intensive operation," Miles said very authoritatively.

"Then you go in there and tell that woman who would rather die than spend the rest of her life without the man she loves," Rachel said as her mean streak surfaced. Miles couldn't help succumbing to her request and beauty.

"Don't worry. I don't break hearts," he said, as he took her hand and placed it into his talented ones. "I mend them." Suddenly Rachel realized this man was making her body tingle in places Stanley had yet to discover.

Chapter Fourteen

Around one o'clock that afternoon, a knock came at the door of Hilda Carr's house.

"Do you want me to get that for you, Hilda?" Alice asked. She was a good friend and Hilda's Christian sister.

"Would you?" Hilda shouted from upstairs. "It's probably my forgetful husband. Bless his old, tired soul. He must have forgotten his keys again," Hilda said as she put Stacy's boys down for their nap.

Alice went to the door, opened it, and found a young man standing there.

"Good afternoon, ma'am. I was wondering if I could speak to Stacy Carr," Kelvin said with a friendly smile, still hoping Chauncy hadn't cheated him out of a hundred bucks.

"And whom shall I say is asking?" Alice asked. Hilda came down the stairs slowly, but a couple of the steps still creaked with age.

"Who is it, Alice?"

Alice turned to Hilda. "It's a young man looking for your daughter," she said as Hilda approached the screen door.

"Yes, can I help you?" she asked.

"I sincerely hope so. I was wondering if Stacy Carr lives here."

"Oh, my Lord! Did something happen to my baby?"

Hilda asked. Kelvin saw the fear in her eyes at the thought of something happening to her daughter.

"No, ma'am. She's fine, I suppose. I just wanted to speak with her if she's available," he said. Hilda noticed his clean-cut looks and business suit. She wondered where her daughter had met such a distinguished gentleman. That was one secret Stacy had failed to tell her mother, Hilda thought.

"Are you a member of Bethel A.M.E?" she asked with a curious expression. Kelvin smiled and answered her shyly.

"No, ma'am."

"Please come in," Hilda invited. While he looked around and saw all the photos of obvious family members, he noticed one in particular. It was a picture of Stacy, with two small boys in her arms.

"Is that your daughter?" Kelvin asked, as he held the framed picture in his hand.

"Yes, it is. Those are my two precious grandsons," she said proudly. "Is this visit about a bill? I'm sure she has put the check in the mail already," she went on.

Kelvin smiled. "No, ma'am. I'm not a bill collector. I just wanted to see her and talk to her. I rarely get to talk to her anymore," he said. "Being a counselor for inner-city youths leaves very little time for socializing." Kelvin placed the picture back on the mantel and prepared to leave.

"Well, if you'd like to leave a message for this visit, I'll see that she gets it. Is there anything I can help you with?" Hilda continued to question him. Nothing would do more to make her day than to have total control of her daughter's life and personal business.

"Maybe I can come back some other time. That is, if it's fine with you, ma'am?" Kelvin asked, showing respect for Hilda and her home.

"Certainly. I just wish Stacy had more friends who are as caring and considerate as you are," Hilda said. She saw the young man to the door. "If you don't have a church home, Stacy would be happy to have you as a visitor on Sunday morning." She couldn't resist. That was one reason Stacy was always upset with her mother. She seemed to push her religion on her friends.

"Thank you, ma'am. I appreciate the invitation." Kelvin opened the door, shook Hilda's hand, walked down the fire redbrick walkway to his car, and got behind the wheel. Since taking the counseling job, Kelvin had found himself working far more hours than the forty per week he was paid for. Up to this point Kelvin had gladly donated his time, remembering the moral debt he owed to the counselor who had rescued him from the wrong path he had started down as an inner-city youth. As he struggled to deal with a particularly difficult boy, he often reminded himself, "There but for the grace of God . . ." Recently, though, he had come to believe that to keep his perspective, he must have a life outside of his work. Knowing no girls in San Diego, he found himself, out of sheer loneliness for a female voice, turning to a phone sex number. And, wonder of wonders, he thought that he had found a rose among thorns.

Hilda and Alice watched until the car vanished down the hill of their street.

"Who was that?" Alice asked.

"I wish I knew," Hilda said, puzzled.

Chapter Fifteen

The sun had set in the west as seagulls screeched, dipped, and glided in the last rays of warm sunlight above the blue ocean. This was considered to be the best time of the day. The waves slowly lapped against the gray, sun-dried rocks along the pier. As the skies grew dark, a dozen small, flickering lights seemed to dance in the distance. The *Saradina* was on its last outing.

Kris had made this a regular routine since the investigation ended. He had talked his commander into letting him keep the boat for a few more days to unwind. But what he really wanted was to remember the good times he and Lesa had spent together. No matter how he tried to put what happened into perspective, he always came to one conclusion: he was in love and there wasn't a damn thing he could do about it.

He dropped anchor and turned up the CD player that played the soulful sounds of Brian McKnight's "Never Felt This Way About Lovin'." Each note seemed to sway to the ripples in the moonlight. If only Lesa were here, he thought. Her beautiful face would add the perfect touch to the tranquil evening. To Kris, this was just another night. He waited until the air started to chill him, then he lifted the anchor and sped back to shore.

* * *

At the hospital, Rachel made a phone call to Faith.

"Where are you? I've called your office more than a hundred times it seems like. Is everything all right?" she said, relieved to hear Rachel's voice.

"Yeah. Today has just been one of those days. But I have no time to get into it right now. I need your help, Faith," Rachel said.

"Sure. Anything."

"I want you to pick up Nicky for me. He's with Mrs. Jenkins, his day-care teacher. I didn't want to call Stanley because he would just make matters worse," Rachel said, exasperated.

"Rach, you know I don't mind, but where are you now? It sounds like a hospital," Faith said.

"Like I said, it's a long story. I'll fill you in later. Just get my baby for me and I'll see you later on."

"Okay, but you call me if you need me," she heard Faith say before she hung up.

At the 1500 block of Madison and McMechan, Heads Above the Rest Beauty Salon was jumping with customers and excitement. The smell of curling irons and hair spray floated out of the large open windows of the shop and into the streets. Laughter and music accompanied the roaring sounds of dome hair dryers that generated tremendous heat inside the matchbox-sized establishment.

"Come on, Natasha," Kiki said to a young lady who sat in the small waiting area. Her hair sprouted all over her head after Kiki took out more than a dozen bobby pins that helped hold her thick "do." In the rear of the salon two sistahs had a deep discussion from under two hair dryers that sounded more like a shouting match from the T.V. show *Square Off*.

"You mean to tell me that your man came home and told you that he quit his job, withdrew all his money from your account, and said that he was not going to work no more?" Crystal asked, as she devoured a chicken wing.

"Shaniqua, gir-r-l-ll, I think you've been sitting in

here under that damn dryer too long," another said as she sat under the other dryer, skimming through a hair book.

"So what if he quit his job. I want my man to know that he can depend on me for support. He was there for me when I got laid off from my job." Shaniqua defended her man.

"You're only supportin' him 'cause social services is supportin' you," Crystal said as her neck twitched from side to side.

"Look who's talking. Well, at least I got a man."

"Oooh! Who's got the dirt?" a bunch of them said as all ears tuned in on the latest gossip.

"Excuse me. Ex-man," Crystal said.

"From what I hear, Crystal, your man was spotted coming in and out of my complex a few nights ago. And he wasn't alone." Shaniqua snapped her fingers, as if to dis' Crystal in front of everybody.

"You don't know what you're talking about. I don't care what or who he's seeing. Ain't none of my business," Crystal said, as she ignored the looks from her friends.

"Yeah, right. If he walked in here right now, girl, you'd probably snatch every last curler out'cha head and slap on some lipstick real quick." The entire place roared with laughter.

"Go to hell, wench!" Crystal was mad now.

"Rump Shaker" by Dos-In-Effect screamed from the large speakers in the corner of the front walls. Tonya, one of the other beauticians, reached over and turned the volume way up. Fingers, feet, and butts were moving to the rhythm of the hip-hop groove. The buzzer from the door sounded. Dina, the owner, let the customers in.

"Oh, my goodness! Look what the wind blew in. Hey, girl!" Dina said to Stacy as the two old friends hugged each other.

"Hey, what's up? Long time no see," Stacy said to her old college buddy. She hadn't seen her since the last time their high school had its class reunion.

Dina used to do Stacy's hair when she wanted to experiment with new styles and color. Maybe that's why Stacy had not allowed Dina to mess with her head since then.

"What have you been doing to this head?" Dina asked. She walked around observing all the damage.

"Nothing. It's been this way since the last time you saw me," Stacy said, standing there like a statue.

"Yeah, that was last summer. It's just screaming for help," Dina said as a joke. "Come on over here in my chair. I have to put my surgical gloves on for this job." Stacy got a good laugh. Dina was always the funny one out of the little clique she hung with in school. In fact, she was the one who introduced Stacy to Clyde in a roundabout way. The women in the salon started up their gossip corner once again. This time they were whispering about Clyde, who sat in a corner by the front door.

"Who is that? He looks awfully familiar," Crystal said as her eyes zoomed in on him. He looked extra tasty in a pair of khaki slacks with a short-sleeved dark green cotton shirt tucked in, which exposed his firm buttocks and trim waistline. His chest stuck out extra big whenever he wanted to show off his football-player body, Stacy thought.

"I don't know. But if he's here in a roomful of love-starved women, he must be looking for a wife," Shaniqua said as she sat straight up to expose her voluptuous breasts.

"Don't even try it, girlfriend. I saw him first," Crystal said, salivating.

"You're both wrong. He came in with somebody," another said, uninterested.

"So tell me, girlfriend, what's been happening with you? If I remember correctly, you have two kids and you're still single, right?" Dina said. She combed out Stacy's thick, dark brown mane and began to clip the ends.

"Yep. Some things never change," Stacy said. Clyde kept his eyes on her the entire time she sat in the chair.

"At least one thing has changed. Your taste in men. Who is that?"

Stacy gave Dina a dirty look in the mirror. "Are you for real? That is Clyde's dumb ass."

"That's Clyde? I thought he flew the coop."

"Yeah, well, it was a shock to me, too. The last person I ever thought I'd run into would be him," Stacy said, unsure of what to think about Clyde's sudden appearance. What was really behind this déjà vu? she wondered.

"You know I'm not one to gossip, and I don't get into anybody's business. People come in here and sit in my chair and start telling me their whole life story," Dina said. After she washed, conditioned, and dried Stacy's hair, she took long strands of fake hair and braided them into Stacy's own hair. "All I do is listen."

"Is that right?" Stacy helped by separating the strands of hair in her hands.

Dina turned the chair around to face the large mirror in front of them.

"You want me to beg, don't you?" she asked, smiling behind Stacy's head.

"What are you talking about?" Stacy returned with a grin.

"You know what I'm talking about. What's up with you two?" Dina whispered in Stacy's ear.

"I thought you said you don't ask questions, you just listen." Stacy looked at Dina in the mirror.

"Well, I didn't say I was a mute, did I? I see and hear everything in this place, girl. I know who's sneakin' around, who's going to be married, and who's getting a divorce before anyone else does."

"Well, this is one little juicy tidbit you won't get a jump on, because there's nothing to tell," Stacy said as she glanced over at Clyde. She was careful not to say too much, knowing the women around her thrived on gossip and dirt.

Stacy was still unsure why Clyde suddenly appeared out of nowhere. If he was getting away with not paying child support for all this time, why in the world would he show up now? He even insisted on paying for Stacy's hairdo.

Clyde caught Stacy's eye and winked at her sweetly. She gave him an artificial smile back. A sneaky bastard, she thought.

Chapter Sixteen

In the small community of Heather Glenway, Rachel pulled up in front of her house. She parked Stanley's car beside her own and got out, noting her mother-in-law's car parked just below the driveway, on the other side of the street. It was Gertrude's silver Saab, all right, the one Stanley bought for her last year.

What in the hell is she doing here? thought Rachel angrily. Rachel knew she had to confront Stanley, but she was in no mood for his mother, who didn't like her in the first place.

"Two against one. Great," Rachel mumbled as she approached the side door to the house. When her key turned in the door, Stanley and Gertrude were in the living room. He had just gotten off the phone with Reggie. And just in the nick of time, too. Reggie had given his big brother hell. Stanley had been calling practically all over town looking for Rachel. He was worried that she might have found out that he was not with his brother last night but with Benita instead. Stanley was just about to call the hospital when he heard the kitchen door close. He laid the telephone down and rushed into the kitchen.

"Where in the hell have you been? Do you realize I've been like a damn fool around here? I've called just about everybody I know who might have had some idea of your whereabouts," he said in a loud, angry voice. Rachel stood perfectly still for a minute. She calmly unbuttoned her suit jacket and laid it across a chair.

"Stanley, I'm not deaf; you don't have to scream," she said.

"Oh, so that's all you have to say?" he continued. "You couldn't pick up a telephone and call me to tell me what was going on?"

"I'm your wife, not some damn child, but that's funny coming from you, considering you couldn't even find your way home the last couple of days. And don't expect me to say anything? What sort of woman do you think I am?"

"I knew you were going to bring that up again. And where's Nicky? Or did you forget we had a son?"

"I left him with a friend until this matter is resolved," Rachel said as she pushed her way past Stanley into the other room.

"What in the hell is that supposed to mean?" he said as he followed behind her.

Rachel walked into the living room only to find Gertrude there.

"Hello, Rachel. We were worried about you," she said with a tight smile.

"Stanley, I would like to speak with you alone," Rachel said with her eyes locked on Gertrude.

"Whatever you got to say, you can say it in front of Mother. She's a member of this family," Stanley said as he went to the bar and poured himself a drink.

"Well, I could see that if we were in her house, but this is my house, and I want to speak to you alone," Rachel said with clenched teeth.

Stanley gulped down the glass of Hennessy. "For God's sake, Rachel!" He slammed his empty glass down on the lacquered bar.

"No. It's all right, son. Rachel's right. I'll just go into the kitchen," Gertrude said. She left the two of them alone. Rachel looked on with determined eyes.

"Okay, you got what you wanted. Now, what the hell is

so damned important that you had to treat my mother like she was some kind of outsider?" Stanley always felt that Rachel said things in spite of his close relationship with his mother. But Rachel thought it was because of their close connection that she spoke out.

"How stupid do you think I am, Stanley? Did you really think you could get away with what you've been doing practically in my face?"

"What? What is it that I supposedly have done?" he asked.

"This is what I'm talking about." Rachel stormed out into the foyer and returned with her mahogany attaché case and snatched out the bottle of cologne and the Valentine card.

"Explain this." She threw the small box at Stanley, as he tried to act surprised.

"What the hell is this?" he asked. Rachel didn't answer. Instead she read aloud what was on the card: " 'To Stanley. Time has a way of making one forget the past, but it never prepares us for the future. There will always be a special place in my heart for you. Love, Benita.' " Stanley turned his back on Rachel as she read Benita's feelings aloud. All hopes of finding an excuse for the unplanned shock had just flown out the window.

"Oh, Rachel, you're always jumping at the first chance to make a big deal out of nothing. This was a gift," Stanley said. "It means nothing."

"Obviously it meant something to both of you, seeing as you couldn't bring your black ass home. And don't tell me you were at Reggie's all night. You can't even look me in the face to tell me the truth. How long have you been seeing her? A week, a month, what?" Rachel challenged as tears streamed down her face.

Stanley went back over to the bar and made himself another drink.

"Do you want a drink? You look like you need one," he said sarcastically.

"What I need is for you to tell me the truth about your relationship with Benita and her son."

"What about him?" Stanley said abruptly.

"Is Malcolm your son?" Rachel waited for his answer. She folded her arms across her chest tightly, as if to keep it from bursting apart.

Stanley paced in front of the empty fireplace in disbelief. He had no idea that she took the rumor for being the truth, yet he knew it was impossible for her not to. Hell, he wasn't even sure if Benita had told him the truth.

"I can't believe this. My own wife listening to rumors, and, worst of all, believing them. Rachel, I thought you were smarter than that."

"You still didn't answer me. Is Malcolm your son? Is that why you can't seem to stay away from her?"

"Are you crazy? Benita and I are just friends and nothing more. Why don't you go ask her the same question you just asked me. I'm sure she'd get a big laugh out of it as well," he said offensively.

"Why? I asked you. If I thought it would be easier to get the truth out of her, believe me, I wouldn't hesitate," Rachel said with sudden tenacity. For some odd reason Stanley recognized a new strength in Rachel's eyes. If he never took her feelings seriously before, this was one time he should.

"There's no getting through to you. Think what you want to think," he said, frustrated. He was starting to feel the effects of the liquor. "I work my ass off day after day and for what? I can't even look around and see what all the hard work was for. Even my own brother and his friends are living their dreams. Where did I go wrong?" He turned to Rachel with glassy eyes.

"Stanley, this is not about Reggie or his buddies. It's about you and your life, as a father and a husband. Now, if you're having some problem fulfilling those roles, then I think you . . ." Rachel began to say.

"You still don't get it, do you? Rachel, I'm thirty-eight years old, and I feel like I've lost vital years of my life.

Since we've been married, I can honestly say that my life hasn't amounted to much. All the dreams I had are dreams that never came true." Stanley had shown a side of him that Rachel had seen only once when his father died. Stanley felt lost.

"I've done everything a black man can humanly do. But I guess you can't see that," he said. Rachel didn't know whether to laugh or cry. How pathetic, she thought.

"And I suppose Benita knows exactly how you feel, huh?" she said with anger written all over her face. "Tell me something. Does she know the bull I had to go through and still go through because your day somehow didn't start out the way you wanted it to? So you're right. If anyone should be complaining, Stanley, it's me." Rachel was outraged.

"I said I was sorry, didn't I?" Stanley yelled as he threw his hands in the air.

"Yeah. You're sorry." Rachel said sarcastically. Sorry had become the only word in Stanley's vocabulary that ever reflected his life. Sorry, Rachel thought. "Stanley, I've taken all I'm going to take. If you felt like this all this time, how come you've decided to let me know about it now? I mean, we've only been married what, eight years? You're right, I don't understand. You're not going to get any sympathy from me. You want to know why?" Stanley just looked at her blankly. "What you need to do is stop making stupid excuses for your failures and start doing something about it. Benita can't help you. Your mother can't help you, and your friends can't. I don't even know if I can, not unless you let me. Stanley, the only person standing between you and your so-called dreams is you. Not me." She turned and started to leave the room. "Until you can find what it is you're looking for, you're not going to be happy. And neither will I." She wiped the tears from her eyes.

"Where are you going?" Stanley asked in pursuit.

"It's clear that this marriage has become nothing more than a stumbling block for you, and until you find what it is that's missing in your life . . ."

"So you're just gonna walk out, just like that, huh?" Stanley asked. He never felt more scared in his life.

Was this what he wanted? Stanley thought quickly. He stood at the bottom of the staircase. Rachel stopped at the top of the stairs. She could no longer harness the tears that poured from her face full force.

"Somewhere we went wrong, Stanley. There's no room in your heart for me and your son, so how can there be room in this house?" Rachel walked into the bedroom and slammed the door.

From the window Stanley watched the family across the street. They seem so perfect, but they must have problems just like anybody else, Stanley thought, as he continued to watch his neighbors disappear behind their front door. How was it that my father did what he had to do in order to keep his family together when his life was falling apart? Stanley suddenly saw himself as the frightened boy he was long ago. It was the time when he and his father were about to take their first boat ride together one cold and foggy morning. He was ten at the time and he remembered crying and shivering. Not because he was cold from the morning air, but because he was afraid of drowning. Just as the fog had lifted off the ocean, his father had instructed him to pick up his gear and get on the boat. Stanley wanted to plead with his father that he did not want to go out there in something so big, that even his father could not save him if something went wrong. There was too much water even for someone his size to swallow. But his father was brave. That was one thing Stanley really admired about his dad. He wasn't afraid of anything. Stanley never wanted to let his father see him cry. His father used to say that crying was for sissies. He also remembered his father saying, "Son, if you want to sail the world, you gotta have courage to lose sight of the dock." A smile suddenly enveloped Stanley's face because his father always knew just what and who Stanley's nemesis was.

"I miss you, Pop," Stanley said as a tear fell from his eye.

After a few minutes of silence, Stanley's rage reached its breaking point.

"Stanley," his mother said in a soft voice behind him.

"What's happening, Mama? What in hell is wrong with me?" he asked. He felt as helpless as a bird in a storm. "Everything I set out to do crumbles right in front of me," he said, upset over his actions.

"Baby, you listen to me. What you and Rachel went through just now was bound to happen. She was never right for you anyway." Stanley couldn't believe what he was hearing.

"When a man and woman see nothing but the negative things in each other, then you only end up blaming yourself for something that should have never happened in the first place," Gertrude said as she attempted to play on his emotions. She picked up the bottle of cologne. "Now, Benita, she really . . ."

"What are you saying? Do you hate my wife that much to push another woman in my face? My marriage is on the brink of breaking up and all you can do is think about your own feelings. I can't believe you." Stanley was devastated and surprised at his mother's tenacious grudge against his wife. He snatched the bottle from her hand. "My marriage is falling apart. Or don't you really care?" He hurled the gift into the cold, empty fireplace. The aroma soon filled the room. Stanley turned toward the stairs to go after Rachel.

"All right, fine. Go run up there and stop her," Gertrude said in a loud voice. "But before you do, just think about what you could be doing, now that you have this opportunity to get back what was once yours. All your hopes and dreams of becoming that success, the one thing your father and I always wanted for you, son." Gertrude only wanted the best for herself. She still intended to live the rest of her life through his. When she lost her husband to death, she promised herself that she would not lose her sons, especially Stanley.

"If you won't do it for yourself, then do it for your father," Gertrude said.

"Stop it! Just stop it." Stanley raced up the stairs and stood outside the bedroom door. He couldn't bring himself to turn the knob. What was stopping him? He wanted to show his mother that what she said was not the truth. Or was it? His head slowly fell forward against the door and he began to cry softly.

Stanley was at his lowest. He didn't know what steps to take or what to say to Rachel. His head felt as if it had split in two.

Inside the bedroom, Rachel sat in tears, unaware that Stanley was just on the other side of the door.

Why in the hell am I still here? He probably told that witch that this whole thing is my fault, she thought. It's as plain as the nose on my face that he doesn't want to save this marriage or else he would be up here right now. Oh, what's the use? Face it, girl, it's over. They've won. Gertrude, Benita, Stanley, they all got what they wanted. Why am I still holding on? He's not going to come running up here and kick the door down like some phony-ass love story and grab me in his arms and smother me with kisses. Rachel gathered a few things and threw them into a suitcase on the bed. She snatched the bag off the bed and started to walk out. Then she reached up and took a picture of herself, Nicky, and Stanley as they sat happily on a park swing. She stuffed it into a canvas bag and slung it across her shoulder. Was this what her life amounted to, a few inexpensive items stuffed inside a cotton bag? She took a deep breath, closed the door behind her, and went downstairs.

She paused in the open area between the living room and the front entrance. Rachel was despondent and stiff. Stanley hadn't remained upstairs and now stood looking in her direction.

"I'll call you once I get where it is I'm going. I may send someone to pick up Nicky's things."

"Rachel, wait. You really don't have to do this. At least don't take Nicky away from his home," Stanley said.

"What could you possibly say to him that would make him understand that his daddy isn't sure that he wants to be a part of this family anymore? Stanley, you don't even understand it yourself. This would only confuse him. But don't worry, you're still his father and always will be," Rachel said.

Stanley walked up to her and gave her a kiss and a tight embrace. They both didn't want to let go of each other, and the tears were inevitable.

"Good-bye, Stanley," Rachel said in a low, tight voice.

"Rachel, please wait," Gertrude said, as Stanley walked back into the living room. "Won't you reconsider?" Rachel snickered sarcastically at her mother-in-law's request. She didn't mean a word of it, Rachel knew.

"You want to know something? I have to commend you on your persistence in destroying not just my life, but your own son's as well. You finally got what you wanted," Rachel said, scornfully.

"Rachel, it's obvious that you're upset," Gertrude said.

"Why don't you just drop the concerned mother-in-law act? You may think you've gotten rid of me, but this is just the beginning. You see, we're still married and we have something more important than that. We have a son together and there's nothing you can do that will change that."

"Rachel, you really should start owning up to your mistakes. But I tell you what ... if Stanley wants to really rectify his marriage, then I'm behind him one hundred percent."

"Please. The only thing you can do for this family is go to hell," Rachel said before she stormed out of the house.

Gertrude stood in triumph. "The pleasure was all mine, my dear," she said after the door had slammed shut.

Stanley stood at the window as he watched Rachel get into her car and drive away.

Chapter Seventeen

"Do you have the time?" Clyde asked the cab driver. The driver pointed to a self-adhesive miniature clock that was secured to the dashboard of the cab. He and Stacy were on their way to pick up the kids.

Stacy glanced over at a nervous Clyde as he looked out the car window. The objects outside the speeding taxi appeared as mere streaks of color.

"You don't seem to be eager to see your children. Hell, it's only been, what, almost two years now," Stacy said.

Clyde's eyes inadvertently connected with hers. Even though he didn't say so, he was more concerned about facing Stacy's parents than his own kids. All he could think about was the last time he and the good Reverend Carr sat down one day in his spirit-filled home and he told Clyde that there was no reason to disgrace the family any more than he already had. With Stacy dropping out of college, getting pregnant, and then having the child out of wedlock, there was no reason for him to continue hanging around when he had no intentions of marrying Stacy.

What was I to do? Clyde thought at that time. There was no way in hell he was gonna get married because of some baby. Guys did it all the time. One marriage out of a million wouldn't make a bit of difference, Clyde thought. Besides, he had a bright future ahead of him. He thought of himself as not being the marrying type. Yep. A bright future that slowly diminished each time he sat with the reverend. Finally it came down to Clyde being pressured into marriage, whether he was ready or not. And frankly, Clyde wasn't having it.

The next day Clyde left town. But it wasn't soon enough for Stacy, who wound up having his baby alone and humiliated. But no sooner had he heard the news that he had a son, Clyde was back. But it didn't stop there. Clyde hung around a year and before she knew what had happened, Stacy was pregnant with her second child. That was the last time she ever saw or heard from Clyde.

"Are you just going to sit there and say nothing?" Stacy asked, interrupting Clyde's daydream.

"What do you want me to say? I'm sittin' here, ain't I?" Clyde snapped.

"Yeah, you're here all right. But you must have left your mind a few blocks back," Stacy said. She tried to figure out his sudden change in behavior.

"Look, don't start it. We haven't even been together for twenty-four hours yet, and you're already getting on my nerves."

"Well, excuse me. Seeing you've been away on vacation or whatever for the last couple of years, I thought maybe I'd let you in on what I've been going through," she said.

"From the looks of you and your fancy clothes, your Louis Vuitton handbag, glitzy costume jewelry, and designer pumps, you really must have been roughing it," Clyde said, making it a point to finally comment on her rejuvenated wardrobe. "Or maybe you got some other man stashed away somewhere," he added with a crude look.

Stacy laughed. She couldn't believe her ears. Clyde, the once-famous guy on campus, who thought he was the cat's meow, had finally turned green with jealousy.

"Even if I did, it's none of your business."

"If he's trying to play daddy to my kids, you damn right it's my business."

"Please. You haven't been a father to those boys for so long that you shouldn't even consider yourself a father. You're one of those deadbeat fathers whose picture is flashed across the T.V. screen along with 'America's Most Wanted.' "

The taxi pulled up in front of Stacy's parents' house. She opened the door and got out.

"Aren't you coming?" she asked Clyde.

"Look. I don't think that would be a good idea. I'm the last person your parents would want to see walking through their holy door right now."

"I knew this was too damned good to be true. All that talk you've been doing about how you've changed."

"I'm sorry. But I'm not ready for a put-down from your folks. I'm not good enough for you in their eyes and I never will be as far as they're concerned."

"Just forget it!" Stacy said, slamming the car door in his face. "I should have known you were still a punk."

"Hey! Watch your mouth, girl!" Clyde yelled out from the car window, as Stacy stormed up the walkway to her parents' house.

"You make me sick," she mumbled angrily.

"Hey! Hey! I heard that."

The cab driver cleared his throat to indicate that the meter was still ticking. It wasn't like he had anywhere special to go, it was just that he witnessed too many small disagreements that turned into big ones. All he was concerned about was getting his fare.

"Yo, man. You can kill that engine. I'm only paying to get from point A to point B, not gas this tin can up," Clyde said to the cabby in a hostile tone.

"Who is that out there with you? And what in God's name did you do to your hair? All these plaits . . ." Hilda ran her fingers through Stacy's rows and rows of shoulder-length braids.

"Nobody. And I was tired of getting up every morning and trying to find a different way to handle this bush," she said. She bent down and picked up Terrence, while Hilda peered out the front window casually.

"Ty, baby, pick your things up and put them in the bag." Stacy helped her son pick up the toys and clothing and placed everything in the canvas bag. "Mama, would you please stop looking out that window, like you can really see that far without your glasses."

"I can see perfectly well from here. He doesn't look like that nice young man who came looking for you this afternoon," Hilda said.

"Who came looking for me today?" Stacy asked curiously. She really didn't care. She only wanted to divert her mother's attention from the window.

"Some handsome fellow stopped by here. He said that he was in the neighborhood and thought he would just stop by," she said as she stretched her twenty-forty vision.

"Well, who was it; did he say? It probably was some ol' bill collector trying to get money as usual," she said.

"No, that's what I thought, too. But it turned out he was just a friend looking for you. Oh, I give up. Stacy, who is that out in that taxi?" Hilda asked, giving up on her surveillance. "I think he said his name was . . ." She paused, trying to remember.

"Mama, don't worry about it," Stacy said.

"Now, wait a minute. I never forget a name," she said, trying to remember.

"Mama, I have to go. I'll see you tomorrow morning." Stacy opened the door with Terrence in one arm, the baby bag in another, and Tyron holding on to her suit jacket as they made their way to the waiting taxi.

"When I think of his name, I'll give you a call!" Hilda yelled from the doorstep.

"Fine, Mama. You can go back inside now," Stacy said. She didn't even bother to turn around because she knew that her mother was the nosy type.

The door to the cab swung open and, without getting

out, Clyde extended his long arms and pulled Tyron in, along with an overstuffed canvas bag loaded with Pampers, extra clothes, and toys.

"Here we are," Stacy said. She watched Tyron stare at the father he didn't know or remember.

"Hey, buddy. What's up, man?" Clyde said as he play-boxed with him. To Tyron, Clyde was a total stranger.

"And this is little Terrence. Terrence, this is your daddy," Stacy said. She talked to him as if he could understand what she was saying. But Terrence was more concerned with his mother's round gold earrings dangling within his tiny reach.

"Well, Clyde, this is your family." Clyde admired the boys. He could not deny them because the boys looked just like him.

The cab driver proceeded in the direction of Stacy's apartment.

At the Bayside Bar and Grill, adjacent to the Sharp Memorial Hospital, Mattie sat in a dimly lit booth in a depressed state, drowning her sorrows in her second glass of Long Island iced tea. She had drunk somewhat heavily for that time of day. She needed the courage to face Fred in the hospital; his condition had not changed.

Mattie sat and tried to hold back the tears of loneliness, heartache, and just plain anger.

"I need my girl," she said. Mattie reached inside her purse and found her Nancy Wilson cassette, but what good did it do seeing she didn't have her tape recorder. It was in her desk drawer back at the office.

A young woman appeared with a pad and pencil in hand. "Good evening. My name is Karen and I will be your waitress this evening." She placed a pitcher of ice water and a glass down in front of Mattie and took her order.

"Yes. Could I get a refill, please?" Mattie asked in a rather loud voice.

"This makes your third one," she said politely. Karen had seen many customers come through those doors upset and despondent. Having the hospital right across the street didn't help much. In fact, that was the cafe's chief business. Doctors, interns, family members, and close friends of patients made this a stop before going home or to the hospital.

"You're right," Mattie said as she gave the young woman a long glance. "I didn't realize keeping count of how many drinks a customer has was part of the job. Now, I asked for a refill. Would you like to get it or should I?" Mattie said viciously. Karen left the table. She wasn't upset, but she had to take a few minutes to put her own attitude in check.

"Hey, Karen," Miles said as he came in and sat down at the bar.

"Hey, Doc," she said with a less than cordial response.

"Who took the wind out of your sails today?" he asked. Karen's eyes scanned over at Mattie who attempted to get the last drop from her glass. Karen dropped a colorful umbrella and a twist of lemon in the tall glass for decoration.

"Doc, this has been one hell of a day. And it isn't over yet."

"You want to talk about it?" Miles asked as he plunged his hand into a bowl of mints and mixed nuts.

"No. I think she needs a patient ear more than I do," Karen said as she looked over in Mattie's direction. Miles then insisted that he take the drink over.

"Good evening. Ms. Thompson, right?" he asked.

"Doctor." Mattie tried to appear calm and in control. She proceeded to adjust her demeanor although she was not in the mood for any guest, even the nice doctor.

"Is everything all right? I couldn't help but notice you from across the room," he said.

"Why? Does it look like I need company?" Mattie snapped. She had acquired a short fuse.

LOVE'S DECEPTIONS

"No. But I could sure use some. Do you mind?" He waited until he was officially invited to sit.

"Please, have a seat. Maybe before this evening is through, we both will have cheered each other up."

Miles sat across from Mattie in the cozy booth. "I believe this is yours." He slid the drink over to her, but Mattie refused to pick it up.

She knew she wanted it more than anything, but she was feeling the sting of the first two. She was afraid of the condition she was going to put herself in and also she did not want Miles to see her in a drunken stupor.

"Is something wrong with it?" Miles asked.

"No, I think I've had enough for one night. Besides, I can't hold my liquor like I used to," Mattie said surprisingly. "Sometimes I have to remind myself that drinking isn't a substitute for life's little surprises," she said. Miles guessed she was referring to Fred.

"How true. But look on the bright side. There's always tomorrow. I know that may sound a bit old, but it's true. Why worry about today when you can start fresh tomorrow? Life always gives us a second chance. But you've got to have the courage to face it."

Mattie laughed. "Don't get me wrong, Doctor, I'm not laughing at you. It's more so at myself. You have no idea how many times I've told myself that and just when I thought tomorrow was going to be better, well, let's just say that I could have accomplished more if I stayed in bed with the covers pulled over my head." Her fingers glided up and down the frosty glass, tempting her to guzzle it down.

"You're not the only person who's ever felt that way. In fact, it's the most natural feeling in the world. If I didn't have so many patients to see in a day, you best believe I'd be home indulging in the same thing." Miles laughed. He attempted to get Mattie to release her tension just by talking and listening. His second-best talent.

"But we have to get up and face the world for what it is—imperfect; and so are we. Don't keep condemning yourself for what you have no control over. It's all part of life. It's trial and error. We won't know how strong we are unless we have trials and tribulations. That was one thing my mama always told me," Miles said.

Mattie saw that this tall, intelligent black man had more than just a white lab coat and a stethoscope; he had knowledge and wisdom, the one thing the world needed more of.

"I've been holding so much in for so long that I was beginning to think that I was going to take this awful burden to my grave. There is nothing worse than feeling and being lonely. To me this is worse than dying. Having to believe that I may have to spend the rest of my life lonely and a widow is the worst thing anyone has to go through. And when Fred came along, I thought I had finally put those fears to rest," Mattie confessed.

"Well, maybe what I have to say will make you change your mind," Miles said with a grin. "Mr. Wilson will be taken off the critical list in a couple of days. He's finally making progress."

Mattie's eyes lit up like a child's on Christmas morning. There was nothing that sounded better to her ears than to hear that Fred was going to make it. "Death should be the last thing you should be worrying about. Things we have no control over shouldn't be our nemesis. But what you both should be looking forward to is living long, productive, and happy lives," he said.

"Doctor, how can I thank you?" Mattie asked.

"Just sitting here and enjoying this nice conversation is thanks enough for me," Miles said with a warm smile.

Mattie got up and hugged Miles like she would her own son, if she had one.

"Doctor, you are a special young man." Mattie had found a new source of hope and direction thanks to Dr. Miles Jordan.

"He still is under watchful care, but give him a week and he will be as good as new." Just as they were about to depart, Rachel walked through the door of the bar and grill. Miles's eyes locked on to her right away. Her eyes nonchalantly scanned the place until she, too, found her attention directed to where Miles and Mattie stood.

"Rachel, over here," Mattie summoned her. Mattie wasn't the only one who was glad to see Rachel. Miles was also glad.

"I can't talk. I'm on my way to see Fred. But I'll call you later." Mattie smacked a quick kiss on Rachel's cheek and darted out the cafe door.

"What was that all about?" Rachel asked, feeling as if she were caught up in a whirlwind.

"I've just given her some good news about your boss. It seems he's making wonderful progress."

"That's great."

Yes, it is, Miles thought as he stared hopefully into Rachel's eyes.

"What brings you out this way?" he asked.

"I was just on my way to a friend's house and suddenly, here I am," she said as she returned the stare.

Miles escorted Rachel to the same table he and Mattie had shared before she left. The restaurant had slowly filled with other resident doctors and patrons.

"What can I get you?" their waiter asked. Karen had already left. This was the second shift.

"Red wine, please," Rachel said. Miles declined. He still had his glass of Sprite. Rachel felt strange. She was not used to coming to a bar by herself. But she wasn't alone, really. She was with Miles, a much younger man.

I can feel every eye on me, she thought. Rachel was paranoid. She thought everyone in the place knew she was married, lonely, and desperate. She couldn't get comfortable.

"Is something the matter? You seem preoccupied," Miles said.

"Do I? I'm not. It's just . . ."

"You feel uncomfortable being here with me, right?"

What did he think? Rachel looked every bit of forty, and he looked like he had just opened his first tube of Clearasil, she thought.

"I know what you're thinking. You're thinking, What does this young man know about fixing somebody's heart, right?" Miles said, unashamed of his intelligence and age. "Well, I'm not that young. I'll be thirty next year." Rachel laughed. "Look," Miles said, "I bet I can guess your age."

"Oh, really?" Rachel stopped laughing.

"You're thirty-one, right?"

"Burrrmp! Guess again."

"You can't be older than that."

"Is that supposed to be funny?" Rachel asked with a straight face. "Okay. Times up. I'm . . ." Miles attempted to help her spit it out. "I'm thirty-five. Now. I've said it."

"Is that all? I thought you were going to say something else," he said calmly.

"Do I look that much older?" Rachel's voice lowered.

"No. You look great. Really. You don't look a day over twenty-eight."

The day had come and gone. Before they knew it, it was eight o'clock. They had laughed and talked practically half the evening away.

"But seriously, it feels good to get a chance to help my brothers and sisters. I see it like this: my grandparents and my parents saved up every penny they got to put me through medical school, and the least I can do is to try my best to help those who can't afford to help themselves, whether they're black or white because sickness has no prejudices. There are too many of us out here who can't even afford to get sick, let alone afford the rising cost of health care," he said.

"Don't I know it. Here I work for a major health care facility and I can't even afford the astronomical cost." Rachel sipped her wine. Miles watched as her every movement hypnotized him. He was drawn to her like a bee to honey.

"It's been a long time since I had a chance to sit and talk with someone who wasn't discussing medicine, if you know what I mean."

"It can get pretty boring, huh?" Rachel asked.

"Let me put it this way. After a full week of running from patient to patient, I'm the one who needs to see a doctor," he said in a playful spirit. It was getting late and Rachel still had to meet Faith at her condo.

"This was one of the worst days I've ever experienced," Rachel said, as she half finished her glass of wine. "But after talking with you, I'm thinking maybe it's one of the best."

"Good. I'm glad to hear it. I try to make it a rule to let go of all the stresses a day can bring and just relax with good laughs and good conversation," Miles said. He glanced down at his watch.

"Are you due back at the hospital soon?"

"As a matter of fact, I'm off for the rest of the evening." He was hoping that Rachel was free for the rest of the evening, too. "What are your plans after you leave here?"

I asked myself that same question a minute ago, Rachel thought. "I really should be going," she said. Rachel went into her wallet to pull out some money, when Miles interrupted.

"Please, let me." He pulled out a twenty-dollar bill and laid it on the table underneath his empty glass. Rachel was impressed, seeing that the drinks only came to eight dollars.

"I was thinking, if you weren't in too much of a hurry, that we could have a late dinner. I make a mean Greek salad."

"Is that a fact?" Rachel smiled.

"Yep. So how about it? I promise you'll be home before your coach turns into a pumpkin." He had a good sense of humor, too.

"In that case, I should be in for a prince of a meal, huh?"

"That's just a start. I'll have you eating out of my hand," Miles said with a sparkle in his eye.

Rachel was tempted. "Is that a promise?"

"Cross my heart," Miles said, then escorted Rachel out of the cafe and up to his place.

Chapter Eighteen

At her apartment, Stacy and Clyde were in the kids' room. She put the baby in his crib, while Clyde tucked Tyron in.

"Are you really my daddy?" Tyron asked Clyde as he lay in the lower of the bunk beds. Stacy found the beds to be a bargain when she was pregnant with her first. But she never knew just how handy they would be, considering the shock of having another so soon.

"Would you like it if I were your daddy?" Clyde asked. He pulled the sheet up to Tyron's chest.

"Does Mommy like you?" Tyron surprised both of them with that question.

Clyde turned and looked at Stacy laying the baby in his crib. "I don't know. Do you, Mommy?" he asked with a Cheshire cat grin.

"Shhh!" Stacy said. Her eyes rolled up in her head, as if to ignore both Clyde's remark and her son's questions.

"Could you read me a story?" Tyron asked in a tiny whisper.

"Baby, your daddy can't read," Stacy said sarcastically.

"Now, why are you telling the boy that big lie for? Of course I can read."

"Well, excuse me. Then I guess you read all of those child support notices that went to your mother's house. I know you kept in touch with her."

"You never give up, do you?" Clyde snarled. He knew Stacy wasn't going to quit until she knew the whole story behind his sudden disappearance and even more sudden return.

"Mommy, what's child support?" Tyron asked.

"Ty, baby, what did I tell you about grown-up conversation? Close your eyes and go to sleep. Besides, if your father didn't know what it meant, how could a child comprehend it?" She walked over and kissed him on his head. "Your only concern should be childish things."

"Don't tell him that. He's old enough to know what's up with you females, and all the crap y'all put us through. It's better to school him now, before the money starts disappearing from his check for some li'l hottie," Clyde said, being foolish.

"You want to know what's up? I'll tell you what's up. Your time, that's what. I want my money, every last cent," Stacy said. "Tyron, go to sleep. Clyde, come on out so he can go to sleep." Stacy stood at the bedroom door with her hand on the light switch.

"Please don't go. Could you read me a story, please?" Tyron pleaded. Clyde looked over at Stacy.

"Go to sleep, Ty. I read to you last night," she said. Stacy didn't want to raise her voice and wake up the baby.

"I was talking to Daddy." Stacy's eyes widened as her own son, the one she raised practically by herself, except for some help from her parents, told her what he wanted instead of the other way around.

"Now I know for sure that he's your child. His head is just as hard as yours, Clyde." Clyde felt something warm and tingly inside. "That's my boy," he said triumphantly. "What's one little story? You've been telling me how smart he is. Come on, Stace. What's it gonna hurt?"

Stacy sucked her teeth. "You're not here every morning scrambling around to get dressed and then having to dress not one, but three, including myself." She stormed out of the room.

"Good. Now that the warden is gone, what will it be,

partner?" He tickled Tyron on his ribs as the two of them engaged in laughter. Stacy stood just a couple of feet from the door, long enough to hear Clyde continue his antics.

"Once upon a time there was a rabbit who wanted to race against this little turtle."

Stacy, in spite of everything else, stood quietly enjoying Clyde's crazy sense of humor. She could always depend on him to make her smile.

In the kitchen she ran water into the sink to wash out the baby bottles and containers. This part of the night she hated. She kept hoping that Terrence would grow out of wanting the bottle early in his stages, like Tyron did. But for some odd reason Terrence was a "mama's boy," Stacy thought.

An hour had passed and she had finished the dishes, fixed six bottles, and packed the usual stuff to take for the kids to her mother's in the morning. She put the red and white plastic vinyl bag on the kitchen counter, put jars of baby food, juices, grapes, and other stuff that she knew the kids liked into the bag. She also packed Tyron's favorite M&M cookies in a sandwich bag for them to nibble on. She even put in a couple of extra ones. She knew her mother had a terrible sweet tooth. She called it her "stress arrest" mechanism. Maybe that's why Stacy took after her mother and her eating habits. But she sure as hell didn't want to take on her weight as an added bonus. Stacy often commented to her mother about her weight, but Hilda always said the same thing: "As long as I'm pleasing in God's and the good Reverend's eyes, weight doesn't matter to me."

Stacy opened the refrigerator door to place the bag inside when the telephone rang.

"Hello," Clyde said. He beat Stacy to it just as he reached the kitchen's entrance.

"Who? Naw, man, you got the wrong number. Don't nobody named Sheila live here." He hung up the phone.

"Did I ask you to answer my phone?" Stacy asked

sharply. She went to a drawer in the kitchen and pulled out her book that listed all of her clients and the times.

"What's that? Your little black book? You got that many men calling you that you got to keep track?" Clyde asked, more than a bit disturbed.

"It's none of your business who I see or talk to. You left the position wide open, remember?"

"Keep on rubbing it in. But the fact of the matter is that I'm back now. So you can tell your new boyfriends that Daddy is back in town and he's here to stay." Stacy began to laugh at Clyde's authoritative command.

"Clyde, you're in no position to start pulling rank now. You had your chance; now it's somebody else's." Stacy was just teasing him. She was in no way involved with anyone. It was for the money.

"Is that the way you treat all your guests? Or is it just me you don't like?" he asked with one hand on his waist and the other up against the cabinet.

"No, just you," she said, cool and unconcerned. Clyde laughed to himself. Then the phone rang again. He and Stacy practically knocked each other down. Stacy answered, mumbling a few hushed words into the receiver, while Clyde tried to place his ear against the handset.

"Why don't you mind your business?" Stacy yelled. Then she unhooked the handset and placed it in one of the kitchen drawers.

"Now, nobody will pick up the phone." But she knew the one in her bedroom would ring, but not so loudly. She wished that Clyde would just leave because he was definitely ruining her phone time.

"So it's like that, huh?" he asked as he sat at the kitchen table. Stacy kept her back to him. Now he's biting hard, she thought, as she ignored his remarks and advances.

"You better not be giving away that ass to nobody."

"Clyde, you know what? You really should not get too comfortable."

"Why not?"

"You come off like things should just pick up where

they left off. Well, it's not going to happen. My main concern is doing what's necessary to get out of this dump and do what I've always wanted to do, whether it was with you or somebody else. I'm tired of being used and abused for the sake of someone else's feelings. No more," Stacy preached.

Clyde knew the old Stacy was gone. The woman before him was much stronger and liberated. Nothing was going to turn her around or distract her from her mission. Whatever that was, he thought. How was he going to get Stacy to trust him? And most important, how was he going to slide his way back into her heart and hopefully her bed?

"Ah, girl. Stop trying to be so hard," Clyde said, as he got up and grabbed her from behind.

"Get your hands off of me. I didn't tell you to touch me." Stacy turned and pushed him away.

"You know you been wanting me to do that ever since we left the hairdresser's. I saw the way you were looking at me. You want me."

"You're really crazy, you know that?" Stacy laughed. But the thought had been in her head since he showed up at her job.

"Even if that was the case, I don't know where you've been all this time. You could have been laying up with every skirt that passed your way. The last thing I need is some ho for a man." Stacy unbuttoned the top button of her white blouse. It faintly revealed her soft white lace bra. Clyde's eyes zeroed in on the soft sculptured dimensions of her breast. He got a tingle that ran from his chest and made a screeching halt in the center of his pants.

"What the hell are you looking at?" Stacy asked.

"I can't look at you?"

"No. I know that look. That's that old 'I want you' look."

"You're not going to give me a break, are you? I, at least, deserve the benefit of the doubt, so I'm gonna tell you what happened three years ago, and why I'm back now," Clyde said as he rose to his feet. Stacy couldn't be happier. The truth was finally out.

Clyde explained how he saw his future fade away when he lost his big pro ball dream to his injured knee. That was the biggest reason, he said, and the other was settling down as a family man.

"But, Clyde, I never begged you to marry me or anybody else for that matter. Nobody was holding a gun to your head."

"No, but if your father'd had one, you better bet he would have had it to my head and would have probably pulled the trigger."

"But that still doesn't clear up the fact that you came back the second time, and then left again for parts unknown. You never even called to find out if your own kids were okay. How can you expect me to feel sorry for you? You didn't care about me or your family."

"Stace, I'm sorry. I'm sorry. How many times do you want me to say it? If you want me to get on my knees and beg for your forgiveness, then I will." Clyde got on his knees in front of Stacy with his hands up to his chest. She couldn't do anything but laugh. It was either that or drop-kick him in his groin.

"You'll never stop, will you? Everything is a joke to you," Stacy said.

"Does this mean you'll forgive me?"

"Not so fast. I didn't say anything close to that. You still haven't told me what I want to hear first."

"What? There's no more to tell. I left town, got a job, and that's it. End of story."

"Who do you think you're talking to? I'm not one of these naive girls out here who'll believe whatever comes out of your mouth. You forget that I'm a preacher's daughter. I'd know the truth if it came flying in on a hot-dog roll. So, for the last time, where were you?"

Clyde got up off the floor then went back and sat down at the table.

"Okay, truth. You may not believe this, but this is the honest-to-God truth," he said with a serious expression.

You're right; I don't believe you and you haven't even started to explain, Stacy thought.

"I was scared. I was scared that my life would end if I married you. I just wasn't ready for marriage, a baby, or your parents. I was nothing in their eyes and I almost believed them. I wanted my life to myself. The more I thought about it, the more I panicked," Clyde admitted.

"So you took the easy way out. To hell with what I felt, right? How could you have been so selfish? And what made you so sure that I wanted to marry you? I knew I could have done better. You weren't the only man around. Just because I had your child didn't mean my life ended there." Stacy worked her neck like a true sistah. "Marriage isn't the only way to raise a family, but it helps when two people love each other and are there for one another no matter what."

After that sermon, Clyde felt real stupid and a little better. The worst of her anger was finally over. This could be a good time to make a pass, he thought, as he approached her with open arms.

"But this still doesn't mean that you're off the hook, sucker. You have no idea of the humiliation and disgrace brought to my family and friends. They depended on me to make something of my life. But thanks to you, all it's amounted to is an apartment in the projects, a kitchen drawer full of bills, and two children who are growing up in a world that's killing itself on a daily basis. And right now, all the apologies in the world can't make up for all the people you helped me let down."

"How many times do you want me to say it? I'm sorry. I'm sorry!" Clyde said with emotion. He took his fist and fired it into the wall. Stacy's body jerked as fear entered her chest. Then she watched Clyde do something she had never seen him do before. He cried.

God, I didn't realize he was gonna break down like this. All I wanted was the truth, Stacy thought. She wanted to hold him, tell him that it was all right. But she didn't want him to get the wrong signals, and she didn't trust herself in his arms again.

"Clyde, please don't do this. I'm sorry, too. We both are two sorry people together," she said with a smile. She slightly touched Clyde's shoulder. Just her sensitive touch caused Clyde's body to surrender and soon they were in each other's arms.

He grabbed her by her waist and pulled her closer to him. As hard as she tried, Stacy couldn't help but succumb to her own sexual hunger. Stacy's whole body instantly reminisced physically, as Clyde's hands explored regions she had almost forgotten she had. There was nothing or no one in the world who could come between them now. Her eyes were closed as their bodies practically floated to the kitchen floor. Clyde started from her neck and slowly kissed his way down to her aching breasts, her quivering stomach, and then down between her caramel-colored thighs that opened with anticipation.

Stacy's moans and groans grew louder and deeper as Clyde's face dove directly into her hot spot. Her hands hungrily caressed his head and shoulders as Clyde seemed to melt inside her. The mere sensation was one she could not forget.

The night ended with the two of them making love.

"Mmm," Clyde moaned as he fell exhausted on top of Stacy in her bed.

"I know you're not tired," she said, barely keeping her eyes open. She had finally unleashed the pent-up passion and other pressures she had stored up inside of her. There's nothing like getting a good nut; no, a great nut, Stacy thought as she lay limp.

Clyde managed to slide himself off her with the help of his relaxed muscles and manhood.

"Damn. That was good. As tight as you were, that made all the difference in the world," he teased.

"I can't remember you being this excited and head over heels when we made love. You acted like you haven't had any in years," Stacy said, unable to move from that one spot.

"It seems longer than that," he said, belting out a long-awaited sigh. "Wait a minute, is my skin still on it? It feels kind of funny." Clyde felt down on his limp manhood. Stacy reached over, felt it, and chuckled.

"That's the rubber, you fool," she said, as she slapped his rippled stomach.

"I almost forgot I had it on. It's a good thing. We would not want to make any more babies, would we?"

"I don't know. I might want another one," Stacy said as a joke. Clyde started to laugh out loud as he got up and went to the bathroom. Stacy laughed, too. How could she entertain such a thought? She was no way financially or emotionally ready for another child, not to mention Clyde's adamant view that fathering more children was out of the question. She soon put the thought out of her head and concentrated on the sexual aerobic workout she and Clyde had just enjoyed.

When Clyde walked out of the bathroom, the telephone rang. Stacy turned to reach for it, but Clyde beat her to it.

"No, man, you got the wrong number. Look, I told you before, ain't no Sheila here." He slammed the receiver back on its cradle as he sat on the edge of the bed. "You really should look into getting your number changed," he said as he lit up a cigarette. There was no better time than now to tell him what was really going on, Stacy thought, as she leaned over and kissed the muscles on his back.

"Remember I said that I had a part-time job? All these wrong numbers aren't really wrong numbers. Well, they are and they aren't," she said.

"Well, what exactly are they? Are these calls wrong numbers or what?"

Stacy got out of bed, went over to the light switch and turned it on. Her naked body still managed to arouse Clyde, even though he wasn't up to performing.

"I had a second line put in for my clients. I'm what you

may call an escort service, but the only difference is that I don't go out with any of them. I just talk to them on the phone. And before you kirk out, the money is good," she said.

"How good?" Clyde asked, intrigued. When he found out how much money was involved, he wanted to listen.

"The men don't pay me, per se. I get paid through the company I work for. And it's the only job where I can work around my schedule. It's after hours so I can be home with the boys and not worry about being away from them all the time. This job is perfect," Stacy said as she crawled back into the bed beside him.

"So you've been cleaning up, huh? You sure you ain't been giving up anything to anybody, have you?"

"No. Don't be stupid. This is strictly business. Like I said, I'm only doing this so I can move out of this place and into a better one for my kids."

"My kids, too. You seem to be forgetting that," Clyde said, as if his sudden parental emotions meant anything. Stacy laughed. He wasn't fooling her one bit. She knew that Clyde still put money above anything else, except maybe sex. He couldn't have one without the other.

"How long do you plan to do this? Not that you should stop or anything like that."

"So you're saying you're not bothered by this at all?"

"When you got bills to pay, you gotta do what you gotta do," Clyde said. He lit another cigarette. "How much did you say you're pulling in?"

"Enough. I've been considering going back to school and getting my degree. I was thinking about San Diego University," she said. Stacy wanted the life she had always dreamed of. With her degree, she would really be on easy street. But there was still the matter of her two sons and getting a real man in their lives. She had a burning suspicion that Clyde wasn't going to stick around long enough to make that dream come true.

Clyde's attention had drifted off into space. The mere

fact that Stacy was pulling in two paychecks got him thinking.

"Hey," she nudged him in his ribs.

"What?" Clyde asked.

"What are you thinking about? Is it something I said?"

"Yeah," he said, looking at Stacy with a weird look in his eye. "What if I got back in the picture, you know, be a real father and all that?" he asked as he tried to manipulate his way back in the door, which he figured would be a breeze seeing that he'd just found his way back into her bed. With that news, Stacy sat straight up in her bed.

"Are you serious? I mean this would mean so much to Ty." It would mean a lot to her, too, she thought.

"Hold up, hold up. I didn't say I was gonna move in; I just said that I think it would be a good idea if I hung around a little more, that's all. And maybe I'll even think about confronting your family. But don't go making any sudden plans," Clyde said with his chest stuck out like he had just made some grand proclamation.

Stacy was overjoyed. Clyde had said things she thought she never would have heard come out of his mouth. For a minute there, Clyde couldn't believe it either. Stacy wrapped her arms around his neck and smothered him with kisses.

"Wait until they hear about this. They're gonna flip," Stacy said, referring to her parents.

"See, there you go. I thought you were your own woman. Why, all of a sudden, you gotta go and tell Ma and Pa everything?"

"You, of all people, should know what it will mean to me to see their faces when I tell them what they thought would never happen in a million years. They were sure I'd never see you again, let alone reinvolve myself with you. But they were wrong. People do change." Stacy continued showering Clyde with affection until they again surrendered to their passions.

Chapter Nineteen

In the kitchen, the aroma of imported Grand Marnier ground coffee aroused Rachel's sleeping senses. She had awakened to yet another pleasant morning outside of her own home.

Faith had prepared breakfast for the three of them. She really didn't mind, considering she enjoyed having breakfast with someone other than herself. It was a breath of fresh air for her to have another warm body sitting across the table from her for a change, rather than an empty chair as usual.

Faith's sex life wasn't as complicated as her professional life. In fact, she found it difficult to set aside her professional life for her personal life. It was evident that the sensitive egos of her male friends, professional as well as personal, made them feel as though they were no match for her wit and intellect. And no matter how she tried, Faith couldn't find that special man who could get inside of her own head.

"Mmm. What smells so good down here?" Rachel asked as she floated into the sweet smells of freshly squeezed orange juice, fresh-baked danishes, country bacon, eggs, and fresh fruits.

"Good morning, sleepyhead. I thought you could use a hearty breakfast. Are you going to let me in on this big secret you've been keeping?" Faith poured Rachel a cup of coffee as they both sat down to a succulent spread.

Rachel had on an ivory silk robe that Faith had given her as a Christmas gift. She had thought it would put the fire back into her and Stanley's marriage. But unfortunately it didn't work. Stanley went to bed early Christmas eve, claiming the seasonal shopping had exhausted his body and his wallet.

"I'm sorry. I should have been more considerate of your feelings. I don't want to burden you with Nicky," Rachel said as she sipped her coffee.

"Don't be silly. I feel as though Nicky is my own son. I think it's great pretending to be a mother. I can't wait to try it for real one day," Faith said. "But I'm not the issue this morning, you are. So what's the big secret you've been promising to tell me for the past couple of weeks, Rach?" Rachel just smiled in anticipation. If she didn't say something soon, she was going to burst.

"I feel so silly telling you this," Rachel said.

"What? Come on, tell me already," Faith begged. "Whatever it is, it sure has you bubbling over with joy. It's a dramatic change from when you first got here," she said as she bit into a cinnamon danish.

Rachel had finally put all her doubts about her marriage behind her for the moment. This happiness was long overdue.

"Well, are you going to tell me about this man or not?" Faith asked as she nibbled on a peach-filled crepe.

"What makes you think it's a man?" Rachel stuffed a piece of French toast into her mouth.

"You didn't have to. All the signs are evident," Faith said.

"What signs? Just because you can tell what's on a person's mind before they say it doesn't mean you can diagnose my condition by a little smile."

"On the contrary. I can remember in college when you used to run up to me at the lunch table ranting and raving about some guy you met. Then you started to pig out

LOVE'S DECEPTIONS

with not only my food, but everybody else's around you," Faith said.

"So what's that got to do with now?" Rachel had piled a little bit of everything onto her plate. "Are you going to eat that crepe?" she asked before she realized what she had done. Faith sat back and watched, amused.

"I'm doing it again, huh?" Rachel paused in embarrassment. They sat back and laughed.

"Believe me, Rach, it's good to see you in such good spirits. I guess Stanley is feeling pretty good this morning as well, huh?" She just assumed that Rachel and Stanley had talked out their differences and were finally on the road to marital bliss. Faith got up and went over to the white Formica counter and poured herself another cup of coffee.

"What makes you think it's because of Stanley that I'm smiling?" she asked, as the smile disappeared quicker than it had appeared.

"Well, who else could it be? I mean, why else have you been spending those long hours on the telephone at night, not to mention the midnight rendezvous on the beach? You're not seeing another man, are you?" Faith asked her dear friend.

Rachel gave her a cool grin. "I might. You told me—in fact, you ordered me—to get out and have some fun, didn't you?"

"Yeah. But I meant with your husband." Faith was taken aback by Rachel's words.

"What's the big deal? People do it all the time. Look at Stanley. I don't see you chastising him. It's all right for a man to fool around. But when a woman does, it's an awful sin."

"Especially when you're married! The rules haven't changed, Rachel. What in the world were you thinking, that you could get involved with another man just like that?" Faith rebuked. "Well?"

"Well, what?" Rachel said, ignoring Faith.

"Who is it? I'm sure he has a name, right? Or did you pick him up at some bar?" she asked jokingly.

"It's not what you think. And, yes, he's wonderful and young. His name is Miles Jordan. Doctor Miles Jordan."

"How young is young? A couple of months, a year? What?" Faith asked with wide eyes.

"Try five years younger. And before you say it, I know what you're going to tell me, and I don't want to hear it!"

"You're not going to hear anything from me. You're grown. All I'm going to say is don't get burnt. Younger men can create one hell of a fire."

"He's not about that. He's a heart specialist who is dedicated to his patients," Rachel said.

"I can see it now. He's going to fix your broken heart? Give me a break. The only thing he's going to fix is your libido."

"All right. Come on. Let me have it. I know you've got some heavy wisdom to lay on me, so let's have it."

Faith, in her silent state, crossed her legs and sat sipping her cup of coffee before she finally spoke. "Don't take this the wrong way, but how long are you going to pretend? Your marriage is in trouble. Have you even told this man that you're married, first of all?"

"No. And it's really none of his business. Faith, I'm not some child. I know what I'm doing is considered wrong in some people's eyes, but what about me? What about what I feel?"

"And what is that? It's obvious that you're not thinking logically, and if you were, you would end this fling, because that's exactly what it is. What's going to happen when your marriage is reconciled? What are you going to say? It was fun, but my husband and family need me?"

"You make it sound like I'm enjoying all of this. But I'm not. I want my marriage to work, as doleful as it may sound," Rachel said unconvincingly.

Faith looked at her with concerned eyes.

"If that was true, you wouldn't be here."

LOVE'S DECEPTIONS

Rachel sucked her teeth in disgust because Faith was turning more into the shrink and she the pitiful client.

There was nothing the two could not tell one another. Rachel was confident that Faith would not go behind her back and repeat anything that was said between them. Faith knew more about Rachel's life than anyone and that most likely included Stanley as well. Miles was probably everything Rachel wanted in Stanley. But at times, the best person to confide in is a stranger and that's what Rachel assured Faith of. Miles was a good listener.

"Talking your problems out has always been the best antidote. But you should be sharing your feelings with your husband, not Miles. Have you spoken with Stanley at all since you've been here?" she asked in a professional tone.

"Yeah. He wants me to bring Nicky home," Rachel said solemnly.

"And are you?"

"I'm not sure I'm ready to see Stanley right now," Rachel replied.

"Whether you want to believe this or not, Miles is only clouding your judgment. He may not be doing it on purpose, but you have to admit, he's keeping you from Stanley . . ."

"It works for me. Stop looking at me like that. I was just kidding," Rachel said. "I want to go back, but . . ."

"Do you realize that more men and women indulge in extramarital affairs because the lines of communication are not open between two people or the sex is no longer enjoyable? And nine times out of ten, couples would rather have outside affairs than separation or divorce?" Faith said. "But they are never really happy with that. I wouldn't want to see you end up that way, Rach. Go back to your husband. At least give it a try." Faith reached out and held Rachel's hand. "I'll help you get back."

Rachel's eyes began to tear. Faith rose from her seat, hugged her friend, and they dried each other's tears.

"I would like for you to be my guest at a seminar I'm

conducting next weekend entitled: A New Agenda, A New Accountability: Empowering the African-American Woman. Bring a couple of your friends, too."

Rachel sighed deeply.

"What's the matter now?" Faith asked.

"What about my doctor friend? It's every woman's dream to meet a man with the letters D-R in front of his name."

"Honey, that's nothing. It's whether or not the D-R is followed by M-R-S." Faith and Rachel laughed their way out of the kitchen and went upstairs to get dressed.

Chapter Twenty

Weeks passed, and Stacy and Clyde had finally made their living arrangement a permanent one. When Clyde did decide to move in, he begged Stacy not to tell anyone just yet because he wanted to make sure things were really starting to happen for them and that they were finally settled into their new place. Whoever said that love was better the third time around obviously had Stacy in mind.

Clyde had gotten up early and gone down to the local gym to work out. That was his daily regimen ever since Stacy met him. Although he had a job at one of the auto parts stores on the other side of town, he spent seventy-five percent of his time working on himself.

Stacy lay snuggled in one of Clyde's oversized sweatshirts. The telephone rang and she rolled over to answer it.

"Hi, darling. What's the 4-1-1, hon?" the high-pitched voice asked. She laughed as Chauncy's girlish voice tickled her.

"What's up? Long time no speak," she said with her head propped up on two pillows.

"Baby, I've been doing great. Aside from a few cramps, I'm still kicking it," he said. "What about you? I haven't seen or heard from you in a while. When I saw your checks among the outgoing mail, I thought maybe something was wrong, because they were so small," he said, concerned.

"That's real sweet that you were worried about me. But everything's fine," Stacy said.

"Good. So how's it going with your clients? Are they working out okay?" Chauncy asked.

"They're going great. In fact, I've been thinking about taking on a couple more. I need the money. I finally found a couple of places I'm even considering moving into," she said excitedly.

"Sounds like a plan to me," Chauncy said.

"You think so? I hope so. My kids' father is back and with his income and mine put together, we can afford something bigger and better," Stacy said, confident of their relationship.

"I heard that. I'm glad things are finally working out for you. Does this mean you won't be seeing that fine brother?" he asked.

Stacy laughed at his humor and determination to get Kelvin. I guess he found somebody else, she thought, trying not to think about it.

"I don't know," she said. "I'm not sure just yet. It's good to have a backup just in case," she said, jokingly optimistic.

"Look, don't sweat it. If your man is doing right by you, then I wouldn't worry about it," Chauncy said.

"I hope you're right. I would hate to go through the same bull all over again," Stacy said.

"Just remember, if you can't find any use for him, send him my way," Chauncy said, cooing into the phone. Minutes after they hung up, the phone rang again. It was Clyde.

"Babe, what's up? You still asleep?" he asked.

"Nope. I'm lying here thinking about you," Stacy purred into the receiver.

"Are you naked?" Clyde's train of thought took a temporary detour.

"Why don't you come home and find out?" Stacy teased.

"I wish I could, but there's something I have to take care of first. And that's where you come in," he said.

"Like what?"

"You'll find out soon enough. I called to ask if you wouldn't mind having a quiet dinner for two."

Stacy was shocked. Clyde never wanted to do anything that was quiet, let alone sit down to have a normal dinner that didn't include a television sitting in front of him and a bag of chips and a liter of Coke beside him. "Could you get your mother to baby-sit for a few hours?"

"I guess so. I kind of like to give her the weekend off since she has them through the week. But if it's that important to you . . ."

"I think it is," he said.

Clyde gave Stacy instructions on where to meet him downtown after he left the gym. It had been a long time since Stacy had dinner out. In fact, it had been a while since anyone other than her parents had asked her out for anything. This could be it. Maybe Clyde was ready to make his residency legal, Stacy thought.

Stacy called her mother.

"Mama, I need a big favor," she said. She knew she had to get a quick response from Hilda or else she would keep her on the phone half the day.

"What's going on?" Hilda asked apprehensively. "I haven't seen much of you lately and now you want a favor. What's going on over there?"

"Mama, I was just there a couple of days ago. And it's not like I've been away on a trip," Stacy said.

"But we haven't taken the time to sit down and talk. Between you and your father, I hardly see the two of you at the same time," Hilda said.

"Mama, you really should pick up a hobby. You're spending too many hours in that house. I need you to watch the kids for me for an hour or so. I promise I won't be out long."

"That's not what's bothering me. You seem to be preoccupied with other things."

"Mama, if I go into it right now, you'll never let me off the phone. I just need you to say yes. Please. I promise I will sit down with you and Dad and tell you both the good news," Stacy said.

"What good news? Oh, come and tell me," Hilda cried.

"I can't. I have to get ready. I'll be over in an hour." Stacy hung up.

At Mariner Lane, Stanley's car sat in front of Benita's home.

"Gotcha! Beat that score!" Stanley screamed as he and Malcolm sat in the den, playing a SEGA Genesis *Jurassic Park* video game. He had arrived there early to fix Benita's washer. It wasn't draining properly. He had taken a break to indulge in some fun.

"Five thousand points! That's because my Rex ate your Mastodon. See if you can beat that," Malcolm said, as he gave Stanley one of his "I'm bad" looks. This was the most fun either of them had had. This was a welcome change for Stanley because he missed his own son.

"Okay, are you guys ready for a snack?" Benita asked. She was on the sundeck, where a picnic table was spread with cold-cut sandwiches, potato chips, and a pitcher of cherry Kool-Aid. She figured Stanley had worked up an appetite after fixing her washer and after being skunked in the *Jurassic Park* video game.

"Break time," he said to Malcolm, who had beaten Stanley for the third time in a row. "He's good or I must be getting old," Stanley said with a chuckle. He didn't think he could beat Malcolm even if he created the game himself.

"That kid must practice in his sleep," he said.

"Malcolm, go upstairs and wash your hands," Benita said.

"I hope he didn't beat up on you too badly, Stanley. I was meaning to warn you that Malcolm plays that thing every minute of the hour."

"Now you tell me. He shot rings around me in there."

They both laughed. Stanley assisted her by pouring the Kool-Aid into the glasses.

Benita had gotten used to having Stanley around, even if it was only a couple of days out of a week.

"Thanks. Malcolm is a bright boy and very quick when it comes to picking up games. He's been at the head of his class since day care. He has never once flunked in anything. Maybe that's why I overdo it when it comes to things like the SEGA Genesis, and the mountain bike, and all the other stuff I spoil him with," she said, as she nibbled on a kosher pickle.

"He's a good kid," Stanley said, not having much of an appetite. "That's why I have to get my act together with my own kid." Stanley had been feeling awful ever since Rachel took Nicky away. There wasn't a day that went by that he didn't miss them both.

"Have you spoken with Rachel at all since she left?" Of course he has. He hasn't been able to think of anything else since he's been here, Benita thought.

"Yeah. But you know Rachel and I haven't been able to see eye to eye on anything lately. She still insists that I was the cause for her leaving," Stanley said. "Do you blame her?"

"Do you blame yourself? I wouldn't if I were you," Benita said to him. This was the perfect opportunity for her to really sink her claws into Stanley, especially being as vulnerable as he was, but what difference would it have made, seeing that he loved his wife? That was one case she could never win. "Stanley, in all my years as a lawyer, I never took on a case without hearing the facts. I'm always willing to give the accused the benefit of the doubt, and the dilemma facing you and Rachel is no different. As hard as it is for me to say this, all the evidence points to you and Rachel having something going on."

"Nita," Stanley said surprised.

"Hear me out. You've been spending time with me, and your mother has been trying her best to push us back together, which makes it look like you're supporting her actions. If Rachel has any reason for suspicion, you and your mother gave it to her," she said. "If I were Rachel, I'd probably have done the same thing."

Stanley never thought he'd ever hear something like that coming from Nita's mouth. He'd thought at least she would understand where he was coming from, but instead she told him what he already knew from the beginning.

"There's nothing going on between us, you know that." Stanley knew Benita didn't want to hear it, but it was the truth. What was then, and what was now, could never be the same. Stanley momentarily reflected on all the pain he had caused Rachel and the anguish he put on their marriage. He still loved her and he wanted to tell her that right away.

"I still love my wife, no matter what anyone thinks, Nita."

"I know it and you know it, but does Rachel know it? Have you even taken the time to really prove it?"

Stanley just shook his head. He couldn't remember the last time he said the words, *I love you.*

"Sure I did. Many times, in a roundabout way," he said, standing in a far corner of the sundeck.

"You can say one thing, but what goes across to the person receiving it is totally different. I should know. I hear it every day in court."

Stanley's heart longed for Rachel and his son. He knew what he had to do, but was it too late? he thought. Had he already lost her?

"You're right. I could have prevented this mess from blowing up in my face a long time ago. I just hope I did not lose her for good."

"There's only one way to find out," Benita said.

"Could I use your phone?"

Benita could see the color and smile return to his face. What Gertrude, his own mother, had tried to destroy still existed. Benita felt a sense of satisfaction in helping the only man she really cared for restore his marriage.

Stanley returned from trying to reach Rachel by phone. "I tried to reach her, but there was no answer." After Stanley had said that, the silence between him and Benita said more about how they felt for each other than they cared to admit.

"Look," they both spoke at the same time.

"Go ahead," he said.

"All I was going to say is that you're doing the right thing." They both looked into each other's eyes for the last time. Stanley took her by the hand and guided Benita down the steps of the deck.

"I realize that this wasn't what we both expected. I'm not sure how it will go between Rachel and me, but I am sure that it could never be the same between us, Nita." Stanley touched the side of her face with his open palm. "I'll always remember the past, but it's the future I'm looking forward to," he said while brushing away a falling tear from her eye.

"I understand," Benita said. Her heart felt as though it were shattering into a thousand pieces.

Stanley looked up at Malcolm, who was both eating his lunch and playing a handheld version of the video game that was given to him by his mother for getting another good report card. "I got to go, Malcolm. But keep practicing; you may one day be world video champion," he said, walking across the lawn to his car.

Malcolm briefly acknowledged Stanley leaving before his attention was back on his portable game.

Stanley took one final look at Benita, who stood almost as she had when they had parted years ago. "See you around, Nita," he said.

"Let's hope not," she said with a grin. She confirmed the thought in her mind that she would not regret the recent days she and Stanley had spent together. He had walked out of her life for the last time and now it was time for her to get on with her own.

Chapter Twenty-one

Lesa's days were long and lonely. Since the raid, she drifted from one room to the other. She spent most of the day flipping through magazines. She had remained silent about her terrible escapade. Neither friends nor family suspected anything, or noticed the change in her behavior. Lesa was ashamed and too humiliated to talk about it. This thing with Kris bothered her more than she cared to admit.

"I'm getting a damn headache," Lesa complained, as she rubbed her hands over her tired eyes. She tossed another magazine on top of the pile. She got up off the sofa, walked over to the television, and picked up the remote. Lately nothing seemed to hold her interest for long, not since Kris anyway. A commercial advertising a Carnival Cruise flashed on the screen. It made Lesa reminisce about the times she had spent with Kris on deck. All those long days and nights of lovemaking.

I want to spend my whole life making love to you. She heard his words over and over again in her head. Lesa felt sure that where she belonged was with him. At the time, the only obstacle was Tony. There had been nothing between them that could make her change the way she felt about Kris. He was the man she fell in love with and the man she wanted to spend the rest of her life with. At least that's what she had thought.

"And topping today's headlines: In Compton, the DEA has foiled yet another possible drug ring," the black anchorwoman announced, looking like a black Barbie doll. "This has been the fourth drug raid this month. And just a couple of weeks ago, there was a similar surprise bust at a condominium complex in the Imperial Beach area," she said. The front of Lesa's street flashed across the screen again. She wondered if it was ever going to go away. Each time the film clip ran across the television screen, there was Kris giving a statement to the press. She felt that her life was an episode of *Hard Copy*.

It was amazing how news, especially bad news about blacks, seemed to get more coverage than anything else these days, she thought, as she sat straddling the large leather ottoman. Lesa clicked the remote and turned the television off. She allowed her body to fall backward into the matching recliner and shut her eyes.

"I'm not going to think about him. I'm not going to think about him," she repeated over and over again. But she couldn't help it. Kris had managed to get inside every part of her. Suddenly loud music began to filter through the walls of her condo. The neighbors had turned their radio up as loud as it could go. They rarely did it since Tony had approached them about it being so loud when he tried to rest. After that one time of him confronting them about it, he'd never had to tell them again. If she didn't miss anything else, Lesa thought, she did miss Tony's antagonistic appearance. He did look hard sometimes, especially when he dressed up in his "Yo" gear. But since the news was out that he got arrested, the neighbors had been playing their music as loud as they wanted to.

"Give it a rest, will you!" Lesa said, frustrated. But lately her request went unheard. The telephone rang. She still had not felt like talking or even seeing anyone. She had not stepped one foot outside her door except for going to work and to the market. She didn't want to be bombarded with questions from nosy neighbors and friends, especially the ones who considered the arrest past due.

The phone continued to ring and Lesa refused to answer it. She had only heard from Tony once since his arrest. He had begged her to bail him out of jail. But where was she going to get that kind of money? The bail was set at five figures. Tony had asked Lesa to sell some of her things to make bail. But she couldn't come up with the money. Not even his so-called homeboys had that kind of cash lying around. And even if they did, more than likely they'd be sharing a cell next to Tony. Lesa had not spoken to him since.

What if it were Tony calling again? What was she going to say to him? Was he informed of the surveillance? Was her involvement with Kris revealed to him? With all these questions swimming around in her head, she definitely didn't want to pick up the phone. She knew she couldn't avoid him forever. Sooner or later she would have to face Tony. She would much rather wait until later, she thought. With a twenty-thousand-dollar bond over his head, Tony might be sitting in jail a little longer than he anticipated. She had got her wish. Tony was out of her house and life. The only thing missing was Kris.

The answering machine finally was activated after the fourth ring. It was Kris. This was the third time today.

"I know you're still upset, and I don't blame you. We have to talk," he said. Lesa stood looking at the small black machine as his voice seemed to penetrate her body like an arrow. How could listening to what he had to say make up for the humiliation he had caused? Would his apology change the way she felt? she wondered. The bumps and bruises had long disappeared. How come he wouldn't? Lesa asked herself.

"Lesa, please answer the phone. I know you're there. I came by today; I saw you moving around in there," he continued. Her hand trembled when she reached for the receiver. There was a lot she wanted to say to him, but when she heard his voice on the other end of the phone, her mind went blank.

"Lesa, I'm sorry I hurt you. The last thing I ever wanted to do was break your heart. You have to believe me."

"Believe you! All you've managed to do is lie and scheme your way into my life. I never should have trusted you. You have done nothing more than turn my life upside down," she blasted. "Why don't you go back to the rock you crawled out from under and leave me the hell alone!" Lesa slammed the phone down in his ear before she broke down in tears.

The evening turned out to be an unseasonably cool one. The long thick leaves of the palm trees swayed to a music all their own.

"This place is too crowded. There's a ten-minute wait for a table. Let's go," Clyde complained, as he and Stacy walked into their third restaurant after finding the other two too crowded. Stacy noticed that Clyde had been in a strange mood all evening. The B Street Cafe was their third and final attempt to have a quiet dinner. Every place they had been to Clyde found something wrong with it. It was either too crowded, too far out of the way, or everyone and their mother were there.

"Clyde, we're not going anywhere else. This is it. I'm starving." Stacy was adamant about staying. "This is perfect. I hear the food here is good. We're staying." Stacy walked on ahead of him when the hostess finally showed them to their table.

"But . . ." Clyde attempted to give a thumbs-down to this place as well, but Stacy just ignored him.

"Here we are. Table for two." She placed the leatherbound menus in front of them when they sat down. The redheaded hostess poured two glasses of water. "Your waitress for the evening will be with you shortly. Is there anything else I can do for you?" she asked with the complimentary smile. A house policy.

This was the first time in a long time that Stacy had

been out anywhere. This night was going to be one that Stacy would never forget.

"No, thank you," Stacy said to the young woman before she left the table and went back toward the kitchen.

"I've never been here before, have you?" she asked excitedly. Stacy scoped out the surroundings as the background music added a touch of romance. The sound of glasses clinking and silverware being removed from the tables to make room for other waiting patrons echoed around them.

"What's the matter, Clyde? You sure have been acting funny ever since we got here. You're looking around like you're expecting someone to walk up to you any minute."

Clyde was a nervous wreck.

"What was so important that you couldn't tell me over the phone today?" Stacy asked, looking over at him from across the candlelit table that romantically suggested that they were two young people in love. A quaint bouquet of assorted silk flowers served as the centerpiece. Overhead hovered a round ball of light extending from a thick black cord, secured by a hook in the ceiling.

Clyde had a lot on his mind. No wonder he was antsy; every place they went he saw women he knew either by acquaintance or by sexual involvement. But of course, these relationships were after he'd left Stacy.

He reached over and took Stacy's hand.

"Stace, you really look beautiful tonight," he said, complimenting her on the white chiffon miniskirt and double-breasted jacket with chiffon sleeves. That was one thing Clyde admired about her. She didn't have a lot of money to buy what she would like for herself, but when she did, her taste was perfect. She began to blush. She had taken the time before she left the house to put a fresh coat of nail polish on just in case one of her fingers suddenly became occupied by a ring. That was her hope, anyway.

"Thank you. You don't look half bad yourself," she

said to Clyde, who looked good in just about anything because he had that kind of body.

Clyde's coal black eyes seemed to subdue Stacy as she sat waiting for him to pop the big question.

"Stace, I have a confession to make."

Oh, this is it, Lord. He's really . . . she thought. Confession? What confession, she wondered. What kind of proposal is a confession? She hoped she didn't get all dressed up for some testimony! Stacy believed that Clyde wanted to ask her to marry him. She figured that was the main reason for his showing up after all this time.

"Well, I thought you asked me to dinner because you had something really important to say to me, like a proposal maybe," she said, slightly disappointed.

"Proposal! Whatever gave you that idea?"

"Well, today you made it sound so secretive and all. I just assumed."

Clyde chuckled.

"I feel like an idiot," Stacy said.

"Stacy, if I could make that wish come true for you, I would."

"But . . ." Stacy began.

"I'm not the one who can fulfill that wish," Clyde said sadly.

Stacy's entire insides began to scream out. What was the problem? Everything was going so well; what could have happened between them that would cause him to change his feelings toward her? Stacy asked herself. Before Clyde could supply her with an explanation, his eyes grew cold.

"Well, well, well. What do we have here?" a young woman said, as she stood at their table.

"Natasha!" Clyde exclaimed in shock. "What are you doing here?" he asked with a tight face.

"I'm working. What are you doing here? The last thing I remember was you were going out to get a pack of cigarettes and you never came back," she said with a pad and pencil in one hand and the other hand placed firmly on her hip. "And who is this? Another one of your freaks?" The long-legged sistah stood, arms akimbo, not waiting for an order but an explanation.

"Clyde, what the hell is going on?" Stacy asked, trying to keep a pleasant smile on her face. This was the most embarrassing thing that had ever happened to her. "Who is this woman?"

"Who am I? Who are you?" she replied. Clyde was fit to be tied. Not only did he have one woman to explain to, but two; and from the looks of it, there was no way he was going to get out of it.

"Stacy, Natasha. Natasha, Stacy," he said with his head in his hands. The people around them were looking on and whispering to one another. This was something many of them rarely saw when they went out. Not only did they have a good meal to enjoy, but also a good love triangle. In the back of Stacy's mind she knew it was only going to get worse.

The black amazon stood in a short, black spandex skirt, a white cotton poet blouse, and an apron that bore the name of the cafe wrapped around her twenty-inch waist. She had smooth cocoa-colored skin and wavy sculptured hair that looked soft to the touch. This was in no way a mere coincidence.

"Clyde, are you going to tell me what's going on here or do I have to ask her?" Stacy asked with tight lips.

"Stacy ..." That's all he could say before Natasha interrupted.

"You see, this man is my husband and ..."

"Husband!" Stacy's voice shrieked. Suddenly all attention was on them. All who were in viewing distance had turned to see what was going on.

"You are married? Clyde, how could you?" Stacy's eyes filled with tears as the news slowly sunk in. The man she was falling in love with yet again, the one she thought had changed for the better, was still the same creep.

"Stacy, I wanted to tell you," Clyde began.

"Oh, yeah? When? After you made a complete fool out of me?" She rose from the table and Clyde rose with her.

"Don't leave now, it's just getting good," said Natasha. "Did you know he has a daughter who asks about her daddy every day? I bet he didn't tell you that."

Stacy decided she had heard enough. "Excuse me," Stacy said, trying to hold in every bit of anger that had built up in her.

"Stacy, wait," Clyde said.

"Don't worry, your things will be on the corner with the trash in the morning," Stacy said in a venomous tone. She stormed out of the restaurant. Every nerve in her body was on the verge of exploding. Clyde tried to run after her, but Natasha held on to his arm. He had escaped her once; he wasn't getting away a second time.

Stacy stood outside the cafe, trying desperately to catch her breath. She thought she was going to have a heart attack right there on the street. She looked from one end of the street to the other. She wanted to get as far away from him as she possibly could.

When Clyde finally broke away from his captor, he raced outside into the street, but Stacy was nowhere to be found.

The smell of tangy marinara sauce and the pungent scent of garlic and butter inside Miles's condo had escaped his patio entrance. Rachel's appetite as well as her intuition had just been satisfied, and she sat cozy and comfy, waiting for Miles to return from the kitchen. The fire in the fireplace was burning brilliantly while the reddish-yellow flames flickered in her wide brown eyes. Miles entered with two brandy snifters and a bottle of warm cognac.

"Here we are," he said. He handed a glass to Rachel as he sat down beside her on the forest green sofa. "How was dinner? I hope it was to your liking," he said.

"Dinner was wonderful. I'm stuffed," Rachel said, patting her flat stomach. She had acquired a certain rapport with Miles, who had grown to enjoy her company as well.

"Would you believe that I haven't cooked like that in a long time? My eating habits have gone from bad to worse," he confessed.

"You could have fooled me. You're in great shape. I kind of thought you were not only a workaholic, but a fitness fanatic," Rachel said. Miles threw his head back in laughter. She watched as his boyish spirit surfaced. She found him to be intriguing and almost innocent. He had become a refreshing change in her life. She had a hard time facing the fact that after tonight, it would be all over. There was no way she could lead two lives: her marriage with Stanley and her attraction to Miles.

"How about you? I'm sure you're in the health spas every other day, right?" he asked.

Is he kidding? Rachel thought.

"My son keeps me in shape," she said, quickly changing the subject.

"You don't look like you could be somebody's mother."

"And you don't look like a man who can handle himself in the kitchen, either. Your mother must be very proud of how you turned out."

"Well, with four younger sisters, responsibility fell on my shoulders at an early age. Besides, I really didn't mind. My mother is a school teacher, and my father is a retired navy officer. They're always on the go. So you can say that I was a military brat. If you think my cooking is something, you should check out the way I braid hair," Miles said with a wink.

"Believe me, you made the right career decision. I don't think we need any more beauticians in this world."

Whenever the words between her and Miles seemed to cease, crazy notions started to run through her head. Damn. How can one man be so perfect, she thought as she looked in his direction. He was so well-rounded and intelligent in everything. And judging from his surroundings, Miles was every woman's dream. She just wished it was her dream come true; that way she wouldn't need an excuse to sexually attack him.

"Wow! You sure read a lot of books." His bookshelf extended from one corner of the room to the other.

"How many of them have you read from cover to cover?"

"All of them," he said, getting up and grabbing one off the shelf.

"I'm impressed," Rachel said.

"I'm kidding. I've only read half," he joked. "I try to read at least one book a week when my schedule permits," he said. He opened a book of poetry by Nikki Giovanni. "I believe our people should have some, if not all, knowledge of our heritage; ancestors like Harriet Tubman, Langston Hughes and the like are the ones who left behind blueprints for our lives. It shows us where we've been, and where we are going."

Every time he spoke, Rachel was blown away. She was fascinated with his intellect and knowledge of culture. He also was a great humanitarian. Men like Miles were hard to find, but she knew they were out there, especially for women who spent most of their time looking for that one special man. Miles was definitely a diamond, and how brilliantly he did shine, Rachel thought.

Miles read a couple of sonnets from the book. He not only was articulate, but confident in every word he spoke. The goose bumps seemed to rise everywhere on her body. Miles raised his eyes and looked in her direction.

Calm down. He ain't a piece of meat on a plate, Rachel said to herself while her heart beat at an accelerated rate. She couldn't remember the last time Stanley took the time to read to her from one of her favorite books. Hell, he didn't even have five minutes to read to his own son, she reflected. Rachel tried to see Miles as just a man doing what he had to do to make it. In fact, she saw herself being alone with him in his house, sipping on a glass of cognac in front of a cozy fire, as perfectly innocent.

It's not like I'm over here every single day making wild passionate love to a complete stranger, right? Rachel asked herself. The only thing she couldn't figure out was why he didn't make any moves on her. She knew she didn't have bad breath and she used really expensive perfume, so it could not have been that. But she popped a mint into her mouth for good measure. The only explanation left was that he didn't really find her attractive enough, she told herself.

" 'You are more beautiful than the bright stars that blanket the black sky,' " Miles quoted from a book of poetry. He then licked his lips as if to make every word glide off his lips with ease. His mouth had the perfect shape, lips full and brown. Rachel couldn't help but get all warm and tingly. She wondered if his kisses were just as perfect.

" 'Her skin is soft as a whisper in the night. I dare not sleep and miss passion's flight.' " Miles closed the hardback book as their eyes were locked on each other's.

Miles leaned forward and kissed her gently on her lips. Rachel's heart sounded like it was echoing throughout the room. He pulled her into his chest and kissed her with everything he had. She tried to keep what was happening in perspective. But with each breath, her attempts seemed futile. This was what she had been hoping for. He would take her lust and forbidden passion.

His hands cupped her breasts that had ached for his touch. Rachel closed her eyes to search for the answer in darkness. She felt her body being lowered down on the sofa as his lips found their way to her exposed stomach. She could no longer stop the desires she'd held back for so long, the same desires she wished she could share with her husband. She didn't want to do it, but she couldn't hold back. She didn't want to hold back.

Miles lifted her skirt up and his hands found her soft spot. Rachel let her feelings and emotions take charge over her rational thinking. A rush of erotic images seemed to circle in her head. She felt the earth shake as she was approaching a climax.

Suddenly the books on the shelf and the glasses on the cocktail table in front of them trembled disturbingly. It wasn't Rachel's imagination, it was an actual earthquake.

"Oh, my God! It's an earthquake!" she screamed.

Miles rushed to his feet just in time to secure the expensive cognac bottle and glasses.

Of all days and times to have an earthquake! Rachel thought, pissed.

"Somebody up there didn't want this to happen," Miles said, keeping his wits about him as well as his humor.

"You're telling me," Rachel said, as she pulled herself up off the couch and drew her skirt down.

Miles went over to the window and looked out to see people running to and fro. Car alarms were going off and trash cans rolled down the street, impeding traffic in all directions.

"Thank God it was only a tremor." It was obvious to both that the fiery flames of passion had quickly turned into a small pilot light. She grabbed her purse and things and headed toward the door.

"You're not leaving, are you?" he asked.

"Yeah. It's better that I leave before something really big happens," she said. If it had been meant for something to happen between them, it would have. She didn't need an earthquake to make that point more clear. "That was a sign."

"A sign? I don't get it," Miles said, meeting Rachel at the door.

"Miles, you are a wonderful man. Any woman would be crazy not to find you attractive. I just think we should call it a night, that's all."

"I see," he said, not moved by her request. "Well, what do you suppose I should do about what almost happened? Am I supposed to just brush it off like nothing really matters?"

"See? I knew it was going to come to this. What do you want me to say? Let's try it again tomorrow?"

"Why can't we try it right here?" he asked while approaching her where she stood. Rachel suddenly remembered what Faith had told her about playing with fire.

"Don't come near me, okay?" Rachel backed away.

"Why? I'm not going to hurt you. Or is it that you can't trust your own feelings? I know that you're married."

Rachel's face dropped.

"Your ring. It was a dead giveaway," he said, taking her hand into his. Rachel consciously placed her hand to her side.

"So now you know. But that still doesn't change anything. I can't be involved with you in any kind of way. As much as I would like to, Miles, I can't."

"Okay. Fine," he said, shrugging his shoulders and turning his back on her.

He sure is taking it hard, Rachel thought. He was stringing me along just as I was, him. Faith was right all along. But why was he so caring and considerate all this time? He knew I was married; why didn't he confront me with that knowledge in the beginning? Rachel didn't want to go right away; she wanted to know what was behind the charade.

"Tell me something. How come all this?" she asked, raising her hands to the fireplace, the cognac, the whole seduction routine.

"Because first, I'm a man, then I'm a doctor. As a man I saw your needs and I made an attempt to meet them. But as you can see, an earthquake put an end to that plan." Miles started picking up the things around the room that had fallen to the floor.

Rachel laughed. It amused her that he could see her needs just by being with her for only a couple of weeks, but Stanley couldn't see them in all the years they'd been together.

"Am I that transparent?" she asked with her arms still folded in front of her.

"Not really. I've learned how to see beyond a person's exterior to what is really bothering him on the inside. Don't be embarrassed. Could I ask you a question?"

"Sure. I guess so," Rachel said.

"Why did you let me get as far as I did?"

Rachel cleared her throat. She was more embarrassed than she thought. She didn't know if she had the answer to the question. She had just acted on her feelings as a woman.

"I guess I was curious. I've never really seen myself as flamboyant or flirtatious. Maybe I wanted to see what it felt like."

"Was it what you expected it to be?"

"More," she said with a smile.

After she helped Miles get the house back to normal, Rachel was ready to go.

"I'm sorry it has to end this way. But there's no other alternative that I can see. It just wouldn't be worth it to me," Rachel said, as she walked to the door.

"You of all people should know that. I hope you and your husband work things out. I really do," he said, placing his hands on her shoulders. That was nice of him to say, Rachel thought.

"But if ever you decide that your conclusion was premature, you know where to find me," he said before he kissed her lips.

Miles reached out to open the door for her, and Rachel walked out.

Chapter
Twenty-two

There was a heavy silence hovering in the building. Maybe everybody had finally said all they had to say about the arrest of the mysterious rapist. In retrospect, almost all the women could remember times when, for no apparent reason, they had felt ill at ease around Terry. Mattie, more than anyone else, seemed to take the situation to heart, berating herself for being so taken in by Terry that she had previously come to his defense on more than one occasion. Seeing herself as the protector of the young girls she worked with, she was dismayed to think how she had let her girls down. If the situation had been less serious, Mattie might have found humor in the fact that this time the shoe was on the other foot as Lesa was the one doing the counseling and Mattie was the one doing the listening. Lesa had tried to remind Mattie that giving everyone the benefit of the doubt, as Mattie always did, was an admirable character trait, even if it did occasionally backfire. "After all," Lesa had said, "you've got to remember that old proverb, Mattie: 'Hindsight is always twenty-twenty.' None of us expected the rapist to be somebody we actually knew and even worked with."

And so the gossip that had flamed for a while had now died down and everybody was more or less in the routine of their work. On the seventh floor, two who were struggling with the deep silent rage of broken hearts found their work more aggravating than usual.

"I broke another nail," Lesa complained. "I swear. These cheap-ass drawers they have in this place are ridiculous. They need to throw these old-ass things in the dump somewhere." It was obvious that she was in a bad mood. (A little different from the sassy mouth she usually kept.) This time she had more than just an ineffective drawer on her mind. She glanced over at Stacy, whose mind was out in left field somewhere. Her head was buried deep inside a rather large Bible.

"Your weekend was that bad? This is the first time I ever saw you read a Bible. What happened this weekend; did you have some big religious experience or something?" Stacy didn't respond to Lesa's comment right away. She reluctantly pulled her eyes away from the good book.

"Huh? Girl, my mind is somewhere else," Stacy said in a weary voice.

"What's up? That Bible is big enough to kill a vampire."

"You act like you've never read the Bible before," Stacy said as she placed it inside her canvas bag.

"The only thing I can remember about the Bible is 'Thou shalt not commit adultery.' I, for one, agree with that. If I can't be number one, to hell with being number two. But don't get me wrong. I got no problem with it. I just thought with your parents being in the church and all."

"That has nothing to do with it. There are some questions that we just can't find the answers to, and frankly, I don't think anyone has the answers for everything. There are just some things that can only be explained by God," Stacy said in a whimsical mood. "All I know is this book has kept my family safe and together all this time. Maybe there's something in it for me, too."

"I don't think the Bible or any other book can help me with my problem. What I need is a how-to book that's gonna tell me 'how to' not love a man who doesn't love me," Lesa said in a blue mood.

"If that was the case, a lot of us would be spared a lot of bull from jump street. At least we'd know the signs before the crap hit the fan," Stacy said, slamming the drawer to her desk. "At least we wouldn't be left looking like fools."

Tracy, from the data entry office on the first floor, slapped some folders onto Lesa's desk. This woman was a thorn in Lesa's side from day one. Not only could this woman dress, but she had no problem turning the heads of the brothers in the building. It was enough to have a shortage of brothers out there as it was. And now here they come. The brothers thought she had it going on for a white girl.

"Excuse me, Ms. Thang. Don't you see these two black trays sitting here? Since black has become your favorite color. One tray says In and the other says Out. Or can't you read?" Lesa said viciously.

Tracy nonchalantly picked up the folders and placed them in the tray, then she flipped her long black mane across her shoulder, as if to let Lesa's remark roll off her back.

"Thank you, Skeezer," Lesa said under her breath.

"You wanna know what really pisses me off?" Stacy said, still disturbed.

"What?"

"How the black man continues to disrespect and humiliate us."

"It's not all of them and it's not just the brothers. There are some white men who do the same thing. They're just not as open about it, only maybe when they get a six-pack of beer in 'em. But I know they want to see what it's like to have some dark meat. Umph. Once they go black, they'll never go back," Lesa said confidently.

"I'm not worried about some white man; I'm concerned about our brothers. And they wonder why some of us have relationships with other races. It's because our own kind still don't know how to treat us. We hurt and feel pain just like they do." Stacy was on a roll. Lesa didn't know exactly what was going on, but she knew it had to be about Clyde. And since she was mad enough for the both of them, Lesa thought it best not to say anything about Kris and Tony, although Stacy had hit the nail on the head.

"I tell you this much, Lesa. I'm going to make sure that my boys will know what it is to respect women. And they better not bring any babies home and think I'm gonna sit up and take care of somebody else's kids. Hell, no," Stacy rambled on. She was letting the incident she had with Clyde get the better of her.

After Stacy had gotten home from leaving the restaurant and Clyde, she had gone into her bedroom and started pulling out everything that was Clyde's. She piled up a mountain of sweatpants, T-shirts, tennis shoes, weights, and whatever else she could find. What she couldn't get into her arms, she kicked. In between wiping the tears from her eyes and the sweat from her face, Stacy was hurting the worst way possible.

This could have been a beautiful thing, Clyde and me together, she thought. How could I have been fooled by him a second time? Don't I deserve to be happy? What am I going to say to Ty? What am I going to tell a small child about his father, who was here one day and gone the next? All night Stacy had cried in her bed, rolled into a ball with the pillows swallowing her tears. She had gotten up the nerve to call her mother the next day and tell her everything that had happened, right up to the point of the restaurant scene. To her surprise, Hilda was compassionate and understanding. It blew Stacy away. She thought she would have to listen to a long drawn-out sermon from her mother, but Hilda sympathized with what her daughter was feeling and going through. That meant a lot to Stacy, and somehow her adverse situation brought Stacy and her mother closer together.

Clyde had been calling Stacy since that night, but she

had been avoiding him like the plague. If he wasn't calling her at home, he was calling her on the job. Stacy got fed up. She informed the receptionist that she wasn't taking any calls from Clyde. There were a couple of times he tried to disguise himself as a client, but Stacy saw through that and slammed the phone on him.

"Stacy, Stacy. Calm down, girl. They're not even in grade school yet. Don't you think you should wait until they're successfully potty trained first before you put 'em out?" Lesa said playfully. "I can see you now. You be tossing condoms in their lunch boxes alongside a container of Jell-O pudding."

Stacy was right, Lesa thought. She wished that she and her mother had the type of relationship Stacy was building with her kids. But you live and learn, she thought. The only thing Lesa had inherited from her mother was the skill to use a man whenever she could, getting as much out of his pocket as she could.

At lunchtime the women met in the basement cafeteria instead of going out as they usually did.

"What do you have hot and edible today, Chuckie?" Mattie teased the cook behind the counter.

"What's up with the brown bag, Stacy? Your big spending days are over already?" Chuckie asked. Stacy rolled her eyes at his smart remark as she reached up and grabbed a bottle of apple juice.

"I could ask you the same thing since you had those same funky pants on yesterday," she said in retaliation.

"Oh, you wanna go like that, huh?" Chuckie said.

"Look. I'm not in the mood today, okay? So just take your greasy ass back in the kitchen and sling some chicken or something," Stacy said in rare form. Everyone else in the lunch line was laughing and snickering at Chuckie as he got mad and snatched his chef's hat off his bald head, ready to throw it down.

"All right, you two. That's enough," Mattie said between giggles.

LOVE'S DECEPTIONS

Rachel and Lesa were already at the lunch table in the corner of the room awaiting Stacy's and Mattie's arrival.

"What's going on with you, Lesa? You haven't said two words since we sat down. Is something wrong?" Rachel asked. "I was telling Mattie this morning that we haven't seen much of you lately." Before Lesa could respond, Mattie and Stacy sat down at the table.

"What's going on?" Mattie asked everyone. "Not everyone speak at once," she said in response to their silence.

"I'll tell you what's going on with me," Stacy spoke up first. "I just found out that Clyde has another child. And the worst part about it, he left her to come back to me! I was just telling Lesa upstairs that men are still doing dumb, childish stuff." Stacy was fired up.

"Humph. Men have been doing that since the beginning of time. The only thing they've improved on is doing it in our faces instead of behind our backs," Rachel said, as she bit into her turkey sandwich.

"Lesa, you sure are quiet over there," Mattie said.

"That only means one thing," Rachel said. "She's got man trouble, too."

Lesa exhaled a long sigh. She wasn't sure what she wanted to say, or if she wanted to say anything at all. Either way, they knew she wasn't herself.

"Lesa, what's wrong?" Mattie said, as she reached over and took her hand. That did it. Tears began to fall from Lesa's eyes.

"Come now, sweetie. Is it that bad?" Mattie asked. She got up and went over and sat beside Lesa in an attempt to console her.

Lesa tried to suck up the tears welling up behind her eyes, but she had to tell someone before she exploded.

"Tony was arrested two weeks ago," she said. Lesa held a napkin up to her eyes for a second to dry the tears. The last thing she wanted was the whole cafeteria in her business.

"Why didn't you tell me, Lesa? I thought we were friends?" Stacy said, upset because she had rambled on about her problems and failed to see Lesa's pain. Not that Lesa had suffered any more than she had, Stacy thought.

"Are you all right? He didn't hurt you, did he?" Rachel said, afraid Lesa had experienced what she had gone through.

"Well, I'm fine now. But he did put a couple of bruises on me," she said, as her eyes remained low. "If it were not for the cops, I'd probably be dead," she said with a slight snicker.

"I don't see what's so funny. You know he could have succeeded," Mattie said in disbelief.

"What's the difference, my life has been nothing more than a big mess anyway. And to top it off, remember the guy I started seeing not too long ago? Well, it turns out that he works for the Drug Enforcement Agency. DEA. This guy used me to get to Tony." At the table everyone's mouth dropped. "Rachel, you told me that one day I was going to meet my match. Looks like you were right after all," Lesa said with pain written all over her face.

"Lesa, I didn't mean anything by it, I just . . ."

"I knew what you meant. No need to apologize. I guess I had it coming."

"Don't say that. No woman deserves to be treated that way. It's not worth it. Believe me, I know," Rachel said, as she reached over and held Lesa's hand. There was now a bond between them that made them sisters in a sense.

"Why in heaven's name didn't you tell us? We could have done something," Mattie said.

"What could you do? I didn't know what I was going to do. I thought breaking away from a bad situation was the best thing for me. It turned out that Kris was only doing his job."

"When will you get it? The man doesn't make the woman. I try telling these young women walking around here that no matter how much flesh they expose and how short the dresses get, a man is going to see your body first, and hopefully your mind second. That's the last thing they think about. If you really want to keep a man in his place, don't let him into yours. That's the only way you'll gain his respect," Mattie preached. "Nowadays we as women leave very little to the imagination."

"Mattie, you can sit there and say all that. You don't know what it's like not having enough men to go around. If he ain't in jail, he's dead. If he ain't dead, he's hanging on the corner. All I've been hearing is 'You have to find yourself a good man.' Tell me where to look, then maybe I'll find one," Stacy argued.

"Stacy, I'm surprised you said that. You, of all people, should realize that there are a lot of good men in the church."

"Please. Some of them got one foot in the church door and the other foot on the sidewalk. You and my mother say the same thing. I've met some of the men in church, and believe me, they're not all what they're cracked up to be. But don't get me wrong, Mattie. There are some nice brothers there, but how do I distinguish between the two? How do I know who's really into church and who's just playing church?" Stacy asked.

"There's only one way to find out," Mattie said. "You have to be there."

"Mattie, you don't have anything to worry about. You're old. What's there to be worried about? Your pension, health benefits? What?" Lesa said abruptly.

"For your information, there's a lot I worry about. I worry every day about losing the people who mean the world to me. People like you for one, and you, Stacy, and you, Rachel." Mattie went around the table. She cared for all of them a great deal. She saw them as the children she'd never had. "And Fred, who's lying in the hospital. I worry about the young children of the world who are dying every day because of our past mistakes. There's a whole lot we take for granted, but there is also a lot we, as a people, are learning to care about. So yeah, Lesa, I do worry. I worry that people my age could possibly be the only living souls left to do something about it." For once Mattie had Lesa's full attention and everyone else's.

"Be glad that somebody cares about you. Sometimes it's all we can offer," Mattie said.

"That's easier said than done sometimes," Stacy said. "I realized this weekend that it's that antagonism between our cultures that causes us to put our own down and see the faults in somebody else rather than our own faults."

"As hard as it is for me to say this," said Rachel, "I used to blame my husband for the mistakes in our marriage, but I don't anymore. It was never his fault or my fault, it was our fault. And if we don't resolve these mistakes together, we're just gonna keep putting the blame on each other. It's better that we find the solution to the problems instead of adding to them. It took a while for me to see that, but now I know. From now on, the next time I look into the mirror, I'm going to remember it's not just me I see in my reflection, it's all of us, especially now. We have to stop identifying ourselves with fancy clothes, gold this and gold that. We're all in this together."

"I don't know about that, Rachel. I still get excited over well-tailored suits. But you're right, I do have a life ahead of me and I'll be damned if I'm going to waste it on a man. Well, maybe just for today," Stacy said.

"Speaking of life. How would you all like to attend a women's seminar this weekend?" Rachel asked.

"What seminar?"

"My girlfriend who is a public speaker as well as a great psychotherapist, she's speaking on empowering the African-American woman."

"A shrink!" Lesa blurted out.

"She hates that word. Furthermore, she's a real good friend of mine," Rachel said.

"Then what else is she? She sits and listens to pathetic conversations by people who don't know whether they're coming or going, who entrust their personal lives to a complete stranger. No way. You can count me out," Lesa said, shaking her head.

"She's not going to put you onstage and ask you to

spill your guts. Faith is not like that at all. She doesn't go around telling everybody somebody else's problems."

"Yeah, right," Lesa said skeptically.

"How much are the tickets?" Stacy asked.

"Nothing. You all are coming as my guests," she said.

"Count me in, then," Stacy said.

"Y'all can go if you want. I have other things I can do with my time," Lesa said.

"You're one of the main ones who needs to hear what she has to say," Rachel said.

"Don't tell me you're thinking about going, too, Mattie?"

"I might. Who knows? I might even get some answers to some real important questions. It may be very enlightening. I might even get something out of it at my age. Right, Lesa?" Mattie teased Lesa for calling her old.

"Well, if you got the nerve to go, then why shouldn't I?" Lesa finally said.

Chapter
Twenty-three

The week passed quickly. It was time for the women's seminar and the anticipation was felt as cars and taxis pulled up in front of the Doubletree Hotel, one of the most popular hotels in the city. Women entered through the revolving glass doors, leaving husbands, boyfriends, and live-in lovers behind. An undefinable energy filled the air. The lobby of the hotel was flooded with excessive chatter and laughter. The constant rotation of the revolving doors seemed to be a streak of lightning as it spat out female after female.

In the underground garage, Rachel, Mattie, Lesa, and Stacy arrived together.

"Does Faith counsel mental people as well?" Stacy asked suddenly. "Because if she does, she needs to sit down and talk to Clyde. If he thought he could sneak around with two women and not get caught, he has a real mind disorder."

"Stace, Clyde isn't nuts."

"He just suffers from some sort of neurosis called sex," Rachel said jokingly. "I'm just kidding. Why don't you ask Faith once we're inside?"

"Rachel, how come you know so much? Were you one of those people who thought they were going crazy, too?" Lesa said rambunctiously.

Rachel took a deep breath. No one knew it, but she

was once a patient. A long time ago Rachel had been on the verge of a nervous breakdown. Faith helped her get through that crisis.

"It's not like I went around broadcasting my personal life to strangers, but I wouldn't say I was a patient, per se. After I got married to Stanley, things weren't as matrimonial as I thought they would be, and I think I just needed a patient ear and a confidential soul to confide in. Faith has always been there for me when no one else was," Rachel said, not ashamed of her past or the present.

"That's a first. I thought getting married was something we all looked forward to, but I didn't know it caused people to seek psychiatric help," Lesa said bluntly.

"Lesa, how many times do I have to say it? What happened between Stanley and me was something that would either strengthen our marriage or break it. And since he thought we didn't have a problem, when obviously we did, I took it upon myself to seek outside advice." Rachel really didn't want to say as much as she did, but inside, she knew it was good to talk about it.

"Sounds to me like the party was over before it began, huh? Are you sorry you got married?" Lesa asked. Rachel continued to walk in the direction of the garage elevator.

"I love my husband, that's why I married him."

"Then why are you here?" Lesa asked.

"To find out if my 'I do' is still 'I do,' and not 'I don't,'" Rachel said as the elevator door closed.

When the doors opened again they were smack dab in the middle of a multitude of women.

"What the—! I know all these women don't have a marriage problem," Lesa said, surprised.

"I bet every woman in town is here. This man-woman thing must go deeper than any of us had imagined," Stacy cried in amazement.

"Remember. Everybody here isn't necessarily married. Look at you two. You both aren't committed to anyone, but yet, you're here," Mattie said, as she looked on. There were women of all ages. Some her own age.

A large assembly of high-heeled, brown-toned females descended en masse in the lecture hall, leaving the tantalizing scent of women behind. The sound of hands clapping and cheers echoed through the corridors of the hotel as the speaker approached the podium. Faith stood briefly to acknowledge the many faces she recognized from previous orations and the new ones. "Thank you. Thank you one and all. Please sit down." She gestured to the full house to take a seat. All women waited with anticipation to hear what Faith had to say about them and their men, for those who had one. Faith's reputation as an inspirational and motivational speaker had exceeded beyond what she ever imagined. She had told Rachel many times that life was bittersweet, and when life handed you a lemon, you had to learn to make lemonade. That was a rule Faith lived by.

Faith recruited three from the audience to pass out small boxes of tissues to every woman in the room. There wasn't room for one more person. There were rows and rows of women in all shapes, colors, and nationalities. Each woman came with a problem or had been experiencing something other than happiness in her relationship. Whatever the case, every single woman had a story to tell.

"For those who wonder what the tissues are for, just turn to the sister beside you and tell her: 'These are for you, girlfriend.' " Laughter and chatter among the women rose as the energy level in the room escalated.

"Before I tell you the real reason as to why we are all here today, I would just like to take a moment and introduce a very dear and very close friend of mine," Faith said, as she looked down at Rachel in the front row.

Rachel looked up and began shaking her head from embarrassment.

"I would like for Rachel Grier to stand, please," Faith said as she urged the crowd to get Rachel to stand. She hesitantly did a timid wave as if she were some big shot, incognito.

The women gave her warm applause as Rachel casually scanned the expressions on the faces around her. She felt almost comfortable, seeing so many African-American women in one place. Then suddenly one face seemed to stick out from all the rest. Benita. She was there just three rows from where Rachel stood. Rachel immediately took her seat as her heart beat wildly in her chest.

"What's the matter? You look like you just saw the Devil," Mattie said, disturbed by Rachel's expression. Rachel could barely speak.

"I wish it were that simple," she said, stunned.

"Rachel, what is it?" Mattie asked as she attempted to turn around.

"No. Don't look," Rachel said. She clutched Mattie's arm. "I just saw the woman my husband has been seeing right over there," Rachel said, bent out of shape.

"Oh, Rachel," Mattie said with a slight grin. "All these women in here, you might have seen someone who looked like her. Calm down."

"Calm down! Mattie, I know what Benita looks like. Even if I was halfway blind, I'd know her when I saw her," Rachel said, convinced. Mattie tried to sneak a peek.

"Don't turn around, then she'll know I spotted her."

"I don't care what you say. If it was her, there's nothing you can do about it. She paid her twenty dollars just like everybody else," Mattie said. Rachel was angry. Of all times for her and Benita to be in the same room together, at an all-women seminar discussing the one thing they both had in common—men! And Stanley!

Umph. If she had any sense, she'd get up and leave right now, Rachel thought, pissed.

"Just by a show of hands, how many women left a man at home today?" Faith said. She expected the obvious. Just about every hand in the whole place went up. "Fantastic. For once let them sit home and watch the kids, cook and clean, do all the other stuff that they're so used to seeing us do." Faith could hardly hear herself talk above all the cheers and roars that came from the audience. "Because right now, from this moment on is woman's day. Not the one in church, and I'm not talking about Mother's Day, either. Because what we go through as women, period, will take more than a day to recover from." The sound of hands clapping and foot-stomping cheers rose to levels unheard of.

"There will be some things covered and said in here that will make you think twice about letting someone else live your life and dreams other than the person who knows you the best. You! So get prepared for three hours of eye-opening, earth-shaking news that every woman should not be without," Faith said, confidently and straightforwardly. "We are not here to step on anyone's toes, nor are we here to put anyone down. I'm here to give you the 4-1-1 on what it means to be a true African-American woman in the nineties and how to be at peace when everything else seems to be going to hell. Be clear that the reason we're all here is not for a pity party. Oh, no! You all are here because it's time to end the crying, dying, lying, and flying. Before you all walked through the front doors of this place, it's safe to say that you were just existing in relationships, am I right? You were not living in the relationship?" Faith asked, as the response from the audience was agreed upon. There were some "Amens" and "Preach" that came from the congregation of women. Obviously, there were some church folks here as well and that was fine with Faith. She realized that most of the women who were there had emotional holes in their souls so deep that only a miracle from God could fill them. Anyone who walked by the closed doors would have thought it was Sunday morning worship a day early.

"So sit back. Relax. Take your shoes off if you want and put aside all thoughts of housework, dirty laundry, the sink full of dishes you left behind, and get ready to receive your breakthrough. Today is no ordinary day; today is your day—a woman's holiday. A day that will never be found on any calendar."

Before things got underway, time was taken for everyone to talk, mingle, and introduce themselves. Faith walked over to Rachel, who was bewildered and upset.

"Faith, this is not going to work," Rachel said, troubled.

"What's wrong?" Faith asked.

"Benita is here," she said stiffly.

"That's good."

"Are you out of your mind? There's no way in hell I'm gonna sit here and have to look her in her face. Forget it, no way," Rachel said.

"Don't worry about it. This could be what you both need. What better way to get everything out in the open once and for all. Besides, did you ever think that she is here for the same reason? Just look at her, Rachel. Does it look like she's feeling triumphant or the least bit happy?" Faith asked, as she and Rachel looked over at Benita, who sat quietly in her seat. "Looks like she has some pretty heavy stuff on her mind, just like you."

Yeah. But what? Rachel thought, as she took her seat.

An hour passed and now the entire assembly was broken into groups of ten. Faith found this exercise to be very helpful to get the women to verbalize their emotions and break the ice. Lesa and Stacy sat together in one group. There were women their own age and some older.

The women listened intensely as one sister explained why she was there.

"I don't really know why I keep letting him share my bed. I realize that he's a married man, but I can't seem to let him go."

"Girlfriend, get a grip!" said one sister in a gold and white dashiki with matching crown. "Honey, the only thing a man can make a woman do is die and cry," she said, as she worked her neck.

"But I love him. Doesn't that count for anything?" the woman asked.

"The question is, who's doing all the counting? You're only getting the fringe benefits of the relationship, while his wife is getting the paycheck," a broad-shouldered sister said. "Gone are the days of 'no romance without the finance.' If the unemployment rate ain't stifling our black men, we're constantly crying about what we don't have because of the absence of the man in our lives. We're not like our ancestors when they were left alone to fend for themselves. No. We can't even live on our own at times because we're too afraid to bear the responsibility. We've gotten to the point now where we don't even want to sleep in our own beds alone. We just got to have somebody lying right beside us. Whether it's your man or somebody else's," she said.

"A little romance, which only turns out to be nothing but sex when it boils down to it," another woman said.

"If you ask me, we all got to wake up and realize that the man does not make the woman. And we better start standing on our own two feet," Stacy spoke up.

"Would you care to elaborate on that comment?" the leader of the circle said. This was no time to clam up now, Stacy thought as she continued.

"Well, I'm here because I was in a relationship where I was willing to give the father of my kids a second chance at parenting. But the moment I let him back into the house and into my life again, it backfired in my face. He was the same old lying cheat he'd always been, and I'm just fed up with the bull. I don't know about the rest of y'all, but I need a man! But I feel as though I can't trust them." Stacy got a welcome response to her brave speech. "I'm looking for someone who I feel comfortable marrying, who will be a real man and father to my kids. I don't want to raise two children and him, too," Stacy continued. She could feel the weight being lifted off her mind. She could go on for hours, but she decided to give someone else a chance to speak.

"Anybody else have anything to share?" the leader asked. They all looked around at one another. Stacy nudged Lesa, who was not there mentally.

"What?" she said, annoyed.

"Tell them why you're here," Stacy whispered. Lesa

did not know why Stacy wanted her to spill her guts. It wasn't Lesa's style. She thought of better things she would rather be doing than sitting around listening to a bunch of women complain about what they felt, when they felt it, and why they weren't getting what they wanted.

"Come on, Lesa, help me out. You've been in more relationships than all of us put together probably," Stacy said. The two of them continued nudging one another back and forth until the leader intervened.

"I'm just as confused as the rest of the group. I don't have a problem," Lesa said. She was not ready to open herself up in front of a roomful of strangers.

"Honey, ain't nobody's situation that bad that they can't talk about it. That's why we're here," the African queen said.

"Lesa, don't be embarrassed. Look around. We're all naked and not ashamed here. You might be experiencing something that somebody else has already been through."

"I don't think anyone has been through what I've been through. I wouldn't wish this on my worst enemy. I know a few men who have pissed me off. But I guess what I'm trying to say is, what does a woman do when she cares a lot for someone and he constantly tells her that he feels the same way, but he has a terrible way of showing it?"

"What you're asking is how can you love someone who doesn't love you back no matter what you do or try?" another said within the circle.

"Yeah. That's what I meant," Lesa said. The tissue box was on its way around. That question brought tears to several eyes. Apparently Lesa's question struck a few nerves.

In her group, Mattie felt comfortable with women her own age. That way she wasn't behind the times.

Everybody else seemed very young compared to their generation. Most of the women had already traveled down that road. Mattie and most of the older ladies in the place knew what it was like to have loved and lost. Not necessarily to lose their husband to another woman, but to something that guaranteed their man would not return. Death.

"There was a time in my life that growing old was something I looked forward to with my husband. Looking at the behavior of the men today, I'm glad to be where I am," Mattie said. "I see what you young people have to worry about on an everyday basis and here I'm graying constantly every day. I wouldn't ever consider coloring my hair because I want people to see that I am mature and I'm not for no foolishness at my age. I don't even worry as much as you all do anymore. I feel like I have one foot in the grave already. Why should I start worrying about stuff that'll more than likely push my other foot in the grave?"

For Mattie, this was easier than she thought. She had imagined a roomful of single, vibrant young women who practically had all the time in the world, versus the women her age, who couldn't afford to get sick for fear that their secure jobs and positions would be snatched right out from under them. What did her life amount to? Mattie mused. She had experienced so much in her life that she refused to let anything or anyone break her spirits. She was still going strong, and it was only through the grace of God that she had made it this far when at times she wanted to throw in the towel. She was determined to allow herself to live again.

"For me, ladies, it's just the opposite," said Joan. "I still have my husband, thank God. And we love each other very much. But there are times when I get these crazy urges to just indulge in some wild, passionate sex." Laughter broke out among the women. That was a sign that "old" was just a word that had no real significance to them. They did not escape sexual frustrations.

"You telling me," Mattie said. "I had not been sexually active for a number of years, and I wasn't sure if I still had what it took to please a man, or myself, for that matter. I'm trusting you all that what is said here will not go beyond these four walls," Mattie said. The last thing she wanted to hear was her sex life on the lips of strangers.

"I can truthfully say that I had never experienced a miracle, but a miracle happened one day with a very close friend. And, ladies, it's everything I ever remembered it to be," Mattie confessed joyfully. She remembered how her body experienced eruptions that she thought would never be awakened again. With her true confessions, it opened the doors for others to talk about their sexuality. Some women unashamedly expressed passions aflame, just waiting to be quenched.

Others had a man but were not interested in starting the flame or making a little smoke. These woman were satisfied with their lives. They were set in their ways and perfectly happy if they never did it again. Some women said that they didn't think they could deal with a man. They were content being "Mrs. So-and-So" even though their spouses were deceased. To them, today's men were "crazy and selfish." Others felt that after all those years of being older, single women, they were still in transition. Everything was still up in the air for them. More Christian sisters said that they would rather wait on the Lord than have to wait for a man to pass their way.

But that wasn't the only issue that concerned Mattie and the others. Health care and other personal issues were vocalized. Becoming a burden to their families when they could no longer care for themselves on their own. But the bottom line was that older women were satisfied with just being in their prime. They laughed when someone said that she remembered when she used to monitor her menstrual cycle. But nowadays she monitored her hot flashes that always started at her feet and at the wrong time. In church they saw her as a very spiritual woman. And she was. It's just she would always start stomping before the preached word went forth. That was because she had a hot flash in her foot and she tried to stomp it out.

"But we will experience a lot more," Mattie said.

"Good and bad. Before I lost my husband to cancer some years ago, I thought I would never have to spend my life alone. Everything was right. But then he got cancer and died and there I was, a lonely, bitter woman who died mentally when my significant other passed. But that wasn't the end of my life. Someone else came into my life and made me feel good about myself and who I was. We have had good times together and just by living day by day, we came to appreciate each other for who we were. I don't have the body of a young woman anymore, and he certainly can't do most of the things he used to, but we still complement each other with what we got," Mattie said.

"I'm glad you brought that up, Mattie," the group leader said. "If we never see each other again, I want all of you to remember that if you put your very best into life and love, the very best will come back to you. Never stop living no matter how hard life gets. Don't sweat the small stuff, 'cause it's all small stuff." The circle of women clapped their hands to end their session.

Just two circles away, Rachel sat quietly as she listened to two women who were involved with the same man. They found out about each other one day by attending the same spa.

"At first I was angry with her, but then I realized that she was just as much a victim as I was," said Sheila, according to her name tag. The two women sat together the whole time, holding on to each other's hands. If they didn't express the love they both had for this guy, one might have thought they had something going on. But that was the least of Rachel's concerns. She didn't care if they started fondling each other right there. She was more concerned with Benita who, by some strange act of fate, ended up in the same circle.

She was always the quiet type, never saying a word, just listening, Rachel mused. She wondered if she wore a weave or was all that black hair on her head her own? She still had a flair for clothes. Not saying that Rachel did not. Rachel sat and watched Benita with an envious eye. Benita listened attentively. She desperately tried to avoid Rachel's piercing stare but at times their eyes did meet for only a second.

Listening was one of Benita's strong suits. That's what made her an outstanding attorney. She liked to hear a case before she decided to represent a client. Rachel assumed that's what attracted Stanley to her. How can one woman be so smart, yet do something so stupid like sneaking around with my husband? Rachel thought. She sat barely comprehending what had been said around her.

It was now Benita's turn to speak and Rachel was on the edge of her seat. Benita stood and brushed the wrinkles from her jade-colored suit and took a deep breath and let it out real slow.

"I'm sort of nervous," she said so articulately. "You would think I'd be used to speaking in front of a crowd by now because of my profession." Rachel did not take her eyes off her. It was like she knew what Benita was going to say even before she said it.

"As I look at and listen to all of the sisters here bare their souls and openly lay their deepest feelings out before a roomful of strangers, I would like to say that all of you are the true essence of what a real woman should be," Benita said.

What in hell is she trying to do? Rachel thought. That didn't sound like something a cheating, back-stabbing woman would say, especially in a roomful of women whose reason for being there in the first place was probably because of women like Benita, who, incidentally, tried every tactic she could think of in order to avoid Rachel's eyes. But Benita could feel the hard stare that crawled up her body.

"I'm here today because I've experienced the opposite of what you ladies are experiencing. You all have a man to complain about or complain to. I, on the other hand, don't have a man. I mean, I have a man; we're just not together." Now we're getting somewhere, Rachel wanted to say aloud.

"But that doesn't exclude me from expressing what you all may be feeling. Because, you see, the man I married didn't turn out to be the man I thought he was when I married him. And the man I wanted obviously didn't want me. For the first time I am able to admit that to myself, and to a roomful of strangers." Benita's eyes finally connected with Rachel's. There was no mistaking pain and bitterness in her words.

"Although my tag says 'Benita,' there is another name one may call me and that is 'the other woman.'" The expression on Rachel's face as well as the faces of everyone was surprise. No way Rachel could have known that she was going to reveal the truth. "I pride myself on not placing labels on people, but that is one label that I am not proud of," Benita said, as she looked directly at Rachel. "But it's women like you that I tip my hat to, women like yourselves who put up with the real mess and stress of loving your men in spite of the lies, betrayal, and the lonely nights. I'm sorry you had to be the ones who got the bad end of the deal, and I just ask that all of you forgive me." Benita sat down just as eloquently as she had risen. The women around her got up and embraced Benita with open arms. Rachel didn't budge. She sat stiffly in her seat, almost in tears. There was no way in hell she was going to show any kind of sympathy toward a woman who tried to destroy her marriage, even if Stanley had told her the truth.

Rachel stood up to address the group. "I know it's not easy for any of us when we have to leave our safety zones of marriage, family, and home. We try not to invite thoughts of insecurity, mistrust, and infidelity to invade our minds. But there are no safety zones in sight when our own marriages and relationships are not built on a strong foundation," she said, as hand claps boosted her mood. "I can't say that at times I have always been the woman my husband wished I'd be, nor has he been the husband I wish he was. But that doesn't mean I love him any less. But what we fail to realize, just like men, is what we did to get them, what we have to continue doing in order to keep them. Because if we don't, we're only seasoning them up for someone else. And I refuse to give up that which I put my time, feelings, and love into, only to give it away to somebody else," Rachel said with strong conviction. She hoped that Benita had got the message loud and clear.

After the group discussions had broken up and the room was reassembled to its previous position, Benita approached Rachel.

"Rachel, could I speak with you, please?" she asked. This was the first time they had spoken since Rachel and Stanley had been married.

"I know I'm the last person you would ever want to speak to."

"You got that right," Rachel said sternly.

"I just wanted to say that . . ."

"Before you say anything, I just want to say that I know about you and Stanley. And I also know that there is nothing between the two of you, and that Malcolm is not his son. As hard as it may seem, Stanley and I love each other. We may have to learn and grow in this love, but believe me, we've been through too much to throw our marriage away."

"I never doubted your love for your husband or his love for you. Frankly, you two were made for one another," Benita said.

"Good. So we understand each other," Rachel said triumphantly. "And as for my busybody mother-in-law, well, every family has its black sheep," Rachel said.

Faith called the women back to their seats.

"All right. Let's settle down now; we haven't finished yet. I would like the leaders of the groups to come to the front and just give a few concerns that were discussed in each circle."

Faith adjusted the microphones as the leaders came forth. Everything from being sick of men, to sick of being alone, to just sick, period, they heard. She knew that those women were ready for a new agenda, a new authority, and a new attitude toward life and in their lives.

"Girlfriend, it's time! Time to stop getting angry at the other woman, time to start taking responsibility for your own actions and stop blaming somebody else for your own troubles. Time to stop existing in that relationship and start living in it," Faith said. The crowd applauded extensively. "It's time that we realize as women, that loneliness is only a psychological trap that will cause us to lie down in the wrong places, and it has to stop. Now!" The women were all fired up again. It even surprised Rachel. Faith had never talked like that when they were together in the last couple of weeks.

"Why didn't you tell me that she was this awesome?" Mattie asked Rachel, who sat amazed at Faith's depth.

Faith cleared her throat and took a sip of the glass of cool water beside her papers on the podium.

"It's time we tell men and whoever else that fails to see, that we are here and we're not going anywhere. Some of us have become prisoners in our own relationships and that's a real shame. I don't think y'all heard me." Faith sounded like a preacher and the crowd encouraged her to preach on. "It's pretty funny and sad how we keep putting ourselves into a psychological prison. We talked about things we do in the name of love, but how ironic it is that we still want to experience love and that feeling of being loved. No one can live and not be loved or have to experience pain and not overcome it. It goes against all rules of the universe. I know how unquenchable your thirst is for fulfillment. And how love in all of your lives can be so fragile and sometimes mocked by your own best intentions," she went on. Suddenly, the women jumped to their feet. Some shouted, others cried out, while some couldn't even vocalize their emotions.

Faith went on to say that women were descendants of

Eve, the real first lady, mother, and wife. God created women because he knew that man could not survive alone. He presented every animal, fowl, and creature created but nothing suited man. But then God made woman and changed the entire course of life forever.

"Sisters, like I said before, the man does not make the woman. We can't live beyond our breakthrough if we never lived before the breakthrough. Now I don't want any of you to go home to your husband or your boyfriend and say that Faith said in order to get your breakthrough, you have to break up." The crowd laughed. "Oh, no. I did not say that. What I'm saying is, see what needs to be changed in your life and in your relationship. Don't wait until things get so bad that fists and dishes start flying, because nobody deserves to be beaten or verbally abused. And if that's the case, leave. Get out while you still can. You all are God's gift to man. And if God thought you were precious enough to give to a man who uses and abuses, then, girlfriend, he doesn't deserve you. If you think you know when an argument is going to flair up, stop, and reevaluate the situation. Out of every adversity comes an opportunity." Faith had the women sitting on the edges of their seats as she gave them advice that they probably couldn't get from their closest friend. Tips and positive points were written down faster than Faith could spit them out of her mouth.

"I'm going to wrap it up by letting all of you in on a little secret." The moans and groans from the audience indicated to Faith that the women weren't ready to leave just yet. They were so eager to hear more. Faith was touched by their affection.

"For those women who are looking for Mr. Right, that man who would make all your dreams come true, stop looking! He's not coming. You must try to accept that you are not perfect. We're not going to find him, either. We make mistakes and we're gonna keep on making mistakes. The only way you'll ever get on the right road is if you put God at the head of your household and life. Not a man. Then and only then, will He give you your heart's desires. This concludes today's seminar." Faith grabbed her notes and belongings and walked off the stage.

The entire room was on its feet. She received a standing ovation. It was as if their lives had just been changed for the better. Some still had questions they wanted to ask and Faith was kind enough to answer them after the session.

After the women left with new attitudes, a new agenda, and a new lease on life as they saw it, some immediately jumped into their cars or cabs to rush home to practice what Faith had preached, while others hung around to partake of the free buffet.

"Did you all enjoy yourselves today? I know I did," Mattie asked with a brilliant glow on her face. "She even answered some doubts I had in my head about Fred and me. To tell you the truth, I feel very lucky. Whether I have someone to share the rest of my life with or not, I'm content with who I am." They all stood at the buffet.

"I'm just surprised she doesn't have her own talk show. Can you imagine the money she could be making?" Lesa said, as she sampled just about everything on the table. "She could push Oprah's tail right off the map."

"I'm surprised she's not married. What's up with that, Rachel?" Stacy said.

"Faith is too involved with other people's business to concentrate on her own personal life right now. But that doesn't mean she doesn't want a family someday," Rachel said.

"I tell you what. I'm not gonna settle for less anymore. If the brother ain't got it going on when he steps to me, then he might as well step off!" Lesa said with a cherry tomato clenched between her teeth.

"You got that right," Stacy said in agreement. "From now on it's got to be all or nothing. I can do bad by my damn self."

Rachel excused herself as she walked over to where

Faith was being smothered by a swarm of talkative females. She barely escaped the human barricade.

"Thanks for coming," Faith said, as she embraced Rachel.

"No. Thank you. You're awesome. I'm telling you, girl, you really gave these women something to think about," Rachel said.

"And what did you get out of it?" Faith said. Rachel looked at Faith with wide eyes and a grin on her face.

"Don't worry. It's not what you think," she said. "I've decided to give my marriage one more try." Faith lunged forward and gave Rachel a big hug. "Rach, you've made the right decision."

"I'd hold the applause if I were you. I still don't know what my husband has on his mind," Rachel said, not sure if Stanley wanted her back or not. Faith had told Rachel before the seminar that love takes nothing less than everything.

"I just pray that we can trust each other again," Rachel said.

"The only way you'll find out is if you ask him yourself," Faith said. She pointed to the hotel entrance where Stanley stood.

Rachel was surprised.

Stanley stood with Nicky in his strong arms. A picture-perfect vision.

What was he doing there? Rachel thought, as she stood perfectly still. The look on his face didn't change. It was the same hard, serious expression he had seemed to acquire over the years. She waited until her heartbeat finally caught up with her brain. What was she afraid of? Stanley would have to be out of his mind to try anything. Not with all of these sistahs here whose opinion of men was as welcome as the seven plagues. He met Rachel where she stood.

"Since you refuse to come to me, I'll come to you," he said, direct and stern. Nicky practically jumped from his arms straight into her chest.

"I didn't expect to see you here," she said with a straight face. Rachel tried to appear cool and in control. But her heart was pounding in her chest like a mighty drum. She wanted to rush into his arms so badly, but most important, she wanted to know why he was there.

"Look," they both said simultaneously. Stanley insisted Rachel say what she had to say.

"Stanley, I know things haven't been great between us. Hell, there hasn't been much of anything between us. But I don't want to continue on like this. It's too much strain on our marriage. And I don't know about you, but it definitely has been too much on me," she said, as Nicky played with her hoop earrings. Rachel wondered if Stanley felt anything at all. He looked in her eyes and watched the way her lips moved when she spoke. Was he hearing anything she was saying? Rachel wondered.

"Stanley, do you still feel that you need your space?"

"What I need is for you to shut up for a minute. Please." Rachel was stunned. He was actually communicating with some sense. Somewhat. That was a start.

"What I want is for you to come home and be my wife again." That was it? Rachel thought. Faith's speech obviously brainwashed her for real. Or else there was a God and he heard her cry.

"Am I hearing you correctly?"

"Rachel, I haven't been able to think of anything else since you left. And I am not screwing around on you. I was telling you the truth," Stanley said.

"I believe you."

Stanley took a sigh of relief. "You do?"

"Yes. It took some time for it to sink in and some other things. But all that matters is that we can be a family again," Rachel said before Stanley grabbed her up into his thick arms.

"I'm sorry for all the bullcrap I put you through. I just want things to be the way they were."

"Oh, no," Rachel said, quickly pulling away. "Things will never be the way they were. We'll either start out fresh with a new focus and more communication or we don't start at all, and that's including your mother. Stanley, she has got to stay out of our business."

"I've already taken care of that. We will have no trouble out of her from here on out," he said. They held on to each other.

Rachel looked up and saw Benita at the exit. It was obvious that it was over before it began. Rachel had confirmed everything she had said. Benita looked on briefly before she turned and walked out of the hotel. Rachel held on to her man tighter. She felt in her heart that she had won the battle, but keeping her marriage together was a war she looked forward to.

"Let's go home," Stanley said as he escorted Rachel, Mattie, and Stacy to the car.

"How did you find me?" Rachel said as they all walked to the elevator.

"You wouldn't believe me if I told you." Stanley smiled.

"Try me," Rachel said, as the elevator doors closed.

Lesa declined the offer to get a ride home. She decided to hang around downtown.

Chapter Twenty-four

Rachel dropped Mattie off at the hospital to see Fred, who was out of Intensive Care and doing much better. Stacy asked Rachel to let her off at her mother's house where, to her surprise, she found Kelvin waiting for her.

"Stacy."

"No, if you don't mind, ma'am, I would like to do the honors," Kelvin said to Hilda, who was just as excited as Kelvin was to see Stacy in the flesh.

"What's going on?" Stacy asked as she stood staring at them. Hilda looked like she had a secret bursting to get out.

"Your pictures don't do you any justice. You know that?" Kelvin said, as he held the photograph in his hands.

"I'll just go into the kitchen to leave you two alone," Hilda said as she took the boys in and fed them a snack.

Stacy started gathering the kids' things and barely said two words to Kelvin. She had an idea who he was. She couldn't mistake the soft, sexy voice.

"Are you surprised to see me? I gather you know who I am," he asked. He bent down and assisted her in getting the kids' toys up off the floor.

"First of all, should I be? Second, yes, I know who you are; and third, thank you, I can do this myself," Stacy said stubbornly. Although she wasn't upset with Kelvin, she wasn't sure if it was going to work between the two of them, especially since her mother had first crack at him. She knew her mother cross-examined him about his life and business. Furthermore, her mother probably revealed Stacy's business, making her seem like a desperate woman in need of a good man.

"I get the feeling you don't like me being here," he said.

"Why on earth would you say that?" Stacy said sarcastically. She tried everything she could think of to give him the cold shoulder. She refused to give him a second look for fear that she would melt in his eyes. Clyde had nothing on this man. He was sharp and could dress his ass off, Stacy thought, as she viewed him from the corner of her eye.

"You really have some great kids. Especially Tyron. He's a very bright little boy."

"Thank you," she said.

"He's very talkative as well."

"I just hope you didn't talk too much to Mother about . . ." Stacy had hoped that he hadn't told her mother that he knew her from the telephone service. That would really cause her mother to flip out.

"No. She would never hear that from me. Besides, what goes on behind closed doors or during a telephone conversation is nobody's business," Kelvin said as he gained at least one point in his favor. Stacy took a minute and acknowledged him properly.

"Thank you. Really. There's a whole lot I haven't told my mother. But someday I will. I appreciate what you just said and I apologize for the way I've been acting," she said with a smile.

"I apologize for popping up here unannounced like this. But I couldn't take the chance of not ever meeting you face-to-face. You have no idea what I had to go through to even get this far," he said.

Stacy laughed because she knew exactly who he had spoken with—Chauncy. She thought about all the things she had been through in the last couple of days. To have her day turn out like this was worth waiting for.

Hilda could hear the laughter floating from the living room and smiled at the thought of her daughter's happiness despite all the other stuff.

"Thank you, heavenly Father."

Chapter Twenty-five

Lesa approached the intersection. The sway of her hips was alluring, and the light breeze caught the tail of her pleated skirt, causing it to reveal more than her long legs. Her beauty seemed to slow up traffic faster than the yellow light. There were whistles, horns, and verbal advances thrown in her direction. But she ignored them all. Before, she would have acknowledged the hormonal taunting by those who found her sexuality more than just visual. This time she didn't even bother to turn around.

She proceeded to walk toward the shopping district of Hillcrest. This wasn't her normal shopping domain, with its wild and outlandish clothing. Sometimes she would find a bargain here and there, but for the most part, the weird and crazy scenes and the people were a sight to behold. This part of San Diego was known for its gay and lesbian crowd.

Lesa walked from window to window, admiring the funky, hippie styles that were back in fashion. She awkwardly tilted her head to view a pair of white stretch bell-bottom slacks and a black leather vest with dangling fringe at the bottom. It looked awesome on the mannequin. She wondered just how it would look on her shapely figure. But her depressed stupor in the last couple of weeks had put a few extra pounds on her hips and she hadn't even bothered to work them off. She stepped back to get a better picture of her reflection in the large window. It wasn't until then that she noticed another pair of eyes fixed on her from behind.

She nonchalantly walked on as if she didn't notice the car following her very slowly. Then she decided to turn around and confront her stalker.

"It's against the law to follow innocent people, you know," she said with her hands on her hips. She didn't care who heard or saw her. But of course she wasn't really mad, since it was Kris who was tailing her in his convertible Mazda.

"I wasn't sure if it was you. But when I recognized those beautiful legs, I knew it had to be you," he said behind a pair of dark shades.

"Now you know. So you can stop following me," Lesa said as she walked on. Kris wasn't giving up that easily. He continued to ride alongside her slowly. Her beauty still affected him in the worst way, not to mention her sassy mouth. He made up his mind that he wasn't leaving without her.

"Do you mind stopping for a minute so we can talk?" he asked. But Lesa didn't respond right away.

"First of all, I don't fraternize with cops, and second of all, I have a hard time believing people who make their living by lying and spying," Lesa said as she sped up the pace. Kris laughed at her stubbornness.

"Okay, if you must hear it, you're right. You are right, Miss Gains. Now, would you please stop making me drive along like this? Please!" he shouted from the car. He zigzagged throughout the traffic in order to keep up with her long strides.

Lesa stopped abruptly. Kris pulled to the curb.

"Look. There is nothing to talk about, nothing you can say that will change what happened between us. As far as I'm concerned there was nothing between us and there never will be." Lesa decided to try out the new attitude she had acquired at the seminar. She hoped that the tips didn't work too well because she really wanted him back.

Kris looked away momentarily and shook his head in disbelief. "Lesa, I'm not gonna beg for your forgiveness. If that's the way you want it then, baby, you got it." He shoved his car in gear and sped off. His tires left skid marks on the street and on Lesa's heart.

Lesa watched as his car recklessly turned the corner out of sight. She started to cry right there on the sidewalk. Lesa felt like a fool. She would never have guessed that one man could infiltrate her hard exterior and get inside her heart, breaking it a second time.

After she cried for a good two minutes, she wiped her eyes, pulled herself together, and tried to catch a cab. She stood on the corner and looked down the street only to see Kris coming in her direction. Lesa's heart began to race as he stopped in the middle of traffic with his motor still on.

"I decided to go around the block to give you time to change your mind." Lesa couldn't hold back the smile that enveloped her face. "Lesa, if I didn't say it before, I love you, and I hope you still feel the same way about me."

Lesa wrapped her arms around Kris's neck and kissed him. "I do! I do!" she said, as they kissed again and again.

She got into the car and they rode off in the direction of his house. She was practically in his lap as they drove down the street.

Late that evening Rachel and Stanley lay snuggled together in their bed. They had just finished making real love. Rachel had finally received that long awaited orgasm and Stanley felt that he had regained his self-worth and the respect from his wife.

"Okay, are you going to tell me how you found me today or do I have to tickle it out of you?" she asked. She and Stanley started to horseplay like teenagers.

"Okay. All right. You win," he said.

"So who was it? Faith? It sounds like something she would do behind my back."

"Nope. It wasn't her."

"Mattie? But I can't see how she could find the time to call you."

"Wrong again. It wasn't Mattie," Stanley said.

Rachel got up and mounted her sultry body on top of his. "All right, I give up. Who tipped you off?" she said, as her fingers parted the hairs on his chest.

"You really want to know? You're sure?" Stanley began to tease her.

"Tell me!"

"Ouch! Okay." She grabbed his hair between her hands. "It was Nita. She told me."

Rachel moved away slowly. After making good love like they just did, the only thing that could spoil it would be her. After all they had been through, he still had her on his mind. "See. That's exactly why I didn't want to tell you. I knew this was going to spoil everything." Stanley sat on the edge of the bed.

"That's where you're wrong, Stanley. No one could ever in a million years know the joy I'm feeling right now. Nothing can spoil this night for us, not even a name," Rachel said, as she snuggled up against his back and started kissing the back of his neck down to the crease of his spine.

Stanley turned around and cradled her naked body in his arms.

"There will never be another woman for me, Rach. You're everything I ever wanted in a woman, and I love you very much. I'm going to do all that I can to make this marriage work. I promise. And I'll never hurt you again."

"I hope you mean that, Stanley." Their bodies fell back onto the bed, their lips rejoined, and they made love over and over again the entire night.

Not once did Miles pop into Rachel's head. A doctor wasn't what she needed. She preferred the sexual healing from the man who knew her best.

Chapter Twenty-six

Two months after Fred was released from the hospital, he and Mattie exchanged wedding vows on August 28 in the backyard of Mattie's house. Rachel was the matron of honor and Lesa and Stacy were the bridesmaids.

"Mattie, you look absolutely beautiful today," Rachel said as she helped herself to another piece of wedding cake. Fred escorted most of the guests, close friends, co-workers, and relatives to their cars out front.

"I feel beautiful and exhausted," Mattie said. She and Rachel were putting on a couple of more pounds by nibbling from the three-tiered cake. Mattie reached up and picked the bride and groom statue from the top.

"This will be a day I will always remember."

"You should. Remember that love is supposed to be better the second time around."

"Speaking of the second time around, how are things between you and Stanley? For the last couple of months we spent most of our time talking about my wedding plans. But it looks like you both found more than just a new love. You've even put on a few pounds. Believe me, I know what love can do. If it weren't for this girdle body-suit, there was no way I was going to fit into this dress. Speaking of which, I can't wait to get out of this damn thing," Mattie said, as she tugged at her off-the-shoulder fuchsia dress that flared out from the waist down to her knees.

"I'm having a baby," Rachel said in a low voice.

"A baby! Rachel, that's wonderful. I can't believe it," Mattie said, as she embraced Rachel happily.

"You? How do you think I felt when I first heard the news? I was afraid to tell Stanley."

"I'm sure he was happy," Mattie said.

"He was. I was shocked. I thought he would hit the ceiling or worse. He's been hoping for a girl," Rachel said. She was truly happy about her pregnancy and the way her and Stanley's relationship seemed to be taking off since they had started seeing a marriage counselor. Plus, thanks to Rachel and Mattie, who talked Fred into turning some of his prominent friends Stanley's way for business, their financial outlook was starting to improve.

Things were finally looking up for both Rachel and Stanley and she had never been happier. Then she ran into Miles at the wedding. They were cordial to each other, and she was not surprised to see an older woman on his arm when he walked in. She was in her late thirties, professional, and very well kept. Miles introduced Bria, an art collector from New York. He went on to explain that Bria came in for a nonroutine checkup because of her constant traveling. She thought she had acquired an irregular heartbeat. After Miles had given her a complete cardiovascular scan, it only turned out that her body was overworked. All she needed was some R&R. She canceled her trip to the Virgin Islands to stay over in California a few more days and that was just what the doctor ordered.

After Miles and Rachel's chat, Bria took his arm and had him all to herself for the duration of the ceremony. Her heart fluttered with joy. Promptly following the ceremony Miles and Bria left. I don't regret a thing, Rachel kept repeating in her head.

As for Lesa and Stacy, they both had embarked on a new relationship with new goals. After Tony's trial, he was sentenced to six years for possession of drugs with the intent to distribute and four years for a handgun violation that would get him a total of ten years in prison. He would be able to receive probation in six years. Kris had pulled some strings so that Lesa would not be called to testify against Tony in court. Kris meant what he said to her when he said that he would never hurt her again. Plus, he didn't want Tony's face to be the last thing she would have to remember about her past. When Tony was sent to prison, Kris and Lesa moved to a town house on the other side of the city in a quiet community.

"You ready to go?" Kelvin asked Stacy. They both had decided to continue to see each other after all. She finally got the new two-bedroom apartment she wanted. It was much bigger and the environment was healthier and cleaner. There was a playground out back and her neighbors were friendly Christians, whom her mother took a liking to right away. And the best part of it all was that Stacy no longer had to get up as early as she did before to get the kids ready to go to their grandparents' house because her father gave her money to get a car. It wasn't anything right off the car dealer's lot; it was a used Toyota that ran like it was new. No more rushing to a crowded bus stop or hailing a speeding cab. Kelvin even pitched in at times and picked up the kids when Stacy had night classes. This was perfect, Stacy thought. She was on her way to fulfilling her dreams.

As for Clyde, he was finally out of her life for good, although she did allow him to see his kids every other weekend when her schedule permitted. Stacy refused to discuss with Clyde her relationship with Kelvin and in return, Stacy didn't ask Clyde anything about his wife or anything pertaining to his marriage. The only reason Stacy let Clyde see his kids was because she didn't want to cheat the children out of knowing their real father. However, Stacy was no longer concerned about Clyde. He only showed up when it was his time to see the boys. As far as she was concerned, Stacy had a new life and it was all because of Kelvin, who made her very happy.

After Mattie returned from her wonderful honeymoon in Hawaii and was back at work, the four friends once more gathered around the same table during lunch break. As they reminisced about the positive changes in each of their lives, they all agreed that there had been dark days during the past few months when they would not have made it without the support they had received from one another. It was Mattie who voiced what all of them were thinking. "Girlfriends, we are family, not by birth but by choice. We've been there for each other and we will be there for each other no matter what new directions our lives take! And take it from one who has lived a lot longer than any one of you, life will continue to take us in new directions." As she finished her sentence, Mattie spontaneously reached out to either side, and then they all were joined in emotional handclasps that said more, physically, than words could ever say.

Now that you've enjoyed *Love's Deceptions*,
look for One World/Ballantine's latest Indigo Love Story:

Shades of Desire
Monica White
May '98

A forbidden love. An unforgiving world. Jasmine Smith and Jeremy Collins have found everything they ever wanted in each other.

What each of them wants, society tells them they shouldn't have—Jazz is black and Jeremy is white.

Jazz and Jeremy each wonder if their abiding passion is enough to prove that love can be both blind and color-blind?

Please turn the page
for a special bonus preview chapter of
SHADES OF DESIRE

Chapter One

It was my twenty-sixth birthday. To celebrate, I was going out with my girlfriends—I hadn't had a date in months, and it was killing me!

Taylor, my roommate and best friend, had actually agreed to go with us, giving up her beloved Cameron for one night, just to be nice to me. I like Cameron and can understand what Taylor sees in him. The only problem is, he's white. Taylor says she doesn't care, that the problems that black woman–white man relationships cause are a small price to pay for love. But personally, I didn't think I could do it.

"Jasmine, you about ready?" Taylor stood at the door to my bedroom, watching me put on my lipstick. "Danielle called. She and Simone are on their way."

"How about you?" I asked. "You're not even dressed. If it were Cameron, you'd be ready."

She smiled. "If it were Cameron, I wouldn't be wearing anything at all."

I felt a flash of jealousy. "I can't believe you're giving him up for tonight."

"For you ..." She let the thought go unexpressed. "Besides, there's nothing wrong with wanting to spend all my time with Cameron. When you find the right man, you'll see." She walked out of my room to finish dressing.

I looked at myself in the mirror. I had spent a lot of money on a birthday gift for myself: a dark, mustard-colored dress with a V-neck that highlighted my full breasts and caramel complexion. Maybe I'll get lucky tonight, I thought. My hair looked good, cut shorter than I had ever worn it (the women at First Federal would be knocked out tomorrow when they saw me), and my makeup was done to perfection, making my brown eyes seem dark, even sultry.

I shouldn't have broken up with Reggie, I told myself, then realized with a stab of anger that it had been the only thing to do. He had been screwing around with every skirt in town, and when he got Anita pregnant, that was it. Still, the thought of him inside me, his hands on my breasts, quickened my breathing beyond control and I was glad the doorbell rang to distract me.

"Where's the birthday girl?" Danielle asked. I walked out of my room to greet her.

"You look great!" she said. "New dress?"

"I call it the man-catcher," I told her. "If it doesn't work, I'll ask for my money back."

Danielle was the wildest of our group; she knew the best places in town. "We're going to the Catnip Club," she announced. "Some friends at work were talking about it. They say the music's out of this world."

"Where's Simone?" Taylor asked, joining us and kissing Danielle hello.

"She's meeting us at the club. Come on. We'll take my car."

The club looked like a small house from the outside. We pulled into the parking lot. "Intimate," I said.

Danielle smiled. "You won't be disappointed."

We got out of the car and walked to the front entrance. A doorman checked our IDs and we entered a courtyard where there was a wading pool with a small fountain and a bar. There was a bunch of people, both black and white, dancing in the fresh air; the music from inside blared from speakers on the eaves. It sounded wonderful. I couldn't wait to get on the dance floor.

"Let's go in," Danielle said, leading the way. Simone was already waiting for us inside. We hugged and kissed one another in greeting. Taylor was the only one of the group with a permanent man; Simone and Danielle, like me, were cruising.

The dance floor was already crowded. Confetti sprayed from the ceiling and fog drifted from the floor. The music—jazz, my favorite—was amplified from ten-foot speakers scattered around the sides of the floor. Couples were dancing on top of all of the speakers.

We got drinks at the bar. Almost immediately, a great-looking guy asked Danielle to dance, so I carried her glass back to a table. "It's my birthday," I muttered.

"You've got to be more aggressive," Simone said. "Look at that guy on the speaker. I think he's cute. I'm going to ask if I can dance on the speaker with him."

"Girl, are you crazy? What if you fall?"

She laughed. "He'll have to catch me."

She walked over to him. He bent down when he saw her coming and helped her up. I couldn't believe her brazenness, and said so.

"While we're standing around, at least Simone and Danielle are dancing," Taylor replied.

Out of the corner of my eye, I saw a nice-looking, older black man walk into the club. He stood for a moment, scanning the crowd, then caught my look and sauntered toward us.

"There's a man I could take home to mother," I said, hoping he would ask me to dance.

"He's cute," Taylor agreed. "But you know me."

"Yeah," I said, "Cameron and only Cameron."

He was approaching. I could feel my heartbeat quicken. He was gorgeous! Six feet tall, the body of an athlete, smooth, chocolate complexion, deep brown eyes.

"Would you care to dance?" he asked in a sensual voice.

I could only nod. He took my hand, leading me to the dance floor; I could feel his heat.

"I'm a little rusty," he whispered.

Rusty? The guy was a klutz! I couldn't believe someone so beautiful could not dance.

He stepped on my toes once, and then again. My brand-new shoes! I tried to smile and prayed that the song would end. When it did, I walked off the floor and he followed.

"That was great!" he said. "How about the next dance?"

"I'm really thirsty," I told him. The least he could do was buy me a drink.

"I'll find you again when they play something slow," he said, ignoring the hint.

Not if I see you first, I thought, turning away. The cheap bastard.

Simone was still up on the speaker, her arms around her partner's neck. She was a quiet, pretty, light-skinned girl, studying nights to be a nurse. She didn't have a chance to go out much, so she was obviously making the most of it.

"Did you get his number?" Taylor asked, coming up and handing me my drink.

"Are you out of your mind? Did you see the way he danced? And he wouldn't even buy me a drink. I don't care if he's the greatest stud since Denzel Washington."

Taylor laughed that throaty laugh of hers and threw her head back. Her shoulder-length black hair fell away from her face, revealing her olive complexion and intense eyes. No wonder Cameron was attracted to her. There was not a man in the world who would not have found her beautiful.

"I hope you won't mind," she said, "but I called Cameron. I was feeling lonely here, with the three of you dancing. He said he'd be here as soon as he could."

"He won't feel out of place?"

"I don't think so. There are plenty of white men here. White girls, too."

Taylor had met Cameron at the insurance company where they worked. She was a claims examiner, he an actuary. At first, the fact that he was white bothered me and most of her other friends. But they had been going together for almost a year, and now we accepted him. I knew Cameron's parents were unhappy that Taylor was black, but despite our closeness she did not confide her feelings about them to me. It was a problem we all pretended did not exist.

I smiled at her. "I'm glad he's coming. I felt guilty not inviting him in the first place."

"Whew, it's hot." Danielle joined us. The man she had danced with was nowhere to be seen. "I saw you out there, Jasmine. Where's your friend?"

"Same place yours is."

Danielle laughed. "Yeah. Men are scum. But hey, you gotta keep trying."

I knew Danielle always would. She worked as an assistant editor at a black magazine. Her aggressiveness got her promoted quickly, but it seemed to eventually turn off her boyfriends. She'd had dozens of affairs, none lasting more than three months. It suited her fine, she said, but I think she wanted one man, just like I did.

A deep voice asked me to dance. I turned around to say no, thinking it was the guy who had first approached me. Luckily, the word stuck in my throat.

Standing before me was the most beautiful man I had ever seen. I figured him to be thirty, four years older than me, but he had the smooth skin of a schoolboy. He wore blue jeans and a jeans jacket, but I could tell he was heavily muscled—he works out, I thought. I looked at his legs: perfection. Just above them—I could only guess—but a telltale bulge made me yearn to know more. He seemed slightly shy, self-conscious, and I liked that. If he knew how gorgeous he was, it hadn't made him arrogant.

He looked at me with friendly green eyes. But he's

white. Before I could think at all, I said, "Yes, I'd love to," and I was out on the floor, in his arms, letting myself melt against him.

"What's your name?" he whispered.

"Jasmine Smith. And yours?"

"Jeremy Collins. Is it okay if I call you Jazz? It's my favorite kind of music."

Jeremy. A white man's name. I knew no one named Jeremy. So what? I thought. Now I did. "Jazz is my favorite music, too."

"You dance wonderfully," he said.

"You, too."

"Do you work?"

"Yes. At First Federal. I'm assistant manager, claims adjustment."

"I'm a freelancer. A writer. Articles and books. Have you heard of *Castro's Children*?"

"I'm afraid not." I was determined to find a copy.

"It's just out. My latest. About what will happen in Cuba after Castro dies."

The song ended. We stood awkwardly for a moment, not touching. "It's my birthday," I blurted suddenly, desperate not to let him go.

His smile produced crinkles at the corners of his eyes.

"Really! That calls for a drink."

He led me to the bar. Danielle and Taylor, seeing us approach, moved away and pretended not to know me. "Have you ever been here before?" he asked.

"No. It's the first time I've gone out in a while, as a matter of fact."

He handed me my drink. "I've been here before. I like racially mixed clubs. But this is the first time it's really been fun."

I wasn't sure whether it was because of me, but I welcomed the sound of it. We stood at the bar, nursing our drinks, talking mostly about our shared passion: jazz.

The music changed to a ballad, and he led me back

onto the dance floor. He had a wonderful scent, and when he took me in his arms and caressed my lower back, I could feel my nipples tighten and I pressed against him, surprised at the openness of my response. He grew hard against me, but he said nothing and did not kiss me. When the song ended, we again moved apart.

"I'd like to introduce you to my friends," I said, a little out of breath.

"I'd be honored."

Danielle and Simone were standing at the bar, talking to each other. "You guys, this is Jeremy," I said.

He offered to buy them drinks, and they accepted. I felt a little jealous, I don't know why. He went to place their order.

"I can't believe it," Danielle said. "Granted, he's gorgeous, but I never thought you'd go over to the other side."

I couldn't tell how serious she was. Did she care? I remembered she had once made a joke about Cameron and Taylor, how no white man could satisfy a black woman, and I wondered whether she was prejudiced or just making fun of her.

"First Taylor, now you. What's the world coming to?" Simone was obviously teasing.

"It's only a dance," I told them.

"Sure," Simone said. "But I saw you out there with him. Anything more, and it'd be X-rated. What if he asks you for your phone number? Will you give it to him?"

"Maybe I will and maybe I won't. I doubt if he'll ask, anyway." If he did ask, and I prayed he would, I knew the answer.

He came back with the drinks, and talked to my friends. Taylor came up with Cameron; if either was surprised by Jeremy's presence, it didn't show. Jeremy asked me if I wanted to dance again, and we went back on the floor. I was hoping they'd play another slow song, but the music was upbeat, and the sense of intimacy that had been so strong now vanished, leaving me unsure of what would happen.

"I've got to leave," Jeremy said. "An early interview tomorrow morning."

My disappointment must have showed, for he took my hand. "I had a really great time, Jeremy. Thanks for the drinks and for dancing with me. You made it a special birthday."

We walked off the dance floor hand-in-hand. "I'd like to see you again," he said. "Maybe we could go out for drinks or something."

He seemed suddenly shy. Is it because I'm black? I wondered. "I'd love to," I said, and we went to where Danielle and Simone were standing to borrow paper and a pen. I wrote down my number; he gave me his.

"I'll call you tomorrow," he said. "Maybe we can do something tomorrow night."

Again, he seemed shy. "Yes, call," I said, hoping he would kiss me good-bye. But he merely squeezed my hand, waved, and disappeared into the crowd.

"I can't believe you gave him your number," Danielle said.

"So what? I was surprised he could dance." Now that Jeremy was gone, I wanted to go home. I saw the handsome black man out on the floor, trampling someone else, and I laughed. If I had continued to dance with him, I'd never have met Jeremy.

"Considering you've never been with a white man before, what did you think?" Danielle asked.

I kept my thoughts private. "I only danced with him. It was no big deal."

"Then take my advice," she said. "Don't make it one."

But I could still smell Jeremy's cologne and feel his hand on the small of my back.

If you enjoyed *Love's Deceptions*,
look for One World/Ballantine's first Indigo Love Story:

Dark Storm Rising
Chinelu Moore
Available now!

When Star Lassiter meets Daran Ajero, angry sparks fly. Will those sparks turn into flames of passion? Or will the cultural divide between Africans and Americans be enough to thwart their desires and dreams?

While Star must decide if Daran is arrogant or merely confident, overbearing or just assertive, Daran's "friend" Cordelia is moving behind the scenes to ensure that Star sees the storm clouds surrounding Daran's many business and professional entanglements. Are these problems all just an illusion or is there a *Dark Storm Rising*?

Please turn the page
for a special bonus preview chapter of
DARK STORM RISING

Chapter One

Starmaine Lassiter stretched her long-limbed body to the sonorous strains of Whitney's "Saving All My Love." She crooned the song's lyrics and laughed when her voice veered off-key. "Yep, the only thing Whitney and I have in common is we sort of look like each other," she said aloud.

She liked to begin her aerobics warm-up with a slow beat and then later switch to a quicker tempo for the rest of her daily hour-long workout. As she used to tell the aerobics students she'd taught at various spas and resorts, "Exercise doesn't have to be a pain. It's all in the way you think about it. After a while, exercise becomes just another thing you do as a part of your daily regimen—like taking a shower or brushing your teeth."

Of course, most people didn't need to work out for an hour a day, but in her job as a fitness designer who developed exercise programs for spas, resorts, and fitness centers, she had to stay in top form.

Star realized it was nearly one o'clock. With any luck, she'd be completely finished with her routine before she heard the baby's lunchtime whimpers coming through the intercom speaker that transmitted all sounds from the nursery throughout the house. Little Nanette always whimpered before she wailed.

Star moved into a wide-legged stance and prepared to do a thigh-firming exercise she'd learned in a karate class in college. As she did this, a large shadow crossed the sun-flecked room. Her head swiveled to the source of the intruding shape.

A man's form parted the dense, tall evergreen bushes that screened the largely glass room. Her hands shaded her eyes to dim the sudden blast of light, but momentarily blinded by the bright sun, she couldn't see his face. She could only tell that he was dark and too tall to be her brother-in-law Larry. Besides, why would Larry be looking through the shrubbery when he could come in through one of the several doors of the house? Could it be a peeping Tom? She'd always assumed they operated at night.

These thoughts flashed through her mind in a split second, and feeling safely enclosed inside the room, she padded across the white sisal-carpet to where the intruder stood, still peering through one of the long windows.

A feeling of extreme annoyance shot through her. Why was he standing there looking into a private home? As she reached the window, she stood to the side so she could see him better. Her super-sensitive eyes were still having trouble adjusting to the light.

"Yes?" she queried without hiding her annoyance.

"I rang the doorbell, but no one answered," he responded.

"Yes?" she tried again.

"I told Larry I would drop off these in-ground lights." His head nodded toward a bag he held. "If I could find them," he shouted in order to be heard through the double-paned glass that separated them.

"Oh," she said, changing her annoyed and suspicious tone to a more pleasant one, even giving him a small smile. "Go around. I'll open the garage and you can put them there."

He smiled and disappeared in the direction of the garage.

As Star slid open the patio door, she heard Nanette's wail. The baby, undoubtedly awakened by the man's shouting, must have already gone through the first stages of her lunch request.

"Auntie's coming," Star called out as she bounded up the stairs to the baby's room. Normally, little Nanette was a happy, gurgling child, but if she wasn't fed on time, she would be uncomfortable and very grumpy for the rest of the afternoon and evening.

Star knew her sister Gail would not be in the mood for a bad-tempered daughter, no matter how adorable—not after dealing with the squabbles and tantrums of the special education students in her class.

She picked up the thrashing baby and cuddled her, talking to her in soothing tones as she quickly brought her down the stairs to the kitchen.

Just as she stuck the bottle with its warmed contents into the furious child's mouth, she heard the front doorbell chime and simultaneously remembered the man.

She hurried toward the door, holding the child in her arms. Opening it, she noticed the irritation on the man's face, but when he saw the baby, his expression became pleasant.

"I wondered what was taking so long." His voice was deep and he spoke with an accent that she couldn't identify. He was thirtyish, good-looking and somehow familiar. Her brow furrowed as she tried to remember where she'd seen him before. His eyes were familiar.

"You're the man from Pathmark!" She suddenly recalled an incident a few nights ago when a galling man in a grimy uniform had pushed her grocery cart out of the line. She'd left it to hunt for some tomato paste and, well, a few other items. When she returned, her shopping cart had been pushed aside and there he stood in its place as the clerk rang up his purchases. Luckily, no one else was in the line, so she pushed her cart almost on his heels.

"Excuse me, but I was in line here," she had snapped loudly.

His head had pivoted toward her, and his eyes had given her a quick once-over before he replied. "No, you weren't in line; a cart was here. If you weren't ready to stand in line, you shouldn't have put the cart in line," he'd said, lecturing her in a foreign accent.

Furious, she had thrown back her head, refusing to look at him as the clerk packed his boxes of garbage bags and giant-sized packages of paper towels.

Before she turned away from him, she'd seen a glint of amusement in his arresting eyes—eyes the color of wine tinged with brown.

What she wanted to do was ram her cart right into him. As satisfying as that might have been, it would have been risky, so she contented herself with silently jabbing him.

He's just a janitor who makes pathetic power plays by jumping lines at the supermarket, she thought as she recalled how he had brazenly looked her up and down. Of course this was to be totally expected of a man so rude. How like such a man! She almost laughed aloud.

Now he stood before her talking about Larry and in-ground lights.

"I stand accused." He laughed, crossing his chest with his arms. "I'm Daran Ajero. I live across the way," he said, indicating a large house backed by acres of farmland.

"You mean over there?" she said, darting her head in the direction of one of the largest homes in the Blueberry Farms development.

The house she referred to was a huge two-story wheat-colored brick structure with shuttered black Palladiun windows and two sets of French patio doors at the back. From the main highway, the back of the house looked awesome in the distance because of its two-tiered patio, which connected the top level to the lower one by a curved black wrought-iron staircase. One could get a glimpse only while driving by, however. Thick clumps of trees shielded much of the house. Actually, the closer you got to it, the less you saw of it.

"Yes, my house was the second house built in this development." As if reading her mind, he continued. "The land was a steal then, so I put a lot of money into building the house I wanted instead of paying triple the price for the land. It would cost me twice as much now."

Star nodded, enjoying the musical cadence of his speech.

"Larry must've told you about me?" he inquired, cocking his head to one side.

"You know how Larry is," she dodged. She smiled and

hoped this reference to her notoriously absent-minded brother-in-law would explain why she knew nothing about this man.

He continued. "It took me a while to convince Larry that buying the land and building his house made the best of sense, especially after he'd become a husband."

Star noticed that his warm, wine-colored eyes appeared to be smiling even when there was no smile on his face. She watched his eyes study her face and swiftly drop to her long, bare legs. She then remembered what she wearing: a hot pink leotard with a scoop neck and an attached flared skirt that accentuated the roundness of her thighs. Normally she felt completely comfortable in the outfit. It was, for her, a typical work uniform. But this man's eyes made her warm. With her free hand, she tugged the short skirt but to no avail.

She surprised herself again when she heard her voice say in the most neighborly tone she could summon, "Why don't you have a seat? I'm Starmaine."

It was a warm late September day and the veranda running across the front of the house was shady. He sat in one of the wooden Colonial two-seaters that flanked the left side of the front door. She eased herself down into a matching one across from him, holding Nanette. The baby's chubby hands still clutched the bottle, though she had finished its contents. Maybe the air will soothe her, Star thought, as she gazed down fondly at her little niece.

"Well, I'll just stay for a minute," he said, his eyes meeting hers directly as he smiled fully for the first time. Star noticed a gap between his front upper teeth. It only enhanced his looks. He folded his tall, muscular body onto the chair and leaned forward, placing his elbows on his thighs, which bulged through his well-cut beige slacks. His salmon-colored polo shirt complemented his dark chocolate skin.

"I'm sorry I missed Larry's wedding—your wedding. It must have been heavenly, considering the bride." She smiled, accepting the compliment. Her eyes inspected him as she spoke.

"Well it was a small affair actually," she said conversationally, omitting that she had not been the bride. She was enjoying the pretense of being Larry's wife. It was only fair. The guy had one-upped her at the grocery store and she was getting back at him. At some future point, the two families would have a good laugh about it.

"How do you like your new home?" he asked, his smiling eyes running down her neck to the bare skin above her breasts.

Star bristled at his marauding eyes. The nerve of him to openly ogle her—a woman he thought was married, and married to his friend, no less! Down, girl, she warned herself as a scorching remark almost spilled from her lips. He is Larry's friend and, evidently, a foreigner. She'd always heard that foreign men were very bold with their hands, and with their eyes too, apparently.

"Oh, it's tons of work, of course. Men don't know what it's like having to find just the right window treatments to match the light and mood of the room, and everything is so expensive," she answered him, repeating what she'd heard Gail say to Larry two nights before on the phone. "Your wife must've had fits decorating your huge place, or did you have a decorator come in?"

He smiled again, showing even white teeth and red gums that contrasted vividly with his dark skin. "There is no wife, and yes, I did have a decorator come in to do some of the rooms. I needed some of them done for my clients."

The fact that he wasn't married both shocked and pleased her. She covered up these emotions by blurting, "Clients? What type of clients?" Her brain thumbed through all the occupations in which one would have clients.

He regarded her quizzically, his gaze resting on her lips, which had parted in surprise. "Larry really didn't tell you anything about me, did he?"

Star's heart lurched. Pretty soon he'd find out she was an impostor. Considering Larry's relationship with Daran, surely she should know more about the guy than she did. She needed to bring this little chat to an end.

She stood up, saying, "Well, you should know by now Larry is extremely absentminded. He's a brilliant engineer, but other things escape him. Besides," she rambled on, "he moved everything in here all by himself. We got here just one day before school opened, and things have been crazy ever since. Settling into a new house is no joke."

Star knew she was babbling and had to force herself to stop. The combination of his probing eyes and prodding questions had put her on extreme alert. Her pulse raced as his eyes caressed every spot on her body. She feared he would soon know the effect he was having on her. The whole situation had become too uncomfortable.

Daran noticed the sudden change in her and the look of alarm that had settled in her eyes. Damn it! He cursed himself. She's nervous. My eyes must have betrayed my thoughts. What a honey-colored beauty! Damn Larry!

Star stood up. "It's certainly been nice chatting with you but I've got to get the baby to bed."

They both looked at the snoozing baby, who could not have been less concerned about her whereabouts. But Star's abrupt movement caused the baby's empty bottle to fall, bounce off Star's bare foot, and skitter beneath the two-seater.

"Let me," he said, bending swiftly to retrieve it before she could move out of the way.

He crouched between her legs and she could not move unless she tried to step over him—a dangerous feat, considering she still held the baby.

As Daran reached for the bottle, his face was within inches of Star's long legs. Legs that curved delicately upward to her firm thighs. He could smell her slightly sweaty female scent wafting through the air around him and he became light-headed and aroused all at once. He closed his eyes and inhaled her, knowing the moment would imprint on his brain. His lips yearned to kiss her calf and travel on up. He clenched his jaw to get control of himself. She was a married woman! Larry's wife! He couldn't help the effect this woman was having on him, but he could certainly restrain himself. He hated adulterers!

Star felt the heat of his breath on her legs and began to sweat. A tingling feeling started at the pit of her stomach and crept down to her toes. Her knees became weak. She felt they could give out at any moment and she would fall, taking the baby with her.

Just as he was rising, she moved slightly and his face brushed the soft flesh of her upper thighs.

She let out a little scream and began to fall backward into the chair. He clutched her arms to break her fall, easing her and the still-sleeping child into the chair.

Closing her eyes, she let out a long sigh, completely shaken.

The riveting impact of the exchange stunned him, too, for a few seconds. Then he became aware of how his muscles ached from holding his body in check. But he recovered himself before she did.

"I'm sorry," he heard himself say. "Are you all right?"

Before she could answer, they both heard the sound of a vehicle on the road near the veranda.

They both turned to see a black pickup truck stop abruptly. A small, buxom woman dressed in a peach-colored dress stepped from it. She beckoned to Daran. "There's an urgent phone call for you. Luckily, I saw your car over here. Hurry!"

As he moved from the veranda, he glanced at Star. His eyes held no laughter now. Instead they contained a look no woman could mistake.

As Star prepared dinner late that afternoon, she still reeled from the day's events and her own puzzling reactions to them. She couldn't wait for Gail to come home. Questions abounded about this neighbor—Larry's good friend Daran.

Gail finally arrived at four-thirty, but instead of bombarding her with questions about the man, Star retreated to safer ground. "When's Larry coming home?" she asked chattily.

Gail sighed, "Not till the end of the month. Can you believe that?" Gail's usually cherubic face was downcast as she raked the last of the meat and vegetable mixture from the blender into a bowl for Nanette's dinner.

Then she shrugged and smiled as she continued, "I tell you, Star. I think that company wants to adopt my husband. First, he was just supposed to oversee the installation of a new food tower in their plant in Ireland. That was two weeks ago! Then the company decided that since he was already over there, he might as well make a quick dip into Africa and inspect their Egyptian facility. He did that. Now guess what's happened?"

"What?" Star asked as she plopped some chicken wings into the microwave to thaw. She could tell from the scowl that ran from Gail's thick eyebrows to her small pointed chin that Larry's employer had reached new heights of audacious behavior.

"Oh, they want him to stay on to discuss some new inspection procedures with two managers who are currently on vacation!" Gail's large, dark eyes blazed as she recounted this last galling bit.

Star chuckled, and her sister shot her a withering glare.

"Really, Star. What's funny about this situation? I got married to have a husband. Not to be a lonely wife and single mother parked out in the country!"

"Well, how much longer does he have to stay?"

"He doesn't know yet." Gail shut her eyes tightly, pressing back hot tears of disappointment.

Realizing there was nothing she could say to make Gail feel less bad about Larry's postponed return, Star busied herself seasoning the thawed chicken. But moments later she broke into laughter and pointed at Nanette. The baby had pulled herself up out of her high chair determined to reach the spoonful of food that Gail, now gazing out the window, held just inches from the child's mouth.

Seeing what was happening and the humor of it all, Gail began to laugh. "See what I mean. Now that company's causing me to neglect my child!" She turned to Nanette and continued to feed her.

Star came over to the counter island and perched on a stool across from her older sister. "Get a grip on yourself, Gail. You're just lonely, and that's caused you to run off at the mouth. You know Larry loves that kind of responsibility, and he's being paid a heck of a lot of money. Both of you knew he'd be traveling sixty percent of the time. The company told you that back at square one. Remember? You told me that."

Gail put her hand on her hip and rolled her eyes at her younger sister. "Whose side are you on anyway, Starmaine?" she asked, only half kidding.

Star knew she ran the risk of getting Gail more upset, but she also knew her sister could make the biggest mountain out of a molehill if she wasn't stopped in time. With this in mind, Star smiled and continued.

"I also remember that Larry had some serious reservations about taking this job, but you egged him on. Furthermore, you and Nanette could be with him. You told me, remember? You told me even before Larry took the job that it had a provision allowing the spouse and children to travel along a certain percentage of the time. That was one of the perks that made him decide to take the job. But you chose to stay here and be aggravated by your darling students." Then mimicking her sister, Star added, "We'll travel with him during the summer break."

A wry expression came over Gail's face. Then she smiled. "Oh, don't remember everything I say, and don't be so darn right all the time," she said, flicking an imaginary piece of food at Star.

"Gailee," Star said, reverting to her sister's pet name, "I know you miss him, but you can't go around here dragging your chin on the floor, feeling sorry for yourself. I know how you are. You are the original Miss Magnify. Pretty soon everything will be so big in your mind you'll think Larry's staying away from home deliberately."

"Okay, little sister, you've made your point," Gail said as she cleaned up the spotty mess from the floor around the high chair. "I know Larry loves me, but sometimes I just need him around to rub my feet and—"

Grimacing comically, Star interrupted. "Kindly spare me all the lurid details."

She slid the chicken into the oven as thoughts of that man with the laughing eyes paraded through her mind again, accompanied by a host of busy butterflies in her stomach. She wondered how she could casually tell Gail about the unnerving events of the day.

Could she nonchalantly tell her that she'd been turned into a mass of panting, quivering jelly by a neighbor who had stopped by? Or would she begin by saying that for the first time she understood why some women had quickies with the deliveryman?

Pretending to check out whether Daran Ajero was Larry's friend or some nut gave her the pretext to open the dam of questions. "Oh, a guy who said he's a friend of Larry's came by today and dropped off some lights," Star began, and then realized she didn't know where the lights were because she'd never gotten around to opening the garage. Had he left them on the front porch?

"A friend of Larry's?" Gail queried, dumbfounded for a moment. "Oh that must have been the African guy who lives over there. Larry's friend, hm? What's his name?"

"Daran Ajero," Star answered, supplying the name.

Gail stood up and rinsed her hands off at the sink in the kitchen island. "Do you know I've never met him? What's he like?" Gail asked.

Before Star could answer, Nanette began choking on her fruit juice. Gail became too busy patting the little girl's back to notice Star's difficulty in answering this simple question.

It wasn't until Gail had the baby soothed and had transferred her to her play area in the family room that she picked up the thread of their conversation again. "So what's he like? What time did he come by?"

Star was relieved she had her back to Gail as she answered. Her voice suddenly didn't sound normal. "Oh, he's tall and on the slim side," she said. But very muscular, she thought as she rubbed and squeezed the smooth flesh of a cucumber under the running water.

"Larry says he's brilliant and a very sharp businessman. He gave Larry some very good investment advice a few years ago, and now my husband—you know how he is—he swears by Daran."

"Hm," Star intoned noncommittally.

"Larry says he's charming—and can talk the skin off a grape!"

A fresh swarm of butterflies attacked Star's stomach as she recalled the way his eyes had moved over her. His lips had mouthed only polite and proper pleasantries, but his eyes had let the real message slip.

"As a matter of fact, if it hadn't been for him, Larry would have never bought this land and we wouldn't be standing in this house right now."

Star gave her sister a puzzled look.

Gail munched on some melon cubes as she explained. "Larry and Daran met at a Black Student Union meeting at M.I.T. and became very good friends. After college, though, they kind of fell out of touch. Then a few years ago, they met again at some sort of conference. It was when Larry had just gotten his first engineering job. That was right before I met Larry. I remember him telling me, maybe on our second date, that he'd recently run into an African friend who'd just been recruited for a high-level engineering position by an oil company in Africa. Larry even said he'd thought about working in Africa himself one day."

Gail paused and a smile flickered over her heart-shaped face. "It just occurred to me that he will be working in Africa, at least for the few days when he goes to Egypt. Anyway, that's why I remember the conversation. It got me to wondering what it'd be like to live and work over there."

"But what's that got to do with Larry buying this land?" Star blurted. She knew it could take her long-winded sister until tomorrow to get to the here and now.

"Okay, I'm getting there," Gail said, gesturing for Star to be patient. "Well, Larry and I got married later that year. And I started noticing that Larry would sometimes get letters from Nigeria, from Daran, and he'd mention to me that Daran was fine and dah-dah-dah-dah-dah. About a year or so later, Larry told me that Daran had left the oil company and started his own business. He wanted Larry to be his consultant and agent over here, since the business involved buying industrial equipment for African businessmen who were setting up manufacturing companies. Well, Larry tried but it didn't work out. He just didn't have the time. Anyway, the next thing I heard was Daran had married an African American who was living in Nigeria. By this time he'd become very successful. But his wife wanted to go back home, since Daran was spending a lot of time on business trips either to Europe or the United States. So they moved to New York, and Daran and Larry would get together whenever Larry was in New York and Daran was in town."

"But why didn't you ever meet him? Didn't you at least talk to him?" Star asked, recalling her early afternoon charade as Larry's wife.

"I talked to him once when he called from Nigeria, but the connection was bad. Our voices were echoing. It was like we were talking through a tunnel. Besides, I knew the call was very expensive, so I quickly gave the phone back to Larry."

Gail was interrupted by the sound of one of the pots on the stove as its lid plopped up and down. She started for the stove.

Star headed her off. "Now you just go sit down. When I'm here all day, I take care of the cooking, remember?"

"Oh honey, you know just what to say to me!" Gail said, as she sashayed to the kitchen's long window seat and lay back daintily.

"Anywa-ay. Let's see. Where was I?"

"You were telling me why you'd never met him," Star prompted, "and how he led you to this lot."

"Oh, once when Larry met him in New York, he told Larry he planned to invest some money in farmland in Delaware. He was just speculating and thought maybe Larry would want to come in with him on the deal. Larry wanted to, but we couldn't afford it at the time. Within a year, Daran had sold ten of the fifteen acres he bought—ones over there around his house. He kept the other five for his own estate."

"Well, I am impressed," Star said, thinking, A hunk with brains, I do declare.

"I think sometimes he uses some of his clients' money," Gail said dramatically in a loud stage whisper, though there wasn't a chance anyone could hear her.

"Well, nobody ever said that making big money is a saintly activity. Look at some of the richest folks in this country now. Some of their ancestors rolled in the dirt to get that money and now . . ." Star stopped, suddenly realizing she sounded like she was defending him.

"Whoa! Whoa!" Gail said and looked at her for a moment. "I don't think he needs a defense lawyer yet. I wasn't accusing him of anything or criticizing him. It was just something Larry told me."

"Don't pay me any attention, Gailee. You know me. I always root for the underdog."

"This guy is no underdog. Nobody takes advantage of him, at least not in business," Gail said, and then she paused.

"What do you mean by that?" Star asked, setting bowls of salad on the table and beckoning her sister over.

"Well, Larry said Daran's wife was real dirty to him. She really hurt him." Gail spooned some blue cheese dressing on the vegetable salad and began to eat.

"Sounds like that's the past. What's going on with them now?" Star asked, recalling his words: There is no wife.

"Oh, nothing, I don't think. They got a divorce." Chuckling, she added, "I can't believe how much I know about this guy and I wouldn't know him from Adam if I met him on the street."

Star was silent. She remembered the buxom woman who'd come to get him earlier. Who was she?

Throughout dinner, Gail chattered on about when and how she and Larry had decided to buy the land and build their home, but Star only half listened. She kept touching the spot on her bare thigh where Daran Ajero's lips had seared her skin. The spot still tingled.